TRINITY STREET

TRINITY STREET

SALLY ODGERS

HarperCollins*Publishers*

HarperCollins*Publishers*

First published in 1997
by HarperCollins*Publishers* Pty Limited
ACN 009 913 517
A member of the HarperCollins*Publishers* (Australia) Pty Limited Group

The Moonstone logo is a registered trademark of HarperCollins*Publishers* Pty Limited

Copyright © Sally Odgers 1997
Cover photograph © MF–Imtek Imagineering

This book is copyright.
Apart from any fair dealing for the purposes of private study, research, criticism or review, as permitted under the Copyright Act, no part may be reproduced by any process without written permission.
Inquiries should be addressed to the publishers.

HarperCollins*Publishers*
25 Ryde Road, Pymble, Sydney, NSW 2073, Australia
31 View Road, Glenfield, Auckland 10, New Zealand
77–85 Fulham Palace Road, London W6 8JB, United Kingdom
Hazelton Lanes, 55 Avenue Road, Suite 2900, Toronto, Ontario M5R 3L2
and 1995 Markham Road, Scarborough, Ontario M1B 5M8, Canada
10 East 53rd Street, New York NY 10032, USA

National Library of Australia Cataloguing-in-Publication data:

Odgers, Sally Farrell, 1957– .
Trinity Street.
ISBN 0 7322 5868 5.
I. Title.
A823.3

Cover photograph supplied by Stock Photos
Printed by Griffin Paperbacks, Adelaide.

9 8 7 6 5 4 3 2 1
99 98 97

For Angela, Tegan's friend

AUSEURO DIALECT

arretez   stop! [French]
auf wiedersehen   goodbye [German]

bitte   good, or please, or agreement [German]

comprehendez nyet   I don't understand? [French / Russian]
comprehendez vous?   do you understand? [French]
contra code sie   that means I would be acting against the code [HI-Q Short Speech / German]

d'accord   I agree (implied; yes, but . . .) [French]
d'accord. Verzeihen sie   I agree and I'm sorry [French / German]
das tut weh!   that hurts! [German]
def-identity?   are you sure you identified them correctly? [HI-Q Short Speech]
de nada   that's okay (implied) [Spanish]

error of caution   you were being too cautious and slow [HI-Q Short Speech]
es macht mir nichts aus   it's all the same to me [German]
Estellita ma amata   Estelle my dear [mangled Latin]
Estellita mia   my Estelle [mangled Spanish]
es verdad   is that so? (implied) [Spanish]

finis   the end [Latin]

have post versiation of Auseuro   I speak a later version of Australian European dialect [HI-Q Short Speech]

im gegenteil   on the contrary [German]
intended zero minus twenty sec   I meant to do it at twenty seconds before the balloon went up [HI-Q Short Speech]

Auseuro Dialect

ja   yes [German]
ja, aye, au caka-va   yes, I do [German / Fijian]
ja, ich verstehe   that is so [German]

langsam   slowly [German]
liebling   sweetheart [German]

mal de mer   seasick [French]
mea culpa   I'm at fault [Latin]
mein leman   my sweetheart [German / Archaic English]
meinen zuletzt   my last [German]
merde   expletive [French]
mit moi   with me [mangled German / French]
moce   sleep, goodbye [Fijian]

nein   no [German]
necessity   I had to do it – I couldn't help it
   [HI-Q Short Speech]
necessity. Attack   I had to. There was an attack
   [HI-Q Short Speech]
nicht wahr   isn't it so? [German]
nicht im geringsten   it isn't [German]
nyet   no [Russian]
nyet, ich   no, I [Russian / German]
nyet. Prob. Ninety. Inex-ops   no, but there is a probability of
   ninety per cent. They were inexperienced operatives
   [HI-Q Short Speech]

reco-frame   the circumstances and focus of a Recovery
   [HI-Q Short Speech]
recovery complicae   the Recovery was complicated by
   circumstances beyond my control [HI-Q Short Speech]
recovery pre-intended   Recovery took place before I intended
   [HI-Q Short Speech]

AUSEURO DIALECT

Sib? Report Camena de Courcey, latwenty? Have?
    Sib, I want to know about Camena de Courcey, of the late twentieth century. Do you have her? [HI-Q Short Speech]
strength/talent, Daichcue Forn. Match strength/integ
    the strength of your talent, Daichcue Forn, must match the strength of your integrity [HI-Q Short Speech]

teur Estellita   dear Estelle [mangled German / Spanish]
tak   thank you [Scandinavian]
timor mortis conturbat me   the thought of death concerns me [Latin]
totoka mana   very beautiful [Fijian]
totoka cina na butobuto   you are a light in my darkness [Fijian]
tres mal a la tete   headache [French]

vale   farewell [Latin]
verzeihen sei   I'm sorry [German]
viel?   many . . . how many [German / HI-Q Short Speech]

yet contra me?   do you still have a grudge against me? [HI-Q Short Speech]

zut   expletive [French]

PART ONE
KISMET

PART ONE

Death is the end. A child is born, and matures to become an exceptional adult. A new child is born. The original subject grows old and dies, leaving the offspring to carry a genetic message to the future. It takes just one living, fertile descendant to carry on the elite heritage. So death is not the end.

Sometimes, through misfortune or wilful irresponsibility, the cycle is interrupted. We at Hub HI-Q pledge that the cycle shall continue. To this end, we have implemented a programme of strategic Recovery. In this fashion we uphold the most basic human responsibility of the human race. The responsibility to the future.

Camena was Tell Clancy's best friend, but for a long time Tell had had to accept the fact that there were places Camena went that she could never follow. Places in the mind.

Tell's mind was a workmanlike tool which performed quite well when given the correct data. Camena's mind was a maze, an electronic wonder. Hard slog to Tell was a playground to Camena, full of games and possibilities. Camena enjoyed her own mind and its precision, but seemed to accept the fact that Tell's was not the same. Tell could understand that, because she found it disconcerting herself. How could things so clear to Camena be so stubbornly opaque to Tell? And how could things which Tell seemed to know instinctively take so long to dawn on Camena? The double mystery was beyond either of them to solve. Tell lacked the means, and Camena lacked the inclination. And yet . . .

They had been friends forever, complementing one another from childhood. Camena was the beauty, dark and dreamy, brilliant but withdrawn. Tell was the doer, the goer, who dragged Camena out of her shell and along to the pool, the shops, the socials. Almost plain, argumentative and abrasive, Tell sparked raw life into Camena and kept her on track. It was Tell who helped Camena to function socially. It was Tell who reminded Camena of what it meant to be human.

In return, Camena calmed Tell's rough edges, tutored her in Maths, provided her with purpose and someone to protect. And Camena needed protection. Not only when she had one of her crippling migraines, but also from her own indifference.

'People will think you're a snob if you're not careful,' said Tell. '*I* know you're just floating around on some other plane, but *they'll* think *you* think you're too good to live!'

'I don't care,' said Camena.

'You ought to care. You have to care! And if you won't, I'll have to do it for you!'

'You shouldn't care so much,' said Camena. 'If they think I'm a snob, that's my problem. And maybe theirs.'

'But how can I *not* care?' asked Tell. 'I can't just switch it off and on! Besides — I like to care.'

'On your own head,' said Camena. She sounded offhand, but her eyes were warm as she smiled at Tell.

At school, St Saviours College, Tell and Camena were accepted as odd, but close, friends. But then, on the first day of Year Ten, Gerhardt Watchman entered their equation, homing in on Camena with all the certainty of an iron filing which has entered the charged field of a magnet.

At first Tell found it diverting, for her friend had never been the type that attracted boys. Her amusement cooled when she realised that in the new order of Camena and Gerhardt there wasn't a place for herself. Gerhardt was always there. Aware, and saying nothing. It made Tell angry and Camena ill at ease. 'See you later, Tell,' she had said more than once, and Tell would walk away, hurt and baffled.

What price friendship? For Tell her friendship with Camena was worth more than anything she had. She felt it was worth more than her casual relationship with her mother Maureen. Much more than her distant association with her father David. Was this a hiccup or the beginning of the end? Tell couldn't be sure without asking, and there are some things you don't ask your best friend. There are some things you don't want to know.

'If you don't like it, you can leave.' David Clancy had said that to his wife once too often, and Maureen *had* left, taking Tell and the spaniel Betz with her. David now saw his daughter on Saturdays and Wednesdays and for a mathematically calculated half of each school holiday.

The new order suited Maureen, but David still seemed peeved and surprised to find himself alone. The whole thing had taught Tell that you shouldn't throw down a gauntlet unless you were willing to have it taken up. And for Tell, it was her friendship with Camena that was at stake.

Gerhardt was an enigma. He had entered the school waters sideways, two dimensionally, as if he had been made of rice paper or a wafer of ivory. Despite his considerable height — he was one Year Ten boy who *hadn't* forgotten to grow — he was practically invisible in class; neither sulky nor smart-mouthed, neither clever nor dim. He had no visible family, belonged to no teams, ventured no opinions, volunteered no answers.

Thoughts of Gerhardt braying off-key in the shower, dropping dirty underpants behind the door or scoffing all the oriental noodles and being scolded by his mum didn't ring true. Tell couldn't imagine Gerhardt with a mum any more than she could imagine him raiding the pantry or picking his nose. Perhaps, she fantasised, he was really a hologram, and vanished when the lights went out.

Gerhardt was a tall boy, with brown hair, dark blue eyes and a strong chin. He had a rather pleasant deep voice and impressive shoulders, but since he was more likely to be found quietly playing solitaire than kicking a football, he made little impact on life at St Saviours College. And as far as Tell could see, he left the school grounds, turned into Sulphur Street, walked home with Camena down Corella and Galah Streets and turned left into infinity. He had to live *somewhere*, but it might as well have been on Mars.

In the beginning, Tell had eyed Gerhardt distantly as she might a wasp in the garden, but by now, over a month into term one, she found a perverse pleasure in watching him as closely as he watched Camena. She hoped she was making him uncomfortable, but after the first few days he seemed to accept her as a sort of semi-detached extension of Camena. Occasionally he'd try to frown her away, but Tell wasn't about to give Camena up without a fight. Not to a boy who'd arrived out of the blue on the first day of term one and might just as easily disappear.

Once Tell stuck out her chin, spots and all, and issued a silent challenge, her version of the evil eye. *You want me out of the way, Gerhardt Watchman, you get me out of the way. Until then, we share Camena and if you don't like it you can climb up Silicon Peak and jump off. Comprehendez vous?*

She thought Gerhardt gave her a secret, astonished glance. 'Ja, aye, au caka-va,' he responded. Or she thought he did, but the strange garbled words must have come from her own imagination, because his lips had never moved at all. Tell felt the blood drain from her cheeks. Hearing things! She was going the same way as *Jeanne d'Arc* . . .

Gerhardt was watching Camena, and his dedication was *not* in Tell's imagination. If Camena read in the library, Gerhardt read there too. If Camena were playing chess, Gerhardt would match her move for move. Occasionally he set out a pack of cards and played solitaire, but if Camena moved away he would sweep up the cards and follow. Tell wondered what he was thinking. She wondered *whether* he was thinking. Occasionally, she felt like taking hold of Gerhardt's ears, one in each hand, and using them as handles to shake his head. Just to see if anything rattled in there. Just to see if he felt normally human and warm. And what if she threw reticence to the wolves and made a move on him? Would he respond, or would his lips be stiff as wood? And *there* was a nasty thought — finding herself in the embrace of a wooden statue.

Kissing Gerhardt Watchman was an interesting fantasy in a squirmy sort of way, but it *was* a fantasy. And she was ashamed of herself.

'Does he ever talk to you?' she asked Camena one day in the privacy of the girls' loo.

'Not much.' Camena seemed surprised at the question.

'He's your boyfriend — isn't he?'

'No,' said Camena. Almost offhandedly, as if it were none of Tell's business.

'You're not related, are you?'

'Not that I know of. But then, being adopted, how *would* I know?'

Tell ignored her plaintive remark. 'Is he a member of Mensa?'

'No.'

'Does he get migraines like you?'

'I haven't asked. Anyway, I hardly get them any more.'

'What *is* he then? Come on, Brain, explain!'

Camena shrugged and wiped her hands. 'A companion.'

'Who doesn't talk to you.'

'Right.'

'Or kiss you. Or — or anything?'

'No. Shut up, Tell.'

'God, I'll need a tin-opener soon just to get the time of day from either of you. You're about as much use as a pair of bloody oysters!' Tell said crossly.

Camena smiled absently and Tell's skin prickled. This was the way Camena treated other people; politely, but not as if they mattered very much. It was *not* the way she had ever treated Tell.

If the two had been having some hot romance, Tell could have understood, even accepted Camena's abstraction. But there was no hot romance between Camena and Gerhardt. There was just this sudden, exclusive companionship, as if they belonged to a secret club.

Who — what — was Gerhardt Watchman, and why was he watching Camena? The questions buzzed in Tell's mind, but she couldn't ask any more. Not without risking an answer she couldn't face.

Silently, they left the loo and, silently, Gerhardt drifted up and fell into step beside Camena. It was eerie, the way no-one else reacted. It was almost as if they hadn't noticed the tall young man lurking by the senior girls' loo. And neither Gerhardt nor Camena said a thing, only exchanged quick glances — *recognising* glances, thought Tell.

Ja, ich verstehe. That is so.

Who said that? Camena? She often quoted snatches in other languages. But the voice had not been hers.

Tell glanced suspiciously at Gerhardt, but his face gave nothing away. And neither did Camena's.

Tell's own face was cold and suddenly stiff. She was hearing things like *Jeanne d'Arc*. Again. One way ticket to the loony bin — or sometimes to the stake. She wouldn't rave, she would simply quietly go insane. And if she did — who would notice? Maureen might, but not Camena, not now.

Camena's strangeness continued out of school. She never wanted to come out with Tell any more. She stayed at home, shut up in her bedroom with her books. What was she *doing*, while Tell went slowly mad?

It crossed Tell's mind that Camena might be undertaking some sort of extension programme, but if so, why the mystery? She had told Tell when she had joined Mensa, so why not tell her this time? Unless the extra study meant that Camena was transferring to another school. She might keep that quiet, for fear of what Tell would say. And what *would* Tell say?

'Don't leave me? Please don't go?'

She wouldn't be so childish, she hoped. She had always known they would be parted sometime, for just as it was certain Camena would go to university, it was equally certain that Tell would not. Tell's marks were no more than respectable, and accusing Camena of elitism would be unfair. Camena *was* elite, and that was that.

'Let's go shopping,' said Tell on Monday. She was clinging to normality by her fingernails by now. 'There are big sales this week.'

'I can't.'

'You're not getting one of your migraines, are you? Your eyes look okay.'

'No. I can't come, that's all.'

'Grounded?'

That was a joke, but Camena didn't laugh. 'Sort of. Sorry, Tell.'

Camena *was* sorry, in a vague sort of way, but just now she hadn't the time and energy to pursue her friendship with Tell. She hoped Tell would still be there for her when this was all over, but she wasn't banking on it. Camena knew how fragile friendship could be. Just like a house of cards.

House of cards. Gerhardt, and his endless games of solitaire.

'You cheat,' Camena had observed, watching him narrowly. 'You're fast, but I saw you nick the queen from underneath.'

'I needed her,' said Gerhardt.

'It's still cheating. Where's the challenge in that?'

'She was locked away.'

'You should have left her there!' she'd told him severely. 'If you must play games of chance you have to leave it to chance. That's only logical.'

'Sometimes her rescue is part of the challenge. It must be done without disturbing the cards dealt later in the hand.

Avoiding paradox.' He'd swept the cards together and shoved the deck in his pocket — it was the deck he always used, slick and new. He never seemed to play anything but solitaire, and he often cheated in that way. This proclivity didn't seem to fit his character. She wished she could discuss it with Tell. Tell would probably put her finger on Gerhardt's reasons right away. She was very good at that.

'You ought to be a psychologist,' Camena had told her once.

'Ugh!' said Tell. 'Too much study. Besides, I read a book by a shrink once.'

'And?'

'And the bloke was seriously nuts. He gave these little kids some play-dough and spied on what they made.'

'So?'

'They made *sausages*,' said Tell. 'And he thought they were making you-know-whats! I ask you! *All* kids make sausages with play-dough. It's sort of a rule of nature.'

Camena almost smiled wondering what Tell's shrink would have made of Gerhardt's habit of cheating. Perhaps it meant no more than the play-dough sausages. Everyone had a vice or two, and if Gerhardt's sins went no further than cheating himself at cards, she could handle that. It wasn't as if it affected her.

'I can't come out.' That's what she'd said to Tell, over and over since the first week of term. If Tell chose to think she was grounded, well and good. Or so Camena told herself, but the unspoken lie was nibbling and chiselling at the foundations of Tell-and-Camena all the same. A chip here, a nibble there. If too much was whittled away there'd be nothing left to rebuild. By the end of term Tell might have stopped making allowances and found another friend. That would be a pity.

Intellectually, she could leave Tell behind, but for intellectual challenge she could always contact Mensa. There was more to a friendship than a meeting of minds. There was warmth and loyalty, support and companionship ... besides, Lindall and Sister Pat would bother her if she had no obvious friends. Lindall would worry because Camena was family. Sister Pat would worry because it was her job and her vocation. Warmth and understanding overflowed from Sister Pat, but Camena wanted none of that. Tell was the one she wanted, because Tell didn't need a reason to care. She just did.

And Tell acted as her interpreter, because Tell understood ordinary people. Not surprising, since she was one of them herself.

Gerhardt wasn't ordinary, and neither was the news he had brought. Sometimes Camena wished she had told him to get lost. Sometimes she woke in the night and panicked about the news, then woke to the morning and wondered at her night-time self. Gerhardt's tale was so totally unbelievable, like something out of a thriller. Things like this just didn't happen. She was living a giant question and the strain was beginning to bow her down.

'Can't I discuss it with Tell?' she'd asked Gerhardt at lunchtime.

'No-one.' He shuffled his cards, and the tiny slithering sound was so familiar she scarcely even noticed it anymore.

'Why not? Are you making it up?' Even to her own ears she sounded hopeful, and Gerhardt gave her a strange glance.

'No. *Ich bedauere sehr.*'

'*Ger*hardt! English! People will think you're showing off. That's what Tell says to me.'

'I am very sorry,' he translated, apparently bored. He spoke English most of the time with a perfect Catholic

College accent, which made the perfection of his German, French and Spanish accents all the more remarkable. There was no telling which language was his native tongue, but sometimes Camena doubted it was English. His vocabulary was a little too correct. He never used the easy slang and profanity of the other boys his age, and she had the impression that when he paused to consider he was translating in his mind. She was fluent in a number of languages herself, and it intrigued her to find someone similarly gifted. Tell used doubtful French and a scatter of German expletives, but that wasn't the same as fluency.

'What's going to happen?' Camena asked Gerhardt more than once.

'I have explained as far as I can.'

'But — how long before it *does* happen? I'm tired of this. I want to get back to normal. Tell must think I'm going almonds or Brazil,' she joked.

'*Comprehendez nyet...*'

'Nuts,' explained Camena. 'She'll think I'm going nuts. How long before it happens?'

'Who knows? We must be ready.' He smiled, as if at an impatient child, and changed the subject, and no amount of asking would bring her more information. Gerhardt was like a stone god, all knowing and no saying, and lashing out at him would only bruise her hands. Perhaps he was lying, perhaps not. She didn't know. Even when she ran all the facts through her internal computer the result was inconclusive. She had insufficient data.

Too much knowledge would be dangerous, according to Gerhardt. She must take care, and wait, and trust, and none of them came easily.

'And I can't put it to Tell?'

'No.'

'Why not, Gerhardt? I don't want to hurt her feelings. I want her to know.'

He frowned, considering. They were leaning side by side on the college fence, and the chain mesh was imprinting the backs of Camena's legs. Gerhardt, in his regulation wool trousers, seemed hardly aware of the discomfort and his arm, where it brushed Camena's, was warm and solid. She moved away a little, not liking the contact. 'Why not?' she asked again, sensing a chink in his stone veneer.

'Dangerous.'

'For Tell? For me? For *you*?'

'For us all. For more folk than you can possibly imagine, Camena . . . and besides, she wouldn't understand. She has a literal mind, and she still gives credence to bureaucracy.'

'No she doesn't. She's always going on about things.'

'*Ja*. Her commonsense tells her something is wrong, or that this official or that politician is lying. Then she thinks; "But if that were so, why has no-one confronted this person?" She turns this around and reasons; "No-one has confronted this person, therefore there can be nothing really wrong." So she accepts what she is told.'

'You've got her all wrong, and you're asking *me* to accept what I'm told,' said Camena sharply.

'Whether you believe me or not, you know it will do no harm to take care, *ja*? If I've told you a lie and you believe it, the worst you will suffer is disappointment. If I've told you the truth and you discount it, you may suffer disaster.'

'What about Tell? Isn't she in danger?'

'Tell is not the target, Camena. You are. If you speak to her, she may make some rash move that will endanger us all.'

That was all he would say. And so, philosophically, Camena allowed the foundations of Tell-and-Camena to be chipped away a little more.

'People will think I'm really horrible if I only go round with you,' she told Gerhardt. 'So will I.'

'You know better than that. As for others, they will think we are so-so —' Gerhardt touched his palms together and rocked them from side to side.

'Get out,' said Camena uncomfortably.

'Is it so difficult to imagine?'

'*Yes*. So don't get any ideas. This is strictly business, Gerhardt,' Camena said, alarmed.

'Have no fear,' said Gerhardt. 'If I harmed you I would be a dead man. *Timor mortis conturbat me.*'

It was an extravagant claim, but it didn't sound as if he were joking. And perhaps, as the Latin phrase implied, it became one of his calling to be aware of death.

After rejecting Tell's invitation to suss out the sales, Camena sat in the garden, her Biology notes open on her lap. 'Blood-and-Guts' she and Tell called Biology between themselves. Camena hated it. Balls and sockets, cells and striated muscle. It was all disgusting, and so was the sheep's lung she had had to dissect. Still warm and steaming with the odour of the abattoirs ... she wished she could take extra Maths or Physics instead of learning about lungs and livers and lobes.

Superstitiously, she looked up and down the footpath outside the garden. Gerhardt was nowhere, but she knew if she set foot outside her garden gate he would be there. The thought was claustrophobic, but oddly intriguing. Her sister was weeding the garden.

'If you cleared the whole bed before you planted you'd save time,' observed Camena.

'I know,' said Lindall gloomily. 'I hate digging out last year's plants, though. You studying *again*, Cammie?'

Camena nodded.

'Why don't you give it a rest and go out for a bit?'

'I don't need a rest.' She supposed she should feel guilty, keeping things from her sister, but Lindall was only an adopted sister, after all.

Lindall frowned and then plopped down in front of the pansy bed, tugging ineffectually at a stand of oxalis.

'Linnie —'

'Mmm?'

'Linnie, do you think there's a chance my birth father will ever look for me?'

'Your *father*, Camena?' Lindall sounded poleaxed. 'Why — why should you suddenly think of that?'

'Just because.'

'I mean,' said Lindall doubtfully, 'I could understand it if you wondered if your birth *mother* ever thought of you, but fathers hardly ever do. Sometimes, they don't even know they *are* fathers, but mothers always know they're mothers. Stands to reason — unless of course they've been told their babies died. You sometimes hear about that happening in the past.'

'Forget it,' said Camena. 'Just forget it, okay?'

Tell went shopping by herself, but even at sale prices the clothes were beyond her means. She had known they would be, but going round the sales was just something she and Camena always did. Tell tried on a narrow slip dress in a brown print; tunic straps; a scooped neckline, a fluid, ankle-length skirt. It would have looked fabulous on Camena, but on Tell it hung apologetically, cruelly outlining her bony hips and slightly rounded stomach.

'Women are *meant* to have rounded tummies.' Maureen said that, but Tell wasn't a woman yet. The models in teenage magazines were often fifteen or so, and they always had flat stomachs. Clear skins and sleek thighs, too. It wasn't fair. If it wasn't natural, why did the magazines bother to pretend?

Sadly, Tell put the dress back on the rack and slunk out of the shop. It was no fun doing the sales without Camena. She might just as well have spent the time revising, but by the time she'd put in six hours slog at school and another two hours of Maths, Blood-and-Guts (with the good bits glossed over) and tenses or sustained development for homework, Tell's brain felt like day-old bread-and-butter pudding. And what good did it all do anyway?

In Community Service Week she had visited a widow, Mrs Granger. One whole wall of Mrs Granger's unit had been lined with wooden carvings, sleek as silk, sensuous and glorious. Tell had caught her breath with admiration, her hands reaching out to touch, to stroke and admire.

'All my husband's work,' said Mrs Granger. 'He's no longer with me, unfortunately.'

But in a way he was. Tell thought he must have put a good deal of his soul into the carving, and she could sense his presence in the room. Not as a ghost. *The deed is the man.* It wouldn't be so bad to die, leaving such a beautiful legacy. Surely the great artists and sculptors were as alive today as they had ever been while they breathed.

Later at home, Tell thought about that. If she died, what would be *her* legacy? She'd spent more than nine years doing Maths and English, Blood-and-Guts, PE and Australian

Studies, Medieval France and all the saints. She had made nothing beautiful, produced nothing original. Her friendship with Camena was the best thing she had, and that was sliding away. And all she had to look forward to was the rest of Year Ten and that was pretty boring.

'Year Ten's exciting,' said Maureen, grimly determined and not believing a word of it.

'Year Ten's a pain,' said Tell. 'I want to live.'

'You get to take Electives, and widen your horizons — you're given added responsibility.'

'It sucks.'

'*Where the bee sucks, there suck I,*' said Maureen. It sounded vaguely obscene, but Tell knew she was only quoting Shakespeare. Instead of capping the quote as she would have done with Camena, she dropped her head down on the kitchen table and moaned. That seemed to make Maureen feel better. Presumably she'd rather have Tell moaning than answering back. 'Why don't you go to the pool with Cammie?' Maureen asked.

'She'll be studying,' said Tell to her inner left elbow. 'Or something.'

'Well — I suppose you can't live in one another's pockets forever.' Maureen sounded brisk but comforting, and Tell felt herself slipping back into childhood. It was odd, the way it sometimes happened. One minute she'd be her usual teenaged self, prickly, bolshie, bored. The next, she'd revert without warning to the time when Maureen had known all the answers and provided them ready-made for Tell's consumption. She plopped her chin on her forearms and looked up under her brows. 'It's weird, Maureen. Camena's stuck inside studying all the time and it's only term one. She wouldn't even come to the sales. And it isn't that essay for

English, because we're not having English Wednesday after all. It's Activity Day — remember — and we're missing the last morning period.'

'Maybe she's doing special extension work.'

Since that was what Tell had concluded herself, there wasn't any way she could disagree. 'I thought you disapproved of elitism?' she said slyly.

'In general, I do,' said Maureen, 'but Cammie doesn't parade it, and it's probably a case of use it, or lose it, with brains. What I *do* disapprove of is these so-called "activities". Swanning off on a yacht — where's that going to get you?'

If Tell had heard Maureen sounding off about activities once she'd heard her twenty times. If she'd explained it once, she'd explained it twenty times. Nevertheless, she tried once more. 'Activities broaden our experience. When else would *I* ever get a chance to get on a yacht?'

'Exactly. So why make yourself dissatisfied?'

'It isn't a posh yacht. It's a training vessel and it offered St Sav's a free trial. They . . . oh,' she finished in a rush of irritation as Maureen's face set, 'what's the use? If you don't want my experience broadened, I'll tell David instead.'

An empty taunt, because David, (who was paying the school fees, after all) wouldn't approve either.

'Seasickness broadens nothing, but study does!' said Maureen. 'Look at me!'

'Night-school's different. You want to go to school. We've got to. You've already done lots of other things.'

'Most of which I regret.'

Like having me, thought Tell. Like getting the dog. Like marrying David. Like getting yourself trapped into playing chauffeur, Saturdays and Wednesdays.

Maureen had found her own answers in divorcing David. She hadn't found Tell's. But Maureen wasn't ready to finish the conversation yet. 'Perhaps study's not the only thing on Cammie's mind. Who's the boy I've seen her with? Tall, blue eyes, nice looking ... Quite a hunk — or is it spunk?'

'His name's Watchman,' mumbled Tell. 'Gerhardt Watchman.'

'Pretty yummy, if you like them intense — though I'd have thought him a bit too old for Cammie. Year Twelve? Or has he left school?'

'Year Ten. And he's a pain,' said Tell coldly. 'He's always *there*.'

'I suppose you feel he's taking Cammie away from you?'

'*Maureen*! Cut it out, okay?'

'It's always rough when your best friend gets a boyfriend, unless you get one first,' mused Maureen. 'I remember when I was in B Class — Year Ten you call it now —'

'He's not her boyfriend,' said Tell firmly. 'He's her companion. Sort of like a dog. A dog that plays cards with himself.'

'Now I've heard it all.'

'Next she'll have him on a collar and lead and she'll be buying him little tartan overcoats and taking him for walkies round the block.'

'Estelle Clancy! You're jealous.'

'I'm not jealous, I'm amused.' She hoped.

'I wouldn't be too amused about that one,' said Maureen. 'He's got that look.'

'Huh?'

'Intense, like I said. Get an idea in that one's head, you'd never get it out. The stake or bust.'

'See?' said Tell smugly. 'I told you he was a *dog*. Get it? *Steak. Dog.*'

Maureen gave up then and Tell was glad. It was only four-thirty, so she decided to go swimming. Might as well wring some more mileage out of her season ticket because the pool closed at the end of March. A pity, for Tell loved to swim. Kestrel Bay was considered dangerous, but in the local pool she could feel like a dolphin, hovering between seabed and surface, fish and humankind. When the swimming season ended she'd be beached and grounded for nine long months.

The route to the pool led past Camena's house in Galah Street. Camena had said she couldn't come, but she might be persuaded, so Tell dawdled a little. Her hopes were rewarded by the sight of Camena sitting on the porch with her book on her lap, idly watching her sister Lindall weed the garden.

'Want to come to the pool?' called Tell.

Camena jumped. 'Sorry, Tell. I can't. I'm —'

'Busy,' said Tell heavily. 'You look it.'

'Yes, go on Cammie!' urged Lindall. She actually got up and brushed off her knees and chivied her sister in to fetch her swimming things. 'I'm glad you dropped by, Tell,' she said with a grin. 'Cammie's driving me nuts, hanging around the house all the time with her nose in that book. If she doesn't watch out, she'll strain her brain.'

Tell mumbled agreement. She felt uneasy with Lindall, who was an adult but not a parent, a bubble blonde in tight shorts who treated her young husband like an amusing pet. Lindall had been a Year Six kid when Tell and Camena had been in Infants, and Tell could remember her always laughing, always flitting about with a flock of other girls, pretty, carefree and popular. She'd hardly changed, despite being orphaned at eighteen and married before she was twenty.

'Too much study's bad for the soul,' continued Lindall. 'No wonder she gets migraines.'

'She doesn't, often,' said Tell fairly.

'She'll probably have ulcers before she's forty.' Lindall went back to grubbing in the pansy bed — a butterfly woman who managed to be content with very little.

Lindall worked part time in the supermarket, where her cheerful manner brightened the days for countless senior citizens. Tell had seen her in action, dealing capably with packages and runaway oranges, swift and efficient but never in a hurry.

If Lindall was a butterfly, Tell thought, then Camena was a moth, dark, secretive, with a bloomy skin and hair that absorbed the light ... Tell shook her head. If Camena was a moth, *she* was an earnest caterpillar, humping grimly along the path laid out for her by the clash of her parents' oddly-assorted genes.

David the perfectionist, cold, clever and abrupt as steel. Maureen the slapdash, mercurial, and untidy. There was enough of David in Tell's make-up to make her impatient with fools, and enough of Maureen to make her goals recede when something more attractive beckoned. Enough of Maureen to make her untidy, enough of David to make her feel guilty about that. Because of her parents, Tell was usually at war with Tell, and, unlike her parents, the two sides of Tell could not file for a divorce and go their separate ways.

Lucky Camena, adopted as an infant.

Bad luck that her de Courcey parents had died so soon, good luck that she still had Lindall, however little they had in common. Without Lindall, Camena might have ended up in foster homes, and she never would have fitted in.

Tell wondered if Camena still daydreamed of finding her *real* parents, as she had in primary school. If so, she kept it pretty quiet. Tell knew she had registered with an adoption information agency a couple of years before, but apparently neither of her birth parents had had themselves listed, so the trail had stopped there.

Camena came out of the house. 'Let's swim,' she said shortly to Tell. 'I want to be back before dinner . . .'

Out of the gate, three paces along the footpath — and Gerhardt Watchman came around the corner and fell into step. Tell scowled. This expedition to the pool was hers — Gerhardt had no part of it. He hadn't been invited. Unless Camena had telephoned him while she was inside getting changed? And where were his towel and swim briefs? And did he know it cost a dollar? Tell had a season ticket, but Camena always paid on the spot, reckoning a ticket would have been false economy since she rarely wanted to swim.

Piss off, Watchman! thought Tell fiercely. She shot him a glance from beneath her lowered brows and was pleased when his feet stuttered on the pavement. The evil eye was at the top of its form. And she wasn't even hearing things today.

Gerhardt picked up the static of Tell's dislike from the beginning and knew she would be trouble.

His brief from Moss had been simple.

(1) *Observe Camena de Courcey.*

It had taken years of preparation, but at last Gerhardt had come back to Cockatoo. Although he had been well-coached in what to expect, there was a gulf between theory and practice, and a practice run would have increased the risks to an unacceptable degree. 'I should meet other Recoverees,' he'd suggested, but Moss had disagreed. None was currently available, said Moss, and, besides, each prospect was unique. Gerhardt had hoped to visit Jens before he left, but Moss had been against that too. Jens might have fostered Gerhardt as a baby, but, said Moss, that was long ago and far away. A garment that was once out-grown would never fit again. The thing to do was discard it and put on a new one.

'Always face forward, Fostern, even when you are going back,' said Moss, and laughed at his own small joke.

And, most of the time, Gerhardt had heeded Moss's advice. Then he had had his encounter with Jens after all, and it had not been at all the way he expected. The meeting had taken place at Moss's unit and had been initiated by Jens himself. It had been highly shocking and unpleasant, for Jens had broken one of the codes he had always taught Gerhardt to hold sancrosanct.

Once at St Saviours, things had fallen into place for Gerhardt. He had located the subject, and had verified a great deal of information about her family and friends. And all of it had served to underline her suitability for his purpose.

(2) *Prepare to Recover prospect.*

Think of it as a rescue, Moss had said, during the later stages of indoctrination. Think of it as a salvage, a kindness to the prospect.

Gerhardt had accepted that part of the brief quite happily, believing it really was for the best. Best for the prospect. Best for his own society. It was not only Moss who said he should always act for the best. Jens had said so too, long ago. And this was the best for everyone.

He had believed that, and he still did believe, and if he felt increasingly uneasy it was no fault of his preparation. Camena de Courcey was just as he had been told, and so was

St Saviours and the wider society. It was just that he hadn't expected everyone to be so *real*. Names on a screen, figures on a chart — each had fitted neatly into the assignment. But now these names were wrapped in flesh. He hadn't expected to like these people. He hadn't expected to feel anything at all. Sister Pat, the sweet-faced nun who taught Personal Development, had come as a real surprise, a rather unwelcome one. Gerhardt could not remember his mother, but if, in his loneliest days, he had yearned for one, he might have chosen Sister Pat. He was too old now. The time for a mother was gone, and he couldn't remember his father either. In all his life there had been just Jens, and then, more lately, Moss. Jens had been kindly, once, but that had changed. Jens had let him down.

The name of the college amused Gerhardt. *He* was a saviour. Saviour of Camena de Courcey and, perhaps, in a small way, of the destiny of the human race. That was the way Moss looked at it, and Moss had been in the business from the very beginning. This Recovery must go well, for Moss's sake as well as his own. The programme was shaky and just one more loss to RI-P would spell its end.

(3) *Establish your identity.*

He had chosen to call himself Gerhardt Watchman. The surname was a harmless conceit, and he chose the first name because it hinted at foreign or partly foreign parentage. Oh, he was foreign all right, more foreign than anyone at St Saviours could possibly imagine, but he had to be accepted in the school community, and his name and its connotations provided him with a ready-made excuse if he said or did something out of line.

Gerhardt Watchman. Fifteen years, ten months. (A lie.) Newly transferred from another school in another state.

(Another lie.) Later, they might try to trace him. They wouldn't have much luck.

(4) *Befriend the prospect. Become her close companion.*

That had been a little more difficult, for he had no experience in making friends. He had tried charm, but Camena de Courcey was not susceptible to charm. She was not attracted to him, and her body language warned that she would not respond to physical overtures. He had had to take the more devious course, and construct a story to account for his presence. Fortunately the facts had been available, and had lent themselves easily to his task. He had mixed a little truth with a lot of lies, and had come up with a story she appeared to accept.

The only one who didn't accept the situation was Estelle Clancy. Tell was the stumbling block, the tenacious terrier-friend who could blow the whole operation out of the water.

The fact that Camena had no blood ties should have made her the perfect candidate for Recovery, but her bond with her friend was abnormally strong. Their relationship was beyond Gerhardt's experience, but since Moss's detailed briefing had touched on the Clancy name only in passing, he regarded Estelle as a certain peripheral. Unfortunately, she declined to stay on the edge.

(5) *Watch and wait.*

Gerhardt was waiting, and he was impatient. Time crawled by and he knew he was growing careless, distracted more and more by Camena's friend. His business here was deadly serious, but it had its lighter moments, and many of them had been provided by Tell's hostility. He knew he should not, but he couldn't resist teasing her. He couldn't resist playing along the edges of her latent telepathy — a telepathy of which she seemed quite unaware. He had been startled to receive her random sendings, and had responded in kind; tossing occasional mental comments in her direction while otherwise impersonating a contemporary Year Ten St Saviours College student in every particular. How could it matter, in the end? Soon, Tell Clancy would be nothing but a memory to himself *and* Camena.

Oddly, considering the trouble she caused him, Gerhardt found himself regretting that. He *must* stop annoying her — but somehow, he could not. He tried to distance her from Camena, but found himself wanting her attention, thinking of her sometimes with regret. And that, for someone of his calling, was dangerous. Peripherals were forbidden game.

(6) *Act.*

He would act when he must. He didn't expect to enjoy it. A job well done was reward enough, for the cause he served was working for the future and had little regard for the personal opinions of its cogs, especially anonymous cogs such as the one who had chosen to call himself Gerhardt Watchman.

'Think of it as a rescue,' said Moss, and Moss knew best.

Urgent! Require final briefing. Options, nyet, to Trinity Street! That was Jens's voice in his head; Jens, whose place was *not* to give orders to him. Not any more.

'His part in your life is over. Ignore him now.' Moss again having the final word. Verbally, since his telepathic powers were limited.

It wasn't far to the pool. Just along three streets lined with wraggle-taggle gardens, leggy and browning in the ambience of early autumn. A few pansies, heavy purple velvet petunias, the roses gone to hips, their leaves faintly touched with rust and mildew. The grass was crisped on the ends but an autumn rain would set it right — that's what Maureen would have said, thought Tell.

David, distrusting nature as he distrusted most things, would have turned the hose on the garden a week ago.

The tip of Silicon Peak, clearly visible beyond the town, was hazy. Maureen was certain that meant rain. David said it meant nothing but smog, which was why he had moved out of town.

Tell put away the thought of her father. If she had to put many more thoughts under wraps today she'd be a howling whirling void empty of thought and — 'Nature abhors a vacuum,' she said aloud, and stepped deliberately onto Camena's shadow-shoulder.

Last year, Camena would have capped the quote with a silly snatch of jingle from a vacuum cleaner advertisement, but today she made no reply. Chastened, Tell returned to her contemplation of the asphalt under her feet. It was so hot it seemed to be melting slightly, as if someone had spilt treacle there the week before, and Tell could hear the faint suck-slap of her and Camena's sandals. She looked spitefully at Gerhardt's shadow, and wished she had the guts to jump on it, hard. It looked almost palpable, as if it would trip her if she tried. Perhaps Gerhardt's shadow was the substance, and if you scotched the shadow Gerhardt would wither and die.

Nyet. Im gegenteil.

The back of Tell's neck prickled and her cheeks drained in the familiar touch of panic. She felt a lurch in the pit of her stomach. She was going nuts and the thought made her physically sick.

The shadow of the old Bank of Perth fell across them and Tell felt the coolness like a phantom wall. The sauna heat of March lingered on her skin, but the bricks had drunk the warmth. When the sun went down they would exhale it, remaining warm to the touch until after nine o'clock. Then they would cool like a corpse and be stiff and chill in the morning. She trailed her fingertips along the bricks, warm and rough and greedy for sunlight. She forced her mind to consider the bricks, to connect with her fingers instead of her guts and the treacherous inner voices.

Perhaps she was too full of dark thought to allow for the automatic process of walking, perhaps the strap of her last-year's sandal (never too reliable) came loose. It was almost as if someone had pushed her — impossible, since they were walking three abreast. Whatever the reason, Tell found one shin inexplicably slapping into the calf of her other leg as she stumbled and sprawled directly across Gerhardt's path. His arm came out to steady her, and she flushed, as if she'd done it on purpose. Her vague fears mingled with a surge of suspicion. There was something weird about Watchman. No other Year Ten boy of her acquaintance would have saved her just like that. All the others would have either sprung aside in terror in case they were seen to be touching a girl, or else they'd have made a job of catching her. Gerhardt had steadied her with the automatic, unthinking gesture of a much older brother.

There was something about Gerhardt that didn't ring quite true, but who was she to cast aspersions on someone else? *She* was the one who was losing her grip on reality. *She* was the one who was hearing things, and losing her best friend.

Limping a little, ears burning as if with an allergy, mind cold with fear, Tell hurried on.

The pool was a disappointment, choked with kids from the primary school. Tell made an enormous effort to jerk herself into gear. She flashed her pass at the gate, and went to change. She twitched irritably at the bottom of her bathers, which were giving her a wedgie. They'd fitted perfectly the week before, but now the cut-out at the front revealed a bulge, so she wrapped a towel around her like a sarong.

Gerhardt and Camena were by the pool, and Gerhardt apparently couldn't be bothered with the change room, for he was simply peeling down to his swim briefs on the edge of the pool. And *briefs* was the word! Tell gave him one horrified look and turned her back. All the other boys were wearing saggy shorts with draw-strings. Gerhardt was like a member of another species.

Camena sat on the edge of the pool and dangled her feet unenthusiastically.

'Come on, wussie!' said Tell, and sprang up and out in a dive. But even as her fingertips cleaved the water she knew she'd been careless. Some tiny shift of balance or angle had gone wrong and she was going to hit the water in a painful and embarrassing belly flop.

Wham! Feeling sick, Tell surfaced, and pressed the water out of her eyes with the heels of her hands. Her stomach and thighs stung fiercely. Who would believe water could be so *hard*? She hadn't made such a clumsy entry in years!

'You okay, Tell?'

'Fine,' said Tell, biting off the word. The shock was passing, so she swam over to the side of the pool and anchored her forearms over the smooth, fibreglass rim, kicking rhythmically, not so much for support as to wear out the still-smarting pain. 'Aren't you coming in, Cam?' She tried to sound conciliatory, to make up for snapping before.

Camena ducked as one of the Year Seven kids dived in from behind, his body flashing over hers as a horse flashes over a hurdle.

'Arretez!' yelled Gerhardt angrily.

A few heads twisted around to look, and Camena gave him an exasperated glance.

Gerhardt knew he was getting sloppy. Teasing Tell Clancy was one thing, blurting out the wrong language aloud was another. But nobody took much notice. Presumably the other swimmers thought he had used a new swear word. Gerhardt smiled tightly, aware that Tell was watching him. Still leaning on her forearms, her legs making oddly graceful patterns as she trod water, she was looking straight at him. Her eyes were a strange green-grey, the colours shifting with reflections from the water. She had excellent bone structure, thought Gerhardt, if you looked beyond the uncompromising brows and the faintly roman nose. Her front teeth were very slightly misaligned and her hair lay on her shoulders like water weed. She had courage, too — he had felt the jar of the explosion of pain as she hit the water but she had contrived to hide it. Just as she contrived to hide the fear that was tugging at her mind.

Tell Clancy . . . his gaze met hers with unwilling respect, and more, and temptation whispered in his mind. During his rare contacts with other HI-Qs he was forced by their attitudes to be circumspect, but here at Cockatoo he was a free agent, acting autonomously, dependent on his own decisions, his own whim.

Camena de Courcey was his priority. He must defend her life, if necessary, with his own, for she had more potential value than he. But Camena, although appealing and pleasant company, could never be more to Gerhardt Watchman than a responsibility.

He could almost wish Moss had sent someone else to Recover Camena, but as Moss had pointed out, he was the logical choice. Of all available operatives, experienced or not, Gerhardt's profile had most nearly fitted the ideal of a fifteen-year-old schoolboy. And his suitability for the role was not an accident. Moss had been planning the snatch for years — certainly since well before he had removed Gerhardt from Jens's control.

Question; what kind of person would be most likely to appeal to Camena de Courcey, while fitting smoothly into life at St Saviours College?

Answer; a middle-class Australian boy of understated intelligence, moderate sporting prowess and aesthetic appeal. That was what Moss had demanded, and that was what Moss had got, taking the raw material of a dazzled ten-year-old and moulding that material into the form required. And Gerhardt knew he performed well in the role, and would continue to do so, as long as he stayed alert and unemotional.

'Emotions are an inconvenience,' said Moss's voice in his memory. 'They have no place in the civilised HI-Q. Leave them to retrogrades like Beta Jens. He is a primary example of how emotions turn sour.'

So Gerhardt had conditioned himself to neither feel nor express personal interest in Camena, but Tell Clancy was another matter. If he charmed Tell Clancy, he might gain unique experience, and so might she. A little warmth, a little happiness to remember. A little of the things his kind never had — should never even wish to have. It was an intriguing thought, but, regretfully, he put away temptation. Not only was it strictly forbidden by the codes and tenets of Hub HI-Q, but it was also unfair. Whatever this girl's destiny, it did not, could not, include a relationship with Gerhardt Watchman.

Deliberately, he turned away from Tell. The less he had to do with Tell Clancy the better, for her, for him and for the programme. And he *must* stop teasing her. *Moce, auf wiedersehen*, he thought, with regret.

Tell blinked. For an oddly intense five seconds she and Gerhardt had stared at one another, she probing, scrambling for a foothold, he considering, calculating. They had stared, she had seen him decide against whatever it was he had contemplated, and turn away.

She told herself she was relieved, but there was some regret as well. There was more to this companion of Camena's than anyone knew and Tell wished she could graze the veneer.

Mad. Nuts. Both of them, probably. She wasn't usually the susceptible type. She never drooled over pretty boy singers or cunningly-lit movie stars. And Gerhardt Watchman had better watch out. He was Camena's friend, and he had no right to look at Tell like that. He had no right to consider, to reject, and to look so disappointed. He had no right to say goodbye before he had even said hello. Mad. Mad. Definitely nuts.

Danger. Tell shivered, and hitched herself out of the water. She felt too shaky to swim properly today. Too shaky and afraid.

She made another effort to tug herself into her normal mind-set. Camena was standing up, wet to the calves, but no more. That was so like Camena; it had happened over and over again. Forever paddling in the shallows while Tell plunged in.

'Wuss,' said Tell affectionately. 'You had no intention of coming for a swim, did you? You ought to learn properly, you know. What if you fall off the boat on Activity Day?'

'Someone would rescue me. Probably you. And since you're getting out, it doesn't seem worth getting wet.'

'Who said I'm getting out?' Tell spun round and tossed a challenge at Gerhardt, addressing him directly for almost the first time. 'Come on Watchman, let's see what you're made of! Race you to the end of the pool.'

'And back,' said Gerhardt.

Tell was so surprised to be answered that she found herself meeting his gaze again. Dark blue eyes, opaque. She couldn't tell what he was thinking. 'You're on!' she said. 'Ready, steady — go!'

She sprang up and out in her best racing dive, aware that Gerhardt was diving beside her, shoulder to shoulder. Excitement gripped her; the excitement of a challenge she faced so rarely. A serious swimmer willing to take her on.

He was taller, stronger; she was almost certain he was older than he said. He had a longer reach, more economical movement — he must beat her, and all she could hope was to escape humiliation. Tell fell into rhythm, straight as a torpedo, shoulders rotating smoothly as her hands planed and scooped the water. She touched the end of the pool and tumble-turned, catching a flurry of green water as Gerhardt tumbled ahead of her. Her hands were level with his heels, and she couldn't lose any more ground, not and keep her self-respect.

But I'll give you a run for your money, she thought.

She had a moment of pure joy, as her body took over. She felt she could swim forever, and perhaps, perhaps, he could swim forever too ...

And then it was over. He had won, and was lifting himself from the water, to sit, breathing easily, on the tiles. Once more his eyes met Tell's, as she shook back her hair. She was aware of her heartbeat, visible beneath the severe navy swimsuit. Almost, she put out her hands to receive his congratulations.

'You swim well,' he said.

Again there was regret in his eyes and a goose walked over Tell's grave.

She had put up a damned good showing. Why should he pity her?

Tell showered, emerging to comb her wet hair in the sun, swearing under her breath because she had cut her thumb on the rough edge of her zip. Camena, who had avoided swimming after all, looked flushed and pretty in a tie-on skirt over her swimsuit and Gerhardt, like any other boy, had simply dragged a sweat shirt over his head.

A little sourly, Tell slung her damp towel around her neck to catch the drips from her hair. Camena's hair shone like a shampoo advert, Gerhardt's was so short and thick and brown it scarcely looked wet at all. Tell was the scruffy one, and resented it, impatient with Camena for agreeing to the outing and then refusing to swim.

Tell's thumb was bleeding, so she blotted it on her damp towel. Probably crawling with microbes, but the chlorine should take care of that ... her hair and skin reeked of the stuff, even though she'd showered. 'You beat me easily,' she said to Gerhardt, trying to speak lightly, trying to regain the feeling she had enjoyed so briefly.

'You swim well,' he said again.

'I don't need your praise.'

'I know.'

Camena glanced at them, surprised.

'You could have beat me by more, if you'd wanted,' said Tell fiercely. 'You were scarcely trying at all. That's why you . . .' *I don't need your pity!*

Gerhardt shrugged.

'What are you playing at, Watchman?'

'Shut up, Tell,' said Camena. 'He beat you and that's that. Given that he's bigger and a male, you should be able to accept it. The ratio of the fastest male swimmer to the fastest female is . . .'

'Shut up!' snapped Tell. 'I don't want to hear!'

They filed out through the turnstile, Gerhardt and Tell, and Camena lagging a little behind.

The attack came out of the shadows as they passed the Bank of Perth.

It was the second attack, but this Gerhardt realised when it was already too late. The first had caused Tell's stumble, before they entered the pool enclosure. It had been a warning, a testing of the water, so to speak. If he had been fully alert at that time, he would have recognised it for what it was and left the pool another way. He could have taken Camena away while Tell was showering, boosted her over the rear fence and followed her, hurrying her home by a circuitous route and risking Tell's wrath at their desertion. If he'd recognised the warning for what it was.

Tell had tripped, before, and he had steadied her, putting it down to her adolescent clumsiness. If Camena had stumbled, he would have been alert, but it had been Tell who had tripped over nothing.

By reflex action he had steadied her. The contact had startled him, distracted him, given him ideas he never should have had; the seconds he should have spent in drawing conclusions from the incident had instead been squandered in a wholly inappropriate physical awareness of Tell Clancy. But what could he have done? It had been so very clumsy, and so very quick. He thought, afterwards, that

that first attack had been bungled as much by the enemy as by himself. It was immaterial that he had been focused on the wrong girl.

There was no bungling this second time. The new assault was swift and sharp. The speed with which it was launched, the certainty of the blow — and the fact that it was directed against Gerhardt himself — these things told him all he needed to know about its source and purpose, and as he fell in a blinding daze of pain, he cursed himself for his arrogance, for his confidence, and for allowing himself to be distracted, even so slightly, by the thing against which Moss had warned. Emotion.

To Tell the thing happened with unbelievable swiftness. The shadows of the Bank of Perth, the chill after the sunlight — her pupils had not yet adjusted to the lack of light, but she knew she saw *something*. Or someone. The person seemed to flicker into view with the speed of a camera shutter. He — or she — delivered a sharp blow to the base of Gerhardt's neck and then darted forward to catch the falling victim.

If Tell had had time to think, she would have realised she stood no chance against someone who could topple Gerhardt Watchman. Having no time, she reacted instinctively, flinging up her hands and pushing, hard. The assailant staggered, there was a gasp and the sound of running feet. Tell and Camena were left standing in the shadows, staring at one another in disbelief. Between them, face down on the ground as if he had tripped, was Gerhardt.

Tell swallowed. 'Do you th-think he's hurt?' she asked. Her voice trembled a little with reaction.

'I don't know.' Camena sounded bewildered. 'Who was that?'

'He's gone,' said Tell. 'Whoever he was.' She looked about for someone capable of dealing with the situation, but apparently no-one had seen the attack. Or else, she thought cynically, any witnesses had backed off, not wanting to become involved.

Tell paused, offering Camena the chance to act, but Camena did nothing at all. Frowning, Tell knelt on the gritty pavement. With any other Year Ten boy she might have suspected him of shamming, and have been wary of a sudden whoop or grab. Since it was Gerhardt, such a possibility never occurred to her. He was dishonest, she thought, but he would scorn to waste time on such petty deception. Whatever Gerhardt Watchman was up to was something big.

You were not supposed to move victims of injury, but it seemed unlikely he had suffered broken bones or internal injuries from that fall. Concussion, perhaps, or even brain damage, but it was more likely he had just been knocked unconscious.

'Keep an eye out, in case that creep comes back,' Tell said briskly to Camena. 'If you see him, scream your head off. Yell "Fire!" You can call for help till you're blue in the face, but people always turn out to see a good fire.' She folded her towel, lifted Gerhardt's head a fraction and worked the makeshift pad between his face and the pavement. She was conscious of a facial roughness that seemed a little out of character for a fifteen-year-old, and also that he must have gashed his cheek, for her fingertips came away shiny and red.

Blood! Hands shaking only a little, Tell wiped her hand on the damp towel before reaching for Gerhardt's left wrist. His pulse seemed reassuringly steady, though a little slower than she would have expected. The pulse in his neck was also regular, and his breathing, so far as she could tell from his prone position, was normal. What now? She could always roll him over and lift his eyelids, but that would be nothing but play-acting. She knew a fixed, dilated pupil meant trouble, but what sort of trouble? And what did one do about it? At least he wouldn't need mouth-to-mouth resuscitation.

Uneasily, she looked up at Camena. 'We ought to call the ambulance.'

'Not if he's just knocked himself out —' objected Camena.

'Been knocked out,' said Tell crisply. 'We can't just leave him here, Cam. That guy might come back for the coup de grace. Help me roll him onto his side.'

With Camena's reluctant help, she arranged Gerhardt in the coma position, then sat back on her heels, pushing her hair out of her eyes. 'Who was that creep, anyway? And why did he go for Watchman? Any ideas?'

Camena shrugged, but her eyes were wary.

'You know something, don't you?' said Tell.

Silence.

'You do. You know — or you think you know — what's going on.'

She hadn't pressed Camena before because she wanted so much to preserve their friendship. But who are you kidding? Tell asked herself roughly. If she's holding back, if she doesn't trust you, what's there to save? 'Come on, Camena!' she said sharply. 'Give! It could be important.'

Camena sighed. 'Oh — all right. But don't tell Gerhardt I told you.'

'Why not? Someone might have killed him just now. Isn't that worth telling secrets? Oh — don't fuss. His pulse is okay and he's breathing normally. I'm almost sure he's all right, but he'll probably have a headache when he wakes up. Got any of your migraine pills on you?'

'I'll tell you,' said Camena resignedly, 'but we've got to get away from here first.'

Tell raised her brows. 'Carrying him? Get real, Cam, I thought you were meant to be bright! He must weigh a good eighty kilos. Even if we *could* carry him we'd look pretty silly trying. Better go back into the pool and rouse someone up to help. Or yell until someone comes.'

Gerhardt solved their immediate problem by sitting up. There were no preliminary groans, no dubious testings of arms or legs. His hands pressed against the ground and he thrust himself up and round, blinking up at Tell as if in surprise.

'Headache, Watchman?' asked Tell pleasantly.

He touched the back of his neck, wincing a bit.

'Your cheek's grazed too,' said Tell. 'You're bleeding.'

'I know.' He pulled his face into a mirthless smile, testing the extent of the injury. 'That's nothing.'

'Very good,' approved Tell. 'Very macho. Are you going to sit there all day or do you feel like getting up?'

Gerhardt got up. 'This towel is yours?'

'Yes, and you've bled all over it — and over me. You — haven't got anything I should know about? Hep. B, perhaps?'

'Infections? Nyet. No.'

'That's all right then. Come to think of it, you do look a healthy specimen. Come on,' she said abruptly. 'Let's go to the park.'

'What for?' asked Camena. 'I want to go home, Tell. I've got to —'

'Study. Sure, Cammie, but not just now.'

As Gerhardt performed his post-trauma exercises, using auto-hypnosis to summon endorphins and to relax overstrained muscles, he was mulling over his problems. An enemy had struck, but there was another complication, closer to home. Before today, Tell Clancy had been uncertain, sullenly determined to stick with himself and Camena, piqued because she was feeling superseded. Now he felt a subtle shift in the balance of power, as if Tell would no longer be content with so little.

'I think I should go home,' he said. He had willed his circulation back to normal, now he directed the blood away from his skin and raised an uncertain hand to his face to draw attention to his pallor.

'To Casualty,' said Tell. 'You've been knocked unconscious, remember. And we ought to report that guy to the police. You got off lightly, the next one he clobbers mightn't be so lucky.'

'I tripped,' said Gerhardt. 'Didn't I, Camena?'

'Someone attacked you. We both saw him, Gerhardt,' said Camena tiredly. 'Oh — why not tell her the truth? Then she'll stop nagging.'

Gerhardt winced and touched his scraped jaw. The autohypnotic pain block was in place, and he could no longer feel the injury, but it wouldn't pay to advertise the fact. 'We should go home,' he repeated.

'All right. We'll talk at your place.'

'The park is nearer.' Gerhardt was exasperated with himself for his failure, and furious with Tell. Presumably it had been she who had short-circuited the attack. Someone must have routed the enemy, or Gerhardt would never have been left to wake where he had fallen.

The enemy. Who was he fooling? It was a RI-P operative who had attacked him, and if he had been taken out of the game at this late stage, it would have been awkward for Moss to replace him. Tell's quick action might have saved the operation, but it didn't make him any more comfortable with her presence. For a peripheral, she was taking on a much too active role.

Camena was frightened. Until now, she had only half believed Gerhardt's warnings of danger. To have seen Gerhardt struck down so easily was upsetting. She had relied on him.

'Do you think we ought to tell the police?' she said, as they entered the tall park gates.

'We're safe here,' said Gerhardt. He sat down on the dingy grass, in plain view of three mothers of toddlers and a flock of navy-clad Brownies with their cheerful leader.

'Better wipe your face,' said Tell remotely. 'You look like a road accident.'

Gerhardt dabbed at the graze. 'Ja?'

'What's going on?' asked Tell.

Camena looked uncertainly at Gerhardt, who made a gesture which, in anyone else, might have been called sulky. 'Tell her, if you must.' He turned a little away, disassociating himself from the girls.

Camena sighed. She had thought he would tell the story if it were told at all. It was going to be very difficult, making Tell believe what she only half believed herself. 'It's like a thriller,' she said nervously, and stalled. 'It's — Tell, you remember when I put down my name with the adoption people?'

'Sure.' Tell looked surprised. 'But nothing came of it, and you never mentioned it again. So what's that got to do with this?'

'Everything.' Camena clasped her knees in her arms. 'It was when we were in Year Eight, remember? Just after Mum and Dad died. I had to get Lindall's permission to register, and then the adoption people said my birth parents had never registered and so there was nothing they could do for me. They'll only help if *both* sides apply.'

'I remember,' said Tell. 'I thought you'd given up the idea.'

'I did,' said Camena. 'But now it turns out my birth father has known about me all along.'

Clearly, this was the last thing Tell had expected.

'He knew where I was,' said Camena. 'He sent Gerhardt to make contact.'

'Why?' asked Tell. 'Why not come himself? Why not register like you did?'

'He had a good reason,' said Camena stiffly. 'My father is a scientist, Tell. Quite famous in his own field, apparently. He didn't want it to get out that he had a daughter. Mad, isn't it? He's married, but not to my birth mother, and I was born after they'd been married quite a while. He didn't want to get mixed up with Lindall and Jus, so he sent Gerhardt to our school to tell me what was going on.'

Tell's mouth moved, but she said nothing aloud.

'It's *not* bullshit,' said Camena, lip-reading without difficulty.

'Not bullshit, then,' said Tell quickly. 'Just — a bit — thin. Bloody thin, in fact. Look, Cam, if all this were true, why has your father waited until now to make contact with you? And why use him as the proxy?' She pointed to Gerhardt, who was turned away, apparently admiring the petunias beyond the Brownie pack. 'You've got to see it just isn't likely.'

'My father has only just heard about what happened to Mum and Dad. While they were alive, he thought it was better to leave me in a settled environment, but now he's found out I'm —'

'Brilliant?' suggested Tell. 'Gifted and orphaned? Worthy of his name?'

'His wife couldn't have children,' went on Camena, 'and Gerhardt says he's afraid she might feel bad if she heard about me.'

'Let's say I can see her point,' said Tell. 'But I suppose it also neatly explains why he doesn't want you to come home to the bosom of the family and inherit millions. Come *on*, Cammie! I could think of a better plot than that with one hand tied behind me. And what about Watchman, here? Where does *he* come in?'

Camena was stung. She knew the story sounded fantastic, but surely Tell didn't believe she had accepted it just like that! 'I could think of a better plot too!' she snapped. 'And Gerhardt is his business partner's son. Don't you think I checked out the story? Don't you think I asked for proof? Listen, I've seen a copy of my birth certificate. And there's a letter from my father. No, two letters.'

'Delivered by Watchman, no doubt. How do you know *he* didn't write them?'

'Because he has nothing to gain,' said Camena impatiently. 'It isn't as if I were an heiress or anything. My father's a scientist, not a millionaire. There's nothing interesting about me at all, except —' She paused. Mentioning her IQ, even to Tell, seemed too much like boasting. 'And he didn't deliver them,' she added. 'They came in the mail.'

'Have you tried writing back to the address? Or ringing up?' Tell still sounded sceptical.

'He asked me not to. His wife might get upset. They've been married twenty years. And I'm only fifteen. But anyway — what's there to write? He might be my father, but I don't know him. That's not a very nice feeling.'

'Oh,' said Tell. 'There are such things as post boxes which his wife wouldn't necessarily open. But of course a PO box could belong to anyone. It isn't like a residential address.' She cleared her throat and went on more gently. 'Look, Cammie — even if this is all true — if your father is interested in you but doesn't want to stir up trouble at home — what's it got to do with the guy who just clobbered Watchman?'

Camena sighed. Tell was too sharp by half.

'Your stepmother wouldn't organise a hit on *him*,' said Tell. 'If anyone, she'd be angry at your old man for sleeping around. Or with you, for existing.'

Tell began to feel afraid. She didn't believe the story. Oh, Camena's father might well be a scientist and he might well know where she was, especially if he had money, an information grid and an old-boy network on which to call. He might even have arranged Camena's adoption in the first place. That would have been illegal, but you heard of such cases, and just because he was brilliant it didn't follow that he was scrupulous. And *was* it unscrupulous to want the best for your kid? Tell didn't know. But the rest of it didn't make enough sense.

Whether she was losing her mental grip or not, Tell could see the flaws in this scenario, loud and clear. If the guy was so afraid of his wife finding out about his illegitimate child he'd be mad to risk contacting Cammie at all, and if he *had* had an attack of conscience, why not set up a trust fund for his daughter instead of disrupting her life? Camena's habitual detachment might make her less vulnerable to this upset than some girls would have been, but *he* wouldn't know that. And if his attack had been of curiosity rather than conscience, he would have visited the school himself. He wouldn't have made contact through a schoolboy, even if Gerhardt was a lot older than fifteen. And why, having delivered his message, was Gerhardt still hanging around Camena?

'This is ridiculous,' she said. 'This is totally nuts.'

'It is, isn't it?' said Camena bleakly.

'So *why* did this guy attack Watchman? It doesn't make sense, unless the two scenarios aren't connected. I mean — maybe Watchman is who he says he is, but maybe he's got some other agenda that doesn't have anything to do with you. I can think of lots of reasons people might want to hurt him.'

'Like what?'

'Drugs?' hazarded Tell. 'Debts? An old girlfriend? Maybe he's using you as a smoke-screen — or as a bodyguard. Probably reckoned anyone out to get him would keep their distance if he was always with a girl. Probably reckons they're *gentlemen*.' She laughed. 'That's nearly as nuts as the other idea.'

'You've got it backwards,' said Camena.

'Huh?'

'*I'm* not the shield, he is.'

'You mean he's a . . .' Tell choked.

'That's right,' said Camena. 'He's a bodyguard. My father sent him to guard me because there's been a kidnapping threat.'

'Why didn't you say so before?' exploded Tell.

'Well — that's all. That's the only bit I didn't tell you.'

Tell took a deep breath. 'God, Cammie, you sure can pick 'em! *Kidnapping*? In *Cockatoo*?'

'*They* picked *me*,' pointed out Camena. 'To get at my father. His wife is safe enough — she has a security system and he can protect her openly — but I'm easy game, for them.'

'*Them* being a Middle East extremist group who have threatened to kidnap your old man's nearest and dearest and hold it to ransom because — because — because he happens to have come up with a cheap alternative to oil, right? Gotta watch those petro-dollars! Lovely, lovely. Real B-grade stuff.'

Camena winced, seeming to fold in on herself like an injured animal. 'Gerhardt was right,' she said. 'You don't believe any of it, do you? I wish I didn't. Oh, I suppose I ought to be pleased I've got a father out there, but I never asked for this. I wish none of it had ever happened. I'm going home.'

She got up, and Tell was ashamed to see her friend's hands shaking as she brushed leaves and bits of grass off her legs. She had done this to Camena with her scorn and disbelief. And she was supposed to be the one who understood! The one who shielded Camena from the ones who didn't understand. And now, in her fright and jealousy, she had spouted like a geyser.

Before she could make a move to retrieve the situation, Gerhardt had come to stand beside Camena. 'Are you ready to go now?' he asked.

'*Yes*,' said Camena.

It was an uncomfortable walk back to Galah Street, and Gerhardt spent most of it trying to come to terms with the day's developments. Camena had lost her usual placidity, and her friendship with Tell Clancy looked shaky. On the face of it, this scarcely mattered, but he found himself increasingly uneasy. Like it or not, Tell had saved his neck, and possibly saved Camena's, but she hadn't accepted the story, not for a moment. He wondered what she would do now. Would she continue to probe, and perhaps try to disprove his claims to Camena? Or would she accept defeat and back off?

What are you really playing at, Watchman?

The silent query came from Tell, and Gerhardt jumped. He had not been broadcasting his thoughts. Had she intercepted him anyway, or was it random chance that had led to that mental comment? It had been both clear and pointed, and had homed in right on target. Presumably, she thought of her sendings as normal thoughts; or perhaps as comments she would have liked to make aloud.

In his experience, around twenty per cent of the people he encountered had some telepathic powers, but few ever realised it. And only a minute proportion ever made intelligent use of their talents. For most, trying to project a thought at a selected target was about as much use as shooting an arrow at an apple in the dark. And here was Tell Clancy spattering mental comments in all directions, and apparently unaware that she was doing so.

It seemed so unusual that he was tempted to respond plainly, to open the channels further, but he remembered his resolve. He must *not* react, whatever the temptation. His abused neck muscles ached with the effort of *not* turning his head, and his mental screens clamped down, just in case.

Gerhardt saw Camena to her door. Lindall gave him an appreciative glance, and then her eyes turned uncertainly to Tell. Obviously, she was wondering which girl was the object of his interest.

'Coming in, kids?' asked Lindall.

Tell and Gerhardt exchanged measuring glances.

'No, they're not,' said Camena bluntly. 'See you, guys.'

It was an unmistakable dismissal, but Tell wasn't moving until Gerhardt did. He paused, obviously hoping she'd give up and go, but she raised her chin. She wasn't going to disappear so meekly, just to suit him. She was going to winkle out the truth, even if she needed to borrow David's shoehorn to do it. 'Going my way, Watchman?' she said.

'No,' said Gerhardt.

'Yes you are. Or I'm going yours. I'm going to stick to you like super glue. Which way?'

'My place or yours. That is the idiom, ja?'

'*Jar* yourself,' she said savagely, mispronouncing it deliberately. 'Come on then. I want the story from you. I want to know what you're up to with Camena.'

'I mean her no harm.'

'Corny. Who writes your scripts?'

'This is none of your affair, Tell Clancy.'

'Camena is none of *your* affair,' corrected Tell. 'Cammie and I have been friends forever and I won't let you wreck that with your stories. Do you get off on winding people up, or what? Who are you really and what do you want?'

'You cannot accept my word for it that I would die before I would allow harm to come to your friend?'

'You sound like a soap opera,' she said roughly.

Gerhardt lifted his hands in a gesture of surrender. 'My name is Gerhardt Watchman,' he recited.

Tell snapped her fingers and stretched out her hand. 'Birth certificate? Student card?'

Gerhardt did the same. 'You say you are Estelle Clancy. Birth certificate? Student card?'

'Point taken,' said Tell. 'What do you want with Cammie?'

'I have been sent by someone who has Camena de Courcey's best interests at heart, to protect her from a threat.'

'This someone being her father?'

'She has already told you that.'

'She told me what you told her,' corrected Tell. 'Why? Why would anyone want to kidnap her?'

'It need not be a normal kidnapping. It could be worse.'

'If that's true, why has her dad sent just you? Why haven't the police been called in? This story of yours has got more holes than Maureen's colander.'

'The police have not the capacity to guard your friend indefinitely. They don't have the resources or the personnel. No crime has been committed. Yet.'

'Nor have you the capacity,' said Tell nastily. 'Why haven't you moved in with her, if you're so concerned?'

'I would, if I could.'

'The police could, if you gave them some proof.'

'Their presence would be embarrassing to her and to her family. It would disrupt her life and draw attention to her whereabouts.'

'And we have only your word for it there's any threat at all.'

'You saw the threat today.'

'Very convincing,' said Tell. 'Except that there was just the one guy, and he didn't have any weapons. If this *threat* of yours had meant business, he'd have popped you off with a telescopic rifle, not frigged about with a Kung Fu across the neck. God, you're so transparent, Watchman! It was a set-up, wasn't it? You had your mate clobber you in front of Cammie and me just to make your story stand up. If he'd really meant to damage you, you'd have been damaged. Like cut or slashed or shot. Haven't you got anything else to say?'

'Aye,' said Gerhardt. 'The attack was real. If you hadn't moved so quickly I would have been taken.'

'Taken where?'

'Away from Camena. After that, who knows? The threat is real.'

'This,' said Tell coldly, 'is an unprofitable conversation. It proves nothing, except that you're a rotten bodyguard. If you *are* a bodyguard. You let yourself get clobbered.'

'That will not happen again.'

For the first time, Tell saw a flicker of anger in his eyes and pressed her advantage. 'Whoever heard of a fifteen-year-old bodyguard?'

'I am not fifteen,' said Gerhardt.

Tell looked at him hard. The low sunlight threw his face into relief and she saw the strong lines of his jaw. There was no childish roundness left. 'How old are you?' she asked, and even to herself she sounded interested rather than hostile.

'Old enough,' he said obliquely.

'Seventeen? Eighteen? Twenty?'

'Old enough.'

'Sometimes, Watchman, I could *kill* you,' said Tell between her teeth. 'Very happily.'

Gerhardt met her gaze and slowly, deliberately, smiled. '*Totoka mana*,' he said.

'Which is?'

'Fijian.'

'For . . . God, you're impossible! I don't believe a word you say. And get this, if you ever hurt Camena I'll assassinate you myself and damn the consequences.'

'Such love,' said Gerhardt, and Tell blushed.

'Get stuffed,' she said.

'Believe me,' said Gerhardt softly. 'The threat to Camena is very real, and it does not come from me. You, too, should be alert for danger.'

It went against his training and against his own instincts to take a peripheral even so far into his confidence, but

Gerhardt was persuaded he had no alternative. If he had tried to shut Tell out of the picture at this stage, she might have done something unfortunate. She might have gone to the police, or the school principal, or even the adoption agency on Camena's behalf. At the very least she would have agitated Camena's tranquillity.

Camena was going to be agitated soon enough, but Gerhardt hoped to keep her calm and rational for as long as he could, for her sake as well as for his. He had become fond of Camena, even above his brief of protection, and that surprised him, and frightened him, a little. Fondness was an emotion he had not felt for many years. He had thought his capacity for such feelings had faded with his memories of his childhood as Moss had promised. Evidently it had not, and he felt instinctively that to give in to such emotions now would bring him pain and danger.

He had done what seemed best, and perhaps Tell's efforts would prove as useful over the next few days as they had in the shadows by the Bank of Perth. Unprepared, she had disposed of a RI-P agent, who, admittedly, would be even less in love with the limelight than he was, so what might she achieve when forewarned? He wished he could advise her on the correct use of telepathy, but that would break the codes and be unwise. If she knew what a potent weapon it could be, she might turn it against him instead of against RI-P.

She gave him one last hard stare and went off down Galah Street, leaving Gerhardt to wait with trepidation for their next encounter, which came about on their way to school the next morning. Tell must have walked out of her way to accost Gerhardt and Camena, and sure enough, she had no intention of making things easy for him.

'Been assassinated lately?' she asked.

'No,' said Gerhardt.

'Not even by international terrorists armed with five lethal fingers?'

'No.'

'Stop it, Tell,' said Camena. 'I wish I'd never told you.'

'But you did. How are you going to explain your face, Watchman?' Her own face was firm with resolution.

Gerhardt touched his scraped cheek. 'No-one will ask.'

'How do you know?'

'No-one will ask,' said Gerhardt softly, again. He became aware that Camena was watching him curiously, and knew he was acting out of character. He never usually spoke much to Tell. He never usually spoke much to Camena, either. 'It will not happen again,' he told her. 'I will stay alert, from now on.'

'Afraid of letting something slip?'

Tell's sardonic enquiry interrupted his thoughts. He *was* afraid of letting too much slip, for he had very little time to repair such mistakes.

Perhaps if he allowed her to see something of his plans, just a little, as if by accident, she would become sufficiently intrigued to wait and see what he would do instead of rushing precipitately into trouble. She might, he thought, be persuaded to wait a week, which meant he had seven days or a little less.

Fortunately, he needed less than two.

On Wednesday at ten-past four the Recovery must take place, and so the game with Tell Clancy would end. A pity, it really was a pity. If this had been a proper game he would have relished the battle of wits.

Vale, Tell, he thought, and again he felt regret. More than regret. It hurt, and he wished he had never come to Cockatoo.

On Wednesdays, Maureen collected Tell from school and

drove her round to David's flat. The routine never varied. Tell greeted her father, had dinner, made polite conversation, watched television, spent the night and left for school next morning. The pattern had started after the divorce, and sometimes Tell thought David was bored by the visits, but he had never suggested she shouldn't come.

Whether he clung to Wednesdays because he liked routine or because he knew Maureen hated it was immaterial to Tell. She knew she would keep her Wednesdays. They were a part of her life and if the pattern were allowed to blur and skip the time would soon come when she would never see her father at all. He might care, a little, but not enough to make the effort to keep in touch, she thought.

I need to know my father, she wrote in Personal Development. *He is half my history. I owe him my past. I owe myself my future.*

That was deep. She hadn't known she felt like that until she put it into words. Maybe PD had a place in her life, after all, or perhaps it was the question mark over Camena's background that made Tell so acutely aware of her own.

Or perhaps, she reflected honestly, it was a childish desire to annoy Maureen, who hated Wednesdays so much that she nearly always contrived to 'forget' her standing duty to drive Tell to the flat and would schedule something else instead.

DAVID!!! wrote Tell on every Wednesday in the calendar one year.

Maureen lost the calendar.

'How can you lose a calendar?' snapped David when he heard.

'Easily,' said Maureen.

Tell shook her head. Impossible to believe her parents had ever decided to marry, had ever shared a bed and midnight conversations and a hope for the future.

It didn't profit Maureen to forget about Wednesdays, for by arrangement, David paid for the car's irregular services and replacement tyres. These payments, Tell understood, were meant to offset the cost of petrol and inconvenience to Maureen in chauffeuring her on the twice weekly visits. It would have been far more practical if David had made a standing arrangement with a taxi firm instead, but presumably he was still trying to organise Maureen from a distance.

This Wednesday began like any other. Tell's alarm clattered at seven-thirty, and she packed her school and Activity Day gear in her bag. Her library book, Walkman, night shirt and embroidery went in a holdall which she stowed in the boot of Maureen's car. 'It's Wednesday,' she reminded Maureen.

'Wednesday? God, is it?'

'Activity Day. David.'

Maureen groaned. 'Damn! I'm having my hair cut at four.'

'I'll get a taxi,' said Tell equably.

'You won't. David would gloat. Why he just can't move into town . . .'

'Fifty cents,' said Tell, which harked back to another of Maureen's civilised arrangements. She had always paid Tell fifty cents every time she gave in to temptation and criticised her former spouse.

'It was at least as much my fault as his that we got married,' she'd said once. 'He didn't change. Neither did I. We just got more like ourselves and less like one another.'

In recent years Tell had had few fifty cent coins come her way. Sometimes she wondered if Maureen's mental block about the Wednesday schedule was a psychological substitute for the criticisms she hardly ever made.

'No, don't take a taxi,' said Maureen. 'Catch the bus down to the salon. No — it doesn't stop. Walk. I'll take you on from there.'

'Okay,' said Tell. 'Maureen — just think! If it weren't for Wednesdays and Saturdays, and my existence, you'd never see David at all.'

'Hmmmm,' drawled Maureen, and narrowed her eyes. 'The thought *had* occurred. I wonder what the penalty for infanticide is?'

'Life sentence,' said Tell. 'It's murder, just the same.'

'You get life sentence when you have the kid,' objected Maureen. 'And why should it be murder? I created you. You're mine. If I painted a picture, would it be a crime if I destroyed it?'

'*Yes*. If you claimed the insurance.'

Maureen nodded with satisfaction. 'I'll remember that.'

'Maureen, you're awful,' said Tell.

Maureen smirked. 'I'll tell you what's awful,' she said. 'Gadding about on a yacht instead of doing Maths and French. *That*'s awful. A waste of David's hard-earned cash.'

Tell caught the school bus. She had walked to St Saviours on Tuesday, intent on Gerhardt and Camena, but today she had too much to carry. Even St Saviours, with its strong and inflexible uniform code, didn't insist that the students went down to the harbour in monogrammed blazers. Tell had brought her old shorts and a shirt of David's, battered sneakers and an ancient polar fleece jacket, as well as the camera her grandfather had given her last birthday. Her school bag looked nine months pregnant, so she had left her current library book with her night things in Maureen's car.

When she disembarked at St Saviours, Gerhardt and Camena were already at their lockers. Unusually, they were arguing in low voices. 'Trouble in Paradise?' asked Tell, and winced. She had really meant to go easy on Camena today.

'Of course not,' said Camena.

'Of course not,' agreed Tell. She glanced at Gerhardt, and was surprised to see a slight flush on his ungrazed cheek. 'Good morning, Watchman,' she said. 'Do you think we ought to go on the water today? Knowing what we know? Kidnappers *love* yachts. They hijack them to Cuba.'

'We shall be safe on the water,' said Gerhardt.

'Hark at the fortune teller. Shall I cross your hand with silver? Will I be travelling over the water and meeting a dark stranger?' In her imagination, her fingertips brushed his palm, and she shivered. *Silver. Silver bullets. Silver; thirty pieces of ...*

'Perhaps,' said Gerhardt.

'And you're not afraid of meeting any assassins?' quipped Tell.

'Tell, I wish you wouldn't!' said Camena.

'Wouldn't what?'

'Needle Gerhardt. You're always giving him a hard time, lately, and it's getting boring.'

'Yeah, yeah.' Tell looked at her friend's flushed face and softened. 'Sorry, Cam. I won't say another word if it bothers you. You don't mind me *thinking* rude things about him, though?'

'Bitte,' said Gerhardt suddenly.

Bitter? Don't you mean sourpuss, Watchman? She managed to contain it to a mental comment, so of course there was no response from Gerhardt. She honestly didn't want to distress Camena, so Tell made just one more mild comment before attending to her own locker. 'Don't you find this school work awfully boring, Watchman?' she asked. 'You must have done it all before.'

The buzzer shrilled for home room, and Tell thrust her books into her locker and jammed it shut, wrinkling her nose at the smell of over-ripe banana; the tail-end of Monday's lunch, forgotten in her haste to get home. 'I'll ditch it later,' she said, half apologetically to Camena. 'After we get back.'

Gerhardt was more tense than he liked or had expected, this morning, but his hand moved calmly over the paper, ruling lines, drawing symbols and numerals. He wore precisely the right blend of expressions; concentration and resignation, with some artistic added uncertainty when he came to a tricky pair of parentheses. He appeared to be engrossed in the sheet and he really *was* doing mathematics — with seven per cent of his concentration. The rest of it was directed towards the end of the afternoon, when the students of Year TenPH would have returned from the excursion and would be dispersing throughout the town.

He knew he must leave the Recovery as late as possible, for there wouldn't be a second chance. Ideally, it should take place at nine minutes and fifty seconds past four, but that left no margin for error. Even if his presence and intent had remained undetected by RI-P that would have been cutting it too finely, and in the circumstances it would be literally suicidal.

RI-P knew he was here.

RI-P knew he was guarding Camena.

It followed that the operatives knew the Recovery schedule as well as he did. They would expect him to act in good time — perhaps at nine minutes and thirty seconds past four. Twenty seconds might have been regarded as a negligible period, but it was time enough for any number of actions. A rifle could be loaded, aimed and fired in less than twenty seconds. A vehicle could accelerate from a stationary start to well over one hundred kilometres per hour. A man could die a dozen times over, in twenty seconds.

The RI-P operatives knew this as well as Gerhardt, so they might step in and make their own move a little sooner. Therefore, he also should act earlier. Or would they allow for that as well?

Gerhardt frowned. It was bad enough trying to predict what Tell Clancy might do today without trying to second-guess the enemy. And he still did not know how Trinity Street came to be part of the picture.

He stole a glance at Tell's face, half visible as she bent over the work sheet. She lifted her pen and bit the end, and he heard the tiny tapping sound of her teeth. She had a wide mouth, well-shaped, with a slight quirk in one corner. Abruptly, piercingly, he wondered if that quirk had been inherited from one of her ancestors.

She glanced at him, brows coming down as if she had caught his sudden sorrow and was puzzled. Her gaze turned to Camena and Gerhardt bent over his work. He must be very, very careful. Thirty seconds to spare might change the whole situation and if Tell ever once got an idea of his real purpose, she would try to interfere. He knew she was uncertain, knew he had disturbed her with his telepathic teasing. No more, he decided. It wasn't fair. And besides, it was dangerous.

He could not afford trouble from Tell, so he decided to act boldly to turn her from a distraction to an asset. It was still unfair to make use of her in this way, but it wouldn't make any difference to her in the long run. Only to himself and Camena. And Camena was the one who must come through.

'Estelle,' he said quietly as they came together in pairs to double-check their work, 'I need to talk with you.'

'Talk then.' She sounded guarded, and he caught a flare of surprise that he had initiated a conversation. A further flare that he had paired with her, and not with Camena.

'Privately.'

'Don't whisper then. Keep it to the mathematical mumble.'

He half smiled at that, opening his ears to the subdued buzz of comment and query and falling in with her suggestion. He regretted, again, that they hadn't time for games. He would like to have come back again, when it was over, but he knew he never could. The world would have moved on by then, taking Tell Clancy out of his reach.

'Graph the six trig functions . . .' he said.

'Sine, cosine, tangent, and the reciprocals are cosecant, secant and cotangent,' responded Tell. 'What's cookin'?'

'RI-P may strike today,' said Gerhardt.

'What the hell is Rye-pee?'

Error! 'The ones we spoke of before,' he corrected himself. 'The ones who might make the snatch.'

'You said it was safe!' said Tell, underscoring one of her workings-out and tapping it with her pen. 'Get your story straight, Watchman.'

'I did,' he agreed. 'That seems safe enough.' He tapped his own pen on her work. 'Safe on the water. But *after* school . . . they may strike in the street. Try to take Camena.' He glowered at the innocent lines of formulae. 'These things can be more difficult than they first appear. Much more difficult. I hate to get them wrong.'

'You take her home another way,' said Tell. 'Make like Joseph and the angel. Trinity Street, maybe?'

If Gerhardt had not trained his face from childhood, his mouth might have opened in astonishment then. Trinity Street. So this is how Trinity Street came to be a part of the picture.

'Trinity Street,' he agreed, and to him the seemingly innocuous words were heavy with doom.

Tell looked directly at him for a second, and he felt a sharp sense of his betrayal. He should have warned her truthfully, if he was to warn her at all. Using her was wrong. Wrong. But warning her truthfully would change too much.

'These answers seem okay to me,' he said.

'Great,' said Tell. 'And how the hell do *you* know? That one isn't even finished.'

Lunch was half an hour early, to make time for the excursion around the harbour.

'How'd you make out in Maths?' Tell asked Camena, scrambling into her shorts. She zipped them up and unfastened the waistband of her uniform. She was already wearing an old green T-shirt under her blouse and blazer. Usually she kept to the rules, but it was worth risking a warning pink slip to save seconds on getting changed. Authority knew perfectly well uniforms could not be hung in lockers, but that didn't make them any more eager to supplement the meagre supply of hanging space in the change rooms. Late changers had to drape their clothes over the seats or on the floor.

Tell dragged her blazer over the hanger and clicked it onto the last few centimetres of rail, just ahead of Liza Lee, who waved a threatening fist.

'The Maths problems were easy,' said Camena. She was wearing a crimson shirt with a glimmer of silver at the soft collar. It would have looked shapeless on Tell.

'Just because you're a brain box. I got stuck on a question, and now I've got a purple tongue. I gotta stop chewing my pen.' She paused, and said loudly, 'Watchman said I'd got it right, as far as I'd gone. I think he was lying.'

'You want me to coach you after school?' Camena offered, half reluctantly.

'Can't,' said Tell. 'It's Wednesday. Unless you and Watchman want to come round to David's?'

'Pass,' said Camena. She turned to the mirror and began to comb her hair.

'Leave it,' said Tell. 'We'll get left behind.'

There was a considerable confusion as twenty-three Year Ten students sorted themselves into the bus. There were actually three times that number of Year Tens at St Saviours, but activities scheduled outside the school had to be staggered throughout the week to allow everyone to have a turn.

The school had been small and select when Tell had been enrolled, but now an ever-increasing tide had turned and parents were queuing up to give their kids a Catholic education.

'Is it really any better than Cockatoo High?' Tell asked Maureen.

'God knows,' said Maureen. Maureen was a republican, an agnostic and a staunch ALP voter — except when her principles rose in revolt and forced her to vote Green. 'If David wants to pay for what he could have for free that's his prerogative.'

'Fifty cents.'

'*No*, damn it! I wasn't criticising. He might be right. Perhaps you do get more attention in a smaller school. It's easy to have principles, but hard to apply them to your own kids.'

'St Sav's isn't small.'

'It was, in the beginning. He has every right to give you the best chance he can.'

'But you don't agree it *is* the best chance.'

'Look,' said Maureen. 'The only way to know that would be to put you through St Saviours for twelve years then zip you back to infancy and put you through a state school for twelve more. Then compare the results. Taking into account the fluctuations in society and the educational system, plus altered expectations, plus . . .'

'You can't re-run history,' said Tell. 'And just as well. If you could, I'd never be born.'

Maureen hadn't answered that directly, but she had given Tell an awkward pat on the shoulder. 'I wouldn't un-wish you, Tell.'

'Well thank *you*.' Tell had wanted to hug Maureen, or touch her hand — anything to express appreciation — but she hadn't been able to any more than she could hug David. Or Camena. She had hugged her dog Betz instead, and she remembered that as she piled into the bus with the others. Funny, how you got out of the habit of cuddling people. Kids cuddled pets and parents without a second thought. As you got older you cut it down — and down — and then, sometime in your teens or twenties, it started up again. And then it was all different. The innocence was gone.

The bus trip was a mere twelve minutes to Kestrel Bay, but that was quite long enough for Tell, squashed painfully between Camena's left hip and the window. Gerhardt was on

Camena's other side, and beyond him some other girls were holding an animated and rather embarrassing conversation as if he hadn't been there. Or was it perhaps for his benefit?

Shall I cross your palm with silver?

Suddenly she became aware of Gerhardt's gaze. It was definitely speculative, almost as if he knew what she was thinking.

Get stuffed, Watchman! thought Tell, uneasily, and was disconcerted to see him smile. She gave him the evil eye, but today her heart wasn't in it. Was it simply good old-fashioned sex hormones that were scrambling her circuits?

All that bore thinking about, but not now, not with the person in question sitting just beyond Camena, and possibly sticking out his invisible antennae to catch her thoughts. Sniffing to detect any stray pheromones. *Creep!* she thought darkly, directing it at him.

The bay was oddly deserted, with a flock of yachts and pleasure boats moored to buoys and stanchions along the marina. The compact shopping centre hummed away to the west, and the other side of the bay was beyond the horizon, but Tell could sense it, hidden in the haze. The national park was over there, hemmed with white sand and pebbles, with dunes, natural forest and fauna. A primitive place, just across the water from the busy little marina.

A brisk wind had blown up and the surface of the water was chopping into tiny flecks of foam. Indiscernible salt blew up from the foam and settled on Tell's lips. She licked it off, looking at the moving decks, the bobbing buoys, and remembering what Maureen had said about sea sickness. *Mal de mer.* Her stomach tilted. Maybe this wasn't a good idea.

'The *Kismet* is over there,' said Mr Blenning. 'She is, as you all know, a new training yacht with auxiliary engines . . .'

'Just as well,' said someone, sotto voce.

'We are very lucky to be the first to try her out. Since she is of limited capacity, you will be taken in turns. Five of you may board now, the rest will visit the Museum of Sail.'

There was a groan, and a concerted stampede towards the ship, just as if they had been Year Sevens.

'Five, I said!' Mr Blenning was an old hand at it all. 'Ward, Jennifer, Joseph, Madeleine, William.'

The five chosen were fitted with life jackets and shepherded aboard the *Kismet*. The wind blew snatches of instruction and explanation, but the rest of the students were herded away towards the museum.

The museum might have been interesting, thought Tell, if she hadn't been so often before. Did St Saviours get a discount for multiple visits? She had been already in Year Three, and Year Seven, as well as with Maureen and her grandfather. 'Should have brought a hand-line,' she told Camena. 'Might have caught a flathead for dinner. David likes fresh fish.'

There was no response from Camena, and Tell glanced warily at Gerhardt. He appeared tense, glancing about at the museum staff, at the other visitors. He seemed to believe in this danger to Camena. Tell looked earnestly at a diagram of a seventeenth century sailing ship. Gerhardt was keyed up, anticipating — something.

Afraid? she wondered, just below a whisper.

Nein. No. He had heard her. And had he spoken? And it wasn't fear that coloured his tone. It was deep regret. For — Tell.

She gaped at him, astonished. *Why? Why? What has this to do with me?* In her own mind she was shouting, but of course no sound came out. And he had turned away, as one with Camena, to admire an antique diving bell. Tell felt snubbed and terrified. Cut off from reality as if she were clamped into that bulbous metal helmet herself.

Camena, Gerhardt and Tell were part of the third group to board the *Kismet*. By then the two crew members, who were acting as guides and instructors, were damp with spray. Rather to Tell's surprise, one was a young woman, tall and handsome. She had very dark eyes and excellent teeth, which she displayed in a smile as she distributed the life jackets. She sounded bright and breezy, and somehow artificial, as if she had learned her welcome-speech by rote. Probably sick of seasick students. Tell's stomach lurched again, which was ridiculous, for they were still at the marina.

'I'm Pris, and my crew-mate here is Red,' pattered the crew-woman. 'He and I are going to take *Kismet* out into the bay. When we're all clear, we'll let you get some hands-on experience. Presently, I'll hand you over to Red, and he'll explain what all the bits are called, but first, I'd like to check your life jackets. Fine — fine — oops — this one isn't quite fastened. Take off your jacket, that'll make it better,' she said to Tell. 'Good. Now the strap goes through the ring and the clasp should click — there! And when you want it off, you pull it just like this. Now we're all set!'

It was mildly interesting, Tell supposed, shivering without her polar fleece, though she couldn't quite see what use a knowledge of sailing was likely to be for her. She hated to agree with Maureen, but sailing was like skiing and parachuting, white water-rafting and touring Skye on a tandem. Just not her. But still — this might be her only chance, so she forced herself to concentrate on the experience instead of her vague fears.

She felt the *Kismet* begin to move. It was smooth enough in the harbour, but as they slipped out beyond the confines of the marina, the sails filled and the craft began to heave gently on the waves. Just as if it were breathing. And who wanted to stand balanced on the chest of a breathing giant?

Odd, thought Tell. Odd that she could feel so at ease when swimming yet so apprehensive with a deck between herself and the water. Or was the apprehension just part of her wider feelings of disquiet? *Enjoy it*, she instructed herself. *It might be your only chance.*

The *Kismet* heeled over and began to tread the waves, moving like a dancer, out and away from the shore, travelling west towards Penguin Point.

'Hey!' said someone as the marina passed from sight, 'the last lot didn't come out this far. Hey, Pris! You're not hijacking us to Queensland, are you?'

Pris chuckled. 'Not at all. We decided to give the engine a little run, that's all. It's been running rough and Red wanted to — oops!'

Kismet had heeled again, so violently that they all staggered and grabbed for the rail. 'Steady!' said Pris, touching Camena's arm. 'Are you okay?'

'Yes, of course.' Camena sounded a little surprised, and why not? The others had all managed to stay upright without assistance.

'Great,' said Pris, clapping her on the shoulder. 'Come over and hang on to the rail over here and you can watch out for dolphins. You two — Liza and Ali — why not go up to the bows? Hey, Red — fire up that engine in a minute!'

'*Arretez!*' exclaimed Gerhardt. 'Stop!'

'What in the . . .' Suddenly, Tell understood. Gerhardt believed the kidnap attempt was going to be made now, here — though how he thought they hoped to get away with such a thing before so many witnesses she couldn't imagine. They wouldn't take *five* of them. 'Come off it, Watchman,' she said urgently, grasping his arm. 'You're paranoid. We're in plain sight —' But as she glanced over her shoulder she realised they were not. *Kismet* had rounded the wing of the bay and the distant shore was covered with trees.

'Let me go!' said Gerhardt, pulling away. 'You don't understand. These are RI-Ps —'

Pris had guided Camena to a place by the rail. Now she was hastening back to Gerhardt and Tell. 'Settle down, kids!' she said. 'Oh,' she said to Tell, 'you'd like to go over with your friend, wouldn't you?' Her voice was peremptory now, with no trace of the former friendliness. Perhaps it was that that helped convince Tell, perhaps it was the flare of anger and self-recrimination she suddenly sensed in Gerhardt. Perhaps it was the hard, sure grip of Pris's fingers through the thin sleeve of David's old shirt.

'Five, Red!' yelled Pris.

Red started the engine.

'*Merde!*' Pris cursed. Tell felt a violent push between her shoulderblades, which sent her staggering towards Camena. And then the *Kismet's* engines blew.

Tell felt everything in slow motion. The blow from Pris's palm, the ballooning, impossible sound of the explosion. She saw Camena wing by like a kite, stiff with surprise and bulky with the life jacket . . . And then she was tumbling in a dive she hadn't made, gulped by the sliding sea.

The salt water rose like a tidal wave, cold and shocking against her face. The life jacket was bulky and uncomfortable, and instead of bobbing her upright like a cork, it seemed to become waterlogged, scarcely supporting her at all. Her nose and ears hurt, her head seemed stuffed with foam. Her arms were leaden and her legs numb . . . it must have been quite an explosion. God, she was starting to sink!

In an unaccustomed burst of panic, Tell kicked out untidily, and fumbled for the ring closures of the life jacket, thankful, even in extremity, that Pris had shown her how they worked.

Life jacket indeed! The bloody thing was useless! Her hands moved to the round collar, which should have supported her head. It was hard and heavy — as if filled with wet cement or sand. Tell wrenched at the fastenings and kicked hard to stay afloat. It was unbelievably difficult, and she went under more than once. She struggled up until her head burst through the skin of water, and air and light rushed into her face. She could see little, and hear nothing, but surely someone was calling her.

Camena. Dear God, where was Camena?

Tell trod water, peering blindly about. The crippled *Kismet* was a long way ahead, two orange figures bobbing beyond it must be Ali and Liza, safely supported by their life jackets. Five hundred metres away? A thousand? She screamed and waved, but they might as well have been on the other side of the ocean. An inflatable life-raft bobbed just beyond them, and on it was Pris, peering wildly about as if looking for survivors. Where was Red? And where was Camena?

Tell cried out again, gulping salt water, her legs still half numb with shock. Her eyes stung, her lungs hurt. She sank in a trough in the waves. Where was Gerhardt? He had been behind her, yelling at Pris, and then Pris had thrust her forward into the explosion, cursing in French. French —

German — even Fijian — Gerhardt spoke them all. Was Gerhardt part of this? Was he still aboard the *Kismet*, enigmatically watching her drown? The life-raft was coming her way, but she had to find Camena.

'Shit!' said Tell violently. Her throat hurt, and she spat into the waves and turned on her back. When she looked again, there was only the distant raft and a scatter of flotsam. The *Kismet* had vanished, and the waves seemed to be carrying Tell away from the deserted distant shore. And the rest of the class would still be in the museum, listening to Mr Blenning boring on about whaling in the nineteenth century.

'Cammie!' shrieked Tell. 'Camena!' She could hardly hear her own voice, but a head bobbed suddenly above the waves, sleek and dark as a seal's. Not Cammie. Cammie could scarcely swim and if her life jacket had been anything like Tell's —

There was a dolphin leap, and the head disappeared, legs flashing momentarily into view.

Gerhardt. And he was diving. Not swimming. Diving. Diving to save Camena?

'Cammie!' shrieked Tell with voice and mind, and began to swim towards the swirl of Gerhardt's disappearance.

Gerhardt gulped air and dived. Anger flared in his mind, for the RI-Ps had been audacious. They had gone against their own precepts, acting ruthlessly to destroy Camena and discourage himself in a seemingly accidental fashion.

They had gone now, thinking they had beaten him, tricked him with their scheming, but he would *not* give in just yet. He opened his eyes, peering through the green salt depths. Tide shadows. The blur of anger. That explosion had ripped into his ears and mind and he had caught only the edge. Camena had taken the full force, and there was an excellent chance she had died before she hit the water. And the killers had meant to make sure, trapping her in that death-jacket. They had replaced the buoyancy pads with something instantly absorbent and very heavy — and how *could* he have been so stupid? He had not recognised the woman named Pris as a RI-P operative. He knew none of Sib's operatives personally, but surely Pris must have given herself away in *some* fashion — if he had been properly alert. But he'd been so sure they wouldn't risk acting until later in the afternoon.

He should cut his losses and return to base, but stubbornly Gerhardt forced himself still deeper. Returning to base might be more than he could manage in any case. Once through the veil he would still face a long, exhausting swim to the Wild Zone.

The salt stung his grazes and he realised he had let his pain block fail. The endorphins were draining, replaced by adrenaline. Good. That left more chance to find Camena. His body hurt, but it was hurting for an excellent cause.

He was far down underwater now, and knew he should have retained his grip on the death-jacket to assist his descent. It had been blind self-preservation which had led him to strip it off and let it sink in the ocean. The killers. They shouldn't much care whether *he* lived or died, but they had weighted the scales against him. Was it malice or efficiency? Or did they simply believe him better dead? Would their additional act of sabotage count against them? Hardly, since their motive had been to prevent his Recovery of Camena de Courcey. It wouldn't matter to anyone if *he* were taken permanently out of the game. Especially if he drowned and his body was trapped under the water.

It was dark in the sea, but his fingers had brushed trailing wet hair. He twined the strands around his hand, lungs aching, and began to struggle towards the surface. It was probably too late, but he fought for it anyway, rearing above the waves in an agony of relief. Camena was abominably heavy, sagging in his grasp, and it took Gerhardt's abused mind some seconds to realise that she still wore the orange jacket. He should have removed it underwater.

Now he fumbled at the clasp, but it was locked fast. He needed two hands to try to coax it free, and two hands to support Camena's body while he did so. He could not do both at once and perhaps it was too late anyway. Was she even breathing? Her lips were blue. He drew her to him in a parody of an embrace and gave her oxygen from his own lungs.

A wail behind made him aware of Tell Clancy. He had forgotten her in the urgency to reach Camena and he felt a strange pang to see that she seemed unharmed. He had expected her to be burned, damaged in the explosion. She too was not wearing a life jacket. That must mean hers had been sabotaged as well, otherwise she would not have abandoned it.

Watchman! Her cry was more from her mind than from her labouring lungs and throat.

Tell. He answered her in the same fashion. It didn't matter now.

You're kissing her here?

Outrage coloured her thoughts, and was probably keeping her alert, because aside from that she seemed tired and stunned. She had escaped her life jacket, but her energy was low. Gerhardt knew she might never make it to shore. Perhaps it would be better if she did not, for Pris was unlikely to leave things as they stood. But Tell was here, and unharmed for the present, so maybe she could help him now.

'Tell,' he said aloud, trying to keep the fear from his voice, 'can you get the . . .'

There was no comprehension in her eyes and he knew she hadn't heard. The explosion must have numbed her ears.

Tell. Camena's life jacket. Can you get it off?

She understood. She was close to him, feebly treading water, and fumbling at the catch of the deadly life jacket. Her head bobbed awkwardly above the waves, for while she worked she was unable to support herself with her arms. She lost rhythm, gulped water and choked, but continued to tug and wrench.

It's locked. Padlocked. God!

The panic in her mind was frightening. If she gave up now he would lose his chance.

All right, liebling. Hold Camena. I shall break the catch.
Gerhardt turned Camena in his arms and thrust her towards Tell, who rolled obediently onto her back to receive the burden. The combined weights of her friend and the jacket were forcing her under, but that would only hasten the inevitable and might be a kindness in the end . . . The life jacket would not come off and Tell's face was underwater now, bubbles streaming from her lips.

Estellita ma amata . . . goodbye.

Her lips parted, but there was no air in reach and no response came from her thoughts to his endearment. Only pain, fear and regret. She had almost ceased to struggle and he knew it was too late. Pris would be along at any moment, intent on finishing what was begun. Death to Camena and almost certainly for Tell. And for himself? More than likely she'd leave him to take his chances. And his chances weren't so good. The dreadful jacket was wrenched off at last, but his legs and arms were dull with creeping exhaustion and if he delayed much longer none of them would survive.

If he had the courage he would finish it for Tell now, not let her wait for Pris to come. But to help Tell was to risk Camena, and that he could not do.

He closed his eyes a moment, summoning the alpha state. The gentle, regular brain waves so at odds with his current situation. Against the backs of his eyelids he could see Camena's blue lips and Tell's drowning eyes and the funny quirk in the corner of her mouth. He wished he could spare something more for Tell, a comfort, perhaps, but drowning was drowning and where was comfort when your lungs were filled with water? But he knew Tell wouldn't be left to die in peace. Whatever was planned, Pris would leave nothing to chance.

Vale, Tell. He reinforced his mental tone with comfort and praise, the way Jens had done when he was small ... *You were and are the best.*

The best? But not to Hub HI-Q. Hub HI-Q wanted Camena and her rare intelligence. Raw regret was in his mind as he summoned the final effort. Regret that Tell Clancy would not, could not, live to pass on her charming, irregular features and her fierce loyalty to her children.

Vale, Tell! Goodbye.

Gerhardt slipped his arms around Camena, drew in a deep, steadying breath, and forced himself and his charge through the veil.

PART TWO
WILD ZONE

Death is the end. A child is born, and matures to become an exceptional adult. A new child is born. The original subject grows old and dies, leaving the offspring to carry a genetic message to the future. It takes just one living, fertile descendant to carry on the elite heritage. So death is not the end.

Sometimes, through misfortune or responsible choice, the cycle is interrupted. Thus, the cycle is judged to be complete. We at RI-P pledge that the completion of the cycle shall be honoured. To this end, we have implemented a programme of Strategic Correction. In this way we defend the rights of the cycle, and the most basic right of the human race. The right to a death.

The water was warmer on this side of the veil. Not a lot, but appreciably. Gerhardt breathed more easily, but it wasn't over yet.

If he'd known the Recovery would have to be made from water, he could have arranged a standby craft. As it was, the RI-P operatives had forced him to act before he was ready, so he was faced with a long and tiring swim to shore. He wasn't sure he could make it, while supporting Camena, but at least the tide was now flowing in the right direction. It meant that if he could keep himself and the girl afloat they would both be carried safely to shore. If she lived. It would be an irony if she died here now, from drowning and the effects of the explosion.

Rolling onto his back he touched the side of her throat. The pulse was rapid and weak and she was beginning to shiver convulsively.

Gerhardt adjusted her against his arm so that her head was supported on his chest and out of water and her body lay half along his. Strange, he had never had much time for girls — not for want of interest, but for lack of opportunity. Hub HI-Q gave, but Hub HI-Q also took away, and the past years had been given over entirely to his immersion in the world of Camena de Courcey. Now he was immersed in the ocean. If all went well he must spend the next few days with her alone, working to regain her confidence. Telling her a new story, and this time a true one, and persuading her to accept new facts. There would be no time for anything but that. The period of misdirection and lies was over, and Gerhardt was relieved. Weaving schemes had its satisfactions, but towards the end he had begun to feel uncomfortable with his own inventiveness. He thought it was because of Tell.

Maybe it should have been Tell he Recovered, and not for Hub HI-Q.

Horrified at the intrusion of that thought, Gerhardt forced it away and concentrated instead on a hope that the second stage of the operation would work out better than the first. He would have passed this stage on to Moss if he could. Moss had pointed out that Hub HI-Q policy called for the same operative to remain with the prospect until a final decision had been made.

'Final decision?' he'd asked.

Surely there was no decision to be made! The choice offered by Hub HI-Q was simple; life, with implied acceptance of certain conditions, or immediate return to the moment of Recovery. Would Camena choose a past when she could have the future instead? The odd thing was that before he left for Cockatoo, Gerhardt had noticed an increasing number of Recoverees seemed to be doing just that. He'd asked Moss about that some time before, but Moss had told him the destiny of the Recoveree was none of the operative's concern. Gerhardt had wanted to argue, but his training had held and he had closed his mouth. He had thought of putting the puzzle to Jens, but Moss would find out, and he despised Jens. Moss always found out everything.

At least Gerhardt and Camena were currently safe from RI-P. The operatives were probably satisfied their ploy had worked.

Sucked in! he sneered, in the idiom of St Saviours College.

Schooling himself not to notice the increasing cramp in the muscles of his left arm, Gerhardt kicked on towards the shore.

Tell was as cold as a fish when Gerhardt took Camena. The relief as the weight lifted from her chest was tinged with fear that she was to be left alone. Gerhardt was saying something and it seemed to be goodbye. Tell wasn't ready for goodbye yet, not ready to be committed to the deep. Ashes to ashes, dust to dust. Full fathom five thy father lies — where the bee sucks, there suck I —

Bloody hell! she thought. That's what Maureen was saying! And what was Gerhardt saying, and why was her mind suddenly behaving like this? If she was mad the world was madder still.

And why would Gerhardt give up on her now? Freed from the burden of Camena's weight there was plenty of fight in Tell yet. Surely they could encourage one another, and both swim to shore? If they knew where the shore was. *Not goodbye.* 'Watchman!' she called, but her throat burned with salt water.

She thought she heard a cry from the life-raft, but before she could locate it, a wave had lifted her like a body-surfer. The cold salt water curled beneath and over her, sealing her eyes and ears, and her mind was suddenly calm. Ripples were spreading through her brain and she was reaching out to touch ... Tell struck out, but her feeble efforts were nothing beside the power of the wave. And she was getting warmer. Did that mean she was freezing to death?

Hypothermia and drowning too — hell! Resentfully, Tell fought her way through the flurry of the wave, homing in on the land. It couldn't be far; there were gulls circling ahead. Or were they vultures, intent on the wreckage of the *Kismet*? Nonsense. Vultures were dry land birds. And if she ever got out of this one, dry land would be good enough for her. No more swimming, no more sailing — her season ticket for the pool (or what remained of it) could rot. *Home is the sailor, home from the sea, the waves are carrying, carrying me. Watchman, you bastard, where are you? How dare you say goodbye?*

Her first brush with land was painful, a sharp pinnacle of rock with a stubble of mussels. Rock and shell scored her thigh through the sodden leg of her shorts, half dragging them from her body. She hoped it was mussels, hoped it wasn't coral, because coral cuts almost always got infected. She had tripped and fallen when she went to Green Island and ended up at the cottage hospital for treatment — David had been annoyed. Tending a festering daughter was not his idea of a fun holiday.

There was no coral near Kestrel Bay.

Not coral then. Mussels. Bearded mussels. Or oysters, with maybe pearls inside. Mad idea, but she deserved the idea of pearls, if she had to get sliced by the reality of oysters.

Tell began a cautious sidestroke, legs and arms moving minimally to avoid any more painful shocks. It was only another hundred metres to go, now, and here came another wave, swelling silently from the ocean, bearing her in its bosom like a salty Abraham.

The gulls were crying, and if she could hear that then her ears could not be badly damaged. No doubt she had water in them and would get swimmers' ear . . . a few drops of paraffin oil would serve to dry them out. And the main thing was life.

The wave dumped her on a beach.

There was no welcoming outcry, no sputter of a motor boat. No sound aside from the sea and the gulls and the mild crunch of the pebbles beneath her elbows. She became aware that her shorts were half down and rolled over to haul them up, exposing a shallow, bleeding gash in her thigh. The skin around it was bluish and scraped. It would hurt when she warmed up.

Where was everyone? Gerhardt? Camena? And Red and Pris — hadn't Red been over by the engine when it blew? Had he been blown to butchers' scraps?

Tell shuddered, almost scared to look about in case she saw a piece of Red washed up on the beach beside her. But when she did look there was nothing and no-one.

No rescue party. That was a bit much. But of course, the *Kismet* had been around the shoulder of the bay. Perhaps the others had swum, floated or been washed ashore at the marina. Sensible of them, if they had contrived to manage that.

Tell got up, shaking and numbed with reaction and awakening pain. A few tears ran down her face. God, Maureen would have something to say about this! Her only daughter blown up, shipwrecked and left to hike back around the point. And that life jacket — useless! It must have been faulty and no doubt the crew of the *Kismet* would be sued for negligence or for failing to maintain their equipment. Free trial indeed! It mightn't be the only kind of trial on offer now. Tell was not normally a vengeful person, but she told herself she wouldn't mind seeing Pris get a life sentence!

Her knees were trembling, blue and orange, but the day seemed warmer than it had been. The wind had died down and the clouds had blown away. How very strange. It was almost like coming ashore to a different day. Perhaps she was on the wrong side of the bay, in the national park.

Tell put the idea away from her and began to crunch along the beach. She still had her old sneakers on. She was glad she hadn't remembered to kick them off when she first hit the water. Even soggy and cold they were better than bare feet if she had to walk very far. She only wished she had worn her socks.

The bush came quite close to the beach and if the worst came to the worst she was only a dozen kilometres from home. Only two or three kilometres from the marina. Less, if she took the Penguin Point walking track. Two summers ago she had walked from the carpark out to the Point and back again and it had taken less than three hours. She was knocked about now — but say two hours, max, to the carpark and ten more minutes to the marina.

She pulled a face, remembering she was due to go to David's tonight. If she missed the bus back to school she'd be stranded ... but that was impossible. They wouldn't just *leave* her here, whichever side of the bay she was on. For now, the best thing was to look for the other survivors, any or all of whom might be somewhere close by.

'Watchman!' Her voice wobbled and husked. Too much salt water. Tell almost laughed, remembering how Maureen made her gargle with warm salt water when she had a sore throat. Obviously, *cold* salt water had an opposite effect.

Watchman! she thought angrily. *Watchman*! *Where the hell are you?*

Gerhardt was watching Camena. He had often pictured this moment, his triumph in the first stage of his first successful Recovery, but always he had expected to be busy, explaining and placating, convincing his prospect that the impossible was true. He had never expected to sit by a half-drowned girl on the pebbles, feeling her warmth through his skin and breathing the silence.

Camena was alive, and, so far as he could tell, undamaged. Her brain waves were inaccessible, for she was resistant to telepathy. Odd, because, despite her intellectual brilliance, she seemed a little suggestible. He ran his hands over her body, and bent to put his ear to her chest. Her breathing sounded reasonably clear, which was good. If she had inhaled too much water and contracted pneumonia he would have had to hurry the disclosure so he could seek treatment at Hub HI-Q.

Her hair was already beginning to dry, and her faintly tanned skin was a good colour. He thought she was sleeping as much as unconscious, but without medical training, all he could do was wait and see. Even if her intellect were dulled by the experience she would still carry the valuable DNA and could pass her genetically-programmed intelligence on to her children. And near-drowning would not be considered a genetic weakness. It could happen to anyone.

Gerhardt sighed. He had succeeded — just. If it had not been for Tell Clancy he would have lost Camena to the ocean. Now she would have a chance to live out her life in comfort. Unlike Tell.

Vale, Tell, he thought. He wished again he had helped her die.

Watchman! Watchman! Where the hell are you?

Gerhardt stiffened. He had had a great deal of experience in believing the unbelievable, but this was beyond disbelief.

Telepathy could *not* carry so far. He could *not* be hearing Tell's despairing mental cries. Tell was dead, ghosts did not exist, and if Tell were crying out for him now it meant his brain paths had been scrambled in the course of the Recovery. By the explosion? The long swim? Or by the veil itself? Recovery was a stressful occupation, and most operatives made no more than two or three in the course of their active careers. A surprising number made one Recovery and relinquished active Hub HI-Q status thereafter, which argued that he wasn't the only one to suffer emotional strain.

Only Moss was different. Moss had Recovered half a dozen prospects and masterminded the research on two more, including Camena de Courcey. Moss had not seemed to feel the strain, but Moss was unique.

And Moss would *not* be pleased with his protégé if he could see him now. Whatever had been the triggering factor Gerhardt knew he'd better get himself back into shape. Emotional instability was a bad gene, and after spending half his life so far with Moss he should have been better able to control his thoughts and feelings.

But perhaps it was not his brain paths but his psyche, and his mind had gone into guilt mode, because he had left Tell to drown. If that were the case, he would need re-indoctrination. Her death by drowning was not *his* responsibility, but that of RI-P.

'You have no reason for guilt or regret.' That was one of the precepts Moss had taught him. 'Your presence cannot do harm and will do only good to the Recoveree and to Hub HI-Q.'

'Say it three times prior to breakfast,' muttered Gerhardt, and blanched. Talking to himself was another unhealthy sign.

Watchman!

It was strange. Tell's tone was exasperated rather than despairing. A ghost or a guilty mental construct would not sound like that. *Tell* would sound like that. Gerhardt went cold. If he were hearing Tell now it was either a miracle — or a sign that he had somehow committed the worst error in the already shaky history of the HI-Q Recovery Programme.

Holding Camena's cold hand, his fingers registering her pulse, Gerhardt heard the faint physical squeak of shingle. For a moment he was tempted to lie low, to pretend unconsciousness along with Camena. If Tell *had* followed him through, she would go off in search of rescue, and that would mean —

At the best, it would mean he had postponed the inevitable, a little. And at the worst, he would have precipitated disaster without giving himself a chance to think of a solution. He must send her back at once. *At once.*

'Tell?' He said it softly, in what Tell herself had termed the mathematical mumble.

Watchman! The word exploded from her mind rather than from her physical voice. Was she aware of her talent now? Her telepathy seemed stronger than ever.

'Here,' said Gerhardt as calmly as he could.

'You bastard!' *You left me!* She seemed shocked as well as angry.

I had to. 'Here,' he said, 'behind the rock.'

You left me.

Gerhardt swallowed. This was going to be even more difficult than he would have expected. He forced himself to continue his answers verbally. The more he could distance himself from her the better it would be. He would take her back through the veil before she came to full understanding — but first, he must find out how much she knew. If she suspected his purpose, she would fight him, and it would be very difficult to Return an unwilling prospect. And how could he do it to her? 'I didn't expect you to follow,' he said truthfully.

'You didn't expect me to follow.' Her voice was hoarse and painful and she had come into sight behind the rock. 'What the hell did you expect me to do, Watchman? Bloody fold my hands and drown?'

'I hoped you were drowning, yes. I thought it was kinder to let you go that way.'

'God!' She sounded blank. 'What *are* you?'

Gerhardt was familiar with the sarcastic idiom she used, but he felt she wasn't being sarcastic now. She really was bewildered. And hurt. Terribly hurt.

'I was so busy with Camena,' he apologised.

'Yes — Cammie — is she okay?' Tell knelt awkwardly in the shingle, and touched her friend's pale cheek.

'Camena is safe,' said Gerhardt. Beneath the coldness of apprehension, another feeling stirred. However difficult she was making this operation, he was really very glad she had had a reprieve. Perhaps she could stay with him a while.

His relief must have shown in his voice, for she flashed him a quick, astonished glance. 'God, you're really something, you know that, Watchman? Weird. But you've saved Cammie, so I'll graciously forget you left me to drown. No — I'll rephrase that. I'll try to believe you thought it was better to save one of us rather than let us both die. And of course you had to help Camena. She's no swimmer, and she'd been knocked out, so she hadn't a chance by herself. Are you sure she's okay? I mean, that was some explosion . . .'

Now her voice had come back, she seemed unable to stop babbling, but Gerhardt let her talk. If she stopped to think, she might go into shock — or begin to ask questions. The questions would come soon enough, and he needed a reprieve himself, to think how he would answer and what he would do. He should send her back, but he could not.

He tried to concentrate, but his thoughts kept skittering off sideways, and he was constantly aware of Tell, who had been doomed and was now alive and wonderfully unharmed. She was no longer kneeling, but sitting on the pebbles with her legs drawn up in the circle of her arms. He noticed a painful-looking scrape along her thigh, and a tear in her shorts. Her voice ran down, and she began to shiver spasmodically. Shock. He reached out to touch her hand, and her fingers folded around his and clung, painfully. The contact was dangerous to his calm so he squeezed her hand gently and removed his own. 'Are you cold?'

'S-sort of,' said Tell. Her teeth were chattering.

'The temperature is quite high, here,' said Gerhardt. 'Try to relax, and your circulation will restore itself.'

She nodded, then unbuttoned the dripping shirt and pulled it off. 'It m-must be after three,' she said prosaically. 'And it's autumn, so I guess it's okay.'

Gerhardt understood she was referring to the risk of sunburn. Most people he knew had little need to trouble themselves about that, but his genetic heritage meant he was mildly prone to it himself. 'Not much danger now,' he agreed. 'What about Camena?'

'Oh, Cammie doesn't burn.' The T-shirt was clinging and sagging with water, but she didn't take it off.

Camena stirred, and opened her eyes. She seemed astonished to find herself lying on the pebbles.

'Careful, Cam,' said Tell. She smiled as well as she could. 'Hey, here's where you say — "where am I?" — or "what happened?" like a good little rescued heroine!'

'Where am I? What happened?' Camena sat up cautiously.

'You're here,' said Tell helpfully. 'On the beach.'

'Neville Shute.'

'Not that beach — I hope!'

'What is it?' asked Gerhardt. 'Are you all right, Camena?'

'She's all right,' said Tell firmly. 'She's talking about a book. It just means her brain's connecting, that's all.'

'What happened?' repeated Camena.

'Accident,' said Gerhardt. 'Recall?' It hardly mattered, now, whether he used her dialect or his own. He had built Camena's trust in him by offering contact with her father, but now he must first destroy and then rebuild that trust — if he could. And with Tell along it wouldn't be easy. He should have dispatched Tell before Camena awoke.

'Of course I remember,' said Camena. 'We were on the *Kismet* and that Pris was being bossy. Where is she, anyway? Are we the only ones here?'

'Yes.'

'How can you be so sure?' put in Tell. 'I thought *I* was the only one until Watchman — until I found you two. What about the others?'

'They are not here, but they will be safe,' said Gerhardt.

At least he was reasonably certain of that. RI-P operatives might be ruthless, but they were efficient and — usually — conscientious about the well-being of peripherals. As he read the situation it was quite possible either Pris or Red would arrive in the Wild Zone to check his status, but it might just as well be someone unknown. The pair of them had bungled matters badly, and were probably being censured by Alpha Sib at RI-P Base. Unless Sib had been a party to the radical change of plan? Sib was unpredictable, full of iron resolve, but given to odd flashes of eccentricity. How far would Sib go to triumph over Moss?

'We should leave here,' he said abruptly.

'I agree,' said Tell. 'The others must be looking for us — unless they think we've drowned. By the way, Cammie — you ought to know — Watchman saved your skin. You were drowning and he dived after you and brought you to the surface alone and unaided. Your hero!'

'I could not have succeeded without your help, Tell.'

'I did it for Cammie, not for you. Just as well, as I didn't get much thanks at the time.'

The air was thick with resentment and Camena was looking from one to the other of them with apprehension. 'Hey you two — don't start arguing again! The main thing to do is get back to the marina. I suppose we *are* on the right side of the bay?'

'I wondered that too,' said Tell. 'It doesn't look right, somehow, and I can't see the walking track.'

'It must be right,' said Camena. 'There's no way water-wizards like you two would have swum the wrong way.'

'I couldn't see a thing,' said Tell frankly. 'I just went where the waves took me. I could have headed for Antarctica, and never realised where I was until I bumped my nose on Heard Island. It was pure luck I made it here. Over to you, Watchman! How did *you* navigate? Have you got a compass in your head like Cam's got a calculator and an encyclopaedia dictionary disc?'

'No.'

'Gerhardt?' said Camena. 'Do you know where we are?'

'How could he?' protested Tell. 'You and I have lived near here all our lives — he's a stranger.'

Gerhardt felt a rebuttal surge up, but it wasn't time for full disclosure yet. If he broke it to them now, this was a bad place to be. If RI-P turned up and found Camena alive, it would be bad enough — if they found Tell in addition, it could be disaster. 'We should leave here, and argue later,' he said mildly, and reached out to help Camena to her feet.

Camena swayed a little as she stood up. She found herself clutching Gerhardt's arm for support and let go in a hurry. 'Sorry,' she said, blinking the black spots from her vision. 'You really rescued me?'

'He really did,' said Tell. 'But don't go all soppy, Cammie. He's your bodyguard, remember. It was his duty to rescue you. Besides — what sort of guy would leave a girl to drown?'

Again Camena was aware of undercurrents in Tell's tone. Presumably Gerhardt had been ordering her around and Tell, who had her bronze medal for life saving, would have resented that. She wondered if she should say something, but in the end she simply shrugged. She was feeling distinctly weak and she didn't like the blurring in her eyes.

'How could I have drowned?' she asked. 'I was wearing a life jacket.'

'It sank,' said Tell coldly.

'*Sank*?'

'It sank itself and it damned near sank you. Mine was a lemon, but not like yours. Dunno about Watchman's — Watchman? I s'pose your life jacket must've been a death-trap too, or you'd have used it for Cammie — right?'

'It was faulty, too,' said Gerhardt.

'But some of them were okay,' said Tell. 'I saw others bobbing about like corks, but they didn't see me. If only I'd had a flare — but you don't bring that sort of thing on a school excursion.'

'Never mind that now,' said Camena. 'We'd better find the others before some idiot gets onto Linnie and Jus — and to your mum and dad, Tell — and puts them in a panic.'

'God, yes,' said Tell devoutly. 'I bet old Blenny's gone ballistic.'

Camena sighed. Mr Blenning was renowned for making bad situations worse. 'I wonder where he is?' she said to Tell. 'Is he standing guard over the rest of them, or chasing the ones that got away?'

'Chasing us,' said Tell morosely. 'Or chasing his tail. Geez, I feel sick.' She did look greenish, but then she hadn't felt well ever since they'd boarded the boat. 'I feel like I swallowed the sea. Octopus and all. They're squirming.'

'Salt water's an emetic,' said Camena, rubbing her forehead with her fingertips.

'Ugh.'

'We should go,' said Gerhardt. 'Can you walk, Camena?'

Camena didn't feel wonderful either. Cold, shaky, nauseated, headachy, sore, and her eyes kept blurring over. But not too bad at all for someone who should have been dead. She glanced at Tell, who was still holding her stomach. A gash in her friend's leg was bleeding sluggishly. 'We're alive, at least,' she said.

'Too bloody right,' said Tell, with a shiver. 'I s'pose they'll give Watchman a medal for bravery.'

'And you.'

'I only rescued myself. That's self-preservation, not bravery.'

'He said you helped with me.'

'I had to,' said Tell briefly. 'It wasn't a matter of choice.'

For Tell, thought Camena, it was seldom a matter of choice. She did what she needed to do. But for Gerhardt, Camena was only a job. Yet they had worked together to save her. They made a formidable team, which was remarkable when she considered how anti Tell was about Gerhardt. Or was she anti? Camena had noticed before that Tell's gaze rested often on Gerhardt. It could have been distrust. Maybe. Or some kind of fascination.

'It's odd,' she remarked. 'Gerhardt was supposed to protect me from being kidnapped, but instead he's rescued me from drowning.'

Put like that, it sounded very melodramatic, and she wouldn't have been surprised if Tell had snorted with disgust. But Tell just shivered, wrapping her arms around herself as if seeking comfort. Camena looked away. If she had been Tell, she would have offered — something. Being Camena, she didn't know how to start.

Gerhardt knew no-one would give him a medal for bravery. Hub HI-Q would be more likely to expel him for bungling his assignment. If they ever found out how he'd been fooled — but that was something he preferred not to consider. Of course he'd have to tell Moss — he owed Moss that — but with luck no-one else need ever know. Especially Jens. Jens would understand too well, and Gerhardt was carrying enough guilt already. And Jens resented Moss, and would not be sorry to hear of one of his projects going awry. Especially this one.

But now, he must concentrate on getting Camena to the disclosure unit for the second stage of the Recovery. And, since the RI-Ps had forced his hand, getting to the unit was going to take a long time.

If things had gone according to plan, the unit would have been mere metres away as they came through the veil. Having made the Recovery on sea instead of land, and been forced to swim to shore with her to a reasonably featureless Wild Zone, he was now faced with the prospect of a long trek during which suspicion might or might not begin to dawn in Camena's mind. And there was Tell Clancy, the wild card. Tell should never have been here at all, but he couldn't bring himself to send her back to *that*. Besides — how could he dispatch her now, in front of Camena, without jeopardising Camena's own state of mind?

Tell wasn't sure how it happened, but Gerhardt seemed to have been elected, or to have elected himself, as leader of their party. Was it because he was a male that she and Camena were subconsciously deferring to him, or simply because he was older?

'How old are you, Watchman?' she shot at him resentfully.

'Fifteen years, ten months,' he said perversely.

'No names, no bloody pack-drill, right? You've got to be at least seventeen, to be a bodyguard.' She was speaking in a mumble so as not to disturb Camena, but somehow he seemed to understand.

'Eighteen.'

'I knew it!'

Forcing this admission made her feel better about following his lead, but for some reason it had been a hollow victory. It shouldn't matter, but she found that it did. An eighteen-year-old was technically an adult, although so many of them were still at school. It made him seem even further out of her league . . .

Horrified, she clapped the lid on that thought, which had crept up slyly through the layers of her mind.

'Kidnappers after Cammie, eh?' she muttered derisively. 'Like who — a corrupt cod? A sinister shark? Or was it Pinching Pris from the *Kismet*?'

Gerhardt didn't respond, so she turned her attention to Camena, and raised her voice to a normal level. 'Cammie, are we going the right way?'

Camena shrugged. 'How should I know?'

'You got an A for Orienteering.'

'That was theory.'

'We're a long way from St Saviours,' put in Gerhardt.

'Who wants to go to St Saviours?' asked Tell. 'We only need to get back to the marina. We can't have been carried all that far out of our way.'

'We may have come farther than you think,' said Gerhardt. 'Wind and current can set up strange conditions.'

'Yeah, yeah.' As she crunched along behind Camena, Tell could scarcely believe the calm of sea and sky. It seemed to be a good two hours or more since the accident — or possibly more — but the afternoon was still warm although the shadows were getting longer. Yet — however little time had elapsed, surely the alarm must have gone up by now. The explosion had happened out of sight of the marina, but the sound had been punishing, and what about Mr Blenning and the rest of the kids still waiting their turn on the *Kismet*? Shouldn't they have started worrying a long time ago?

A radio call would have established that all was not well with the *Kismet*, and the next step should have been sending a motor boat to check up on the status of craft, crew and passengers. And, once the extent of the disaster was discovered, there should have been a concerted search for survivors. Tell couldn't quite remember whose job it was to find people who'd been shipwrecked, but it must be somebody's, and they should have swung into action by now.

'Why don't we stay here and yell?' she asked. 'They're bound to be looking for us.'

'We must go on,' said Gerhardt.

'Yes,' said Camena. 'We might get to the marina and save them all a lot of trouble.' Her voice sounded strained, and she was rubbing one eye.

'Got some sand in it?' said Tell. 'Want me to look?'

'No, it's okay.'

'I don't want to save them any trouble,' said Tell, reverting to the original subject. 'They should have found us by now. And I think we must be walking the wrong way, or else we've wandered off the track. This looks all wrong.'

'Maybe we really *have* hit the wrong side of the bay,' said Camena.

Tell shook her head stubbornly. 'There are dunes there. And I think the sun's in the right direction.'

'Don't worry about it,' advised Gerhardt. 'You've had a shock, Tell, and so have Camena and I. Is it any wonder if we're a bit blurry about details?'

The surroundings continued to puzzle Tell. Gerhardt had provided the obvious explanation for her disorientation, but it didn't feel right. It was like the time she had borrowed Maureen's shoes. They took the same size, but these shoes had been moulded to the shape of Maureen, and retained her ghostly impression when Tell put them on. They had felt wrong, rubbing in one place, too loose in another. She had been glad to take them off.

Something was wrong here, too. She worried at this notion for a time, but before the wrongness could crystallize, Camena stopped abruptly. 'Tell —'

Something in her tone alerted Tell, and when she glanced at Camena she saw that her eyes were strained and glassy. She looked blind. 'Are you getting one of your headaches, Cam?' she asked. Her spirits, already battered, floundered and sank lower still.

'Yes. Sorry,' said Camena jerkily. Her hand came up to cover one eye, as if in response to a blow.

'Now we'll have to rest,' Tell told Gerhardt, catching his arm to reinforce the urgency.

He looked round, bewildered. 'Here? Now?'

'Here and now. Cammie's getting a headache.'

'That's not surprising,' said Gerhardt, tugging away. 'There's a glare on the water and she may have struck her head in the explosion. It is better to get her to a place where she can rest in comfort.'

'It's not that sort of headache, Watchman. It's one of her specials.' Obviously Gerhardt hadn't a clue what she meant. 'It's a migraine,' she said sharply, and tugged at his arm. 'Tres mal a la tete. *Stop walking*, dammit!'

Gerhardt's eyes flickered. 'Camena gets these often? She never told me.'

'So? The thing is, she can't keep on walking. In a few minutes she won't be able to stand. Or talk. She'll just have to sleep it off.'

'How long?' Now he sounded dismayed.

'Ten hours, maybe. Hope you like camping, Watchman.'

'We have to keep on. They'll be looking for us.'

'So they ought to be,' said Tell. 'And I hope they bloody well find us. Unless you fancy carrying Cammie the rest of the way? I warn you — she could throw up any minute, if she runs according to her usual schedule. For God's sake, Watchman, will you just *look* at her?'

Gerhardt turned to Camena. 'Camena? You have a headache?'

Camena had slumped down with both hands pressed to her face and didn't respond.

'Isn't there anything we can do?' asked Gerhardt.

'Oh yes, she has these great pills that cut the duration of the attack,' said Tell heavily. 'She keeps a spare pack in her locker at school.' She paused. 'The only thing to do is have her lie down out of the sun — and cold compresses might help a bit.'

Camena had crumpled down on the pebbles now, still holding her head, and tears of pain were beginning to trickle down her cheeks. Tell knelt and put an arm around her shoulders. 'Come on Cammie — you'll be okay,' she said gently. 'Why don't you stick your finger down your throat? You know you'll feel better after you've thrown up.'

But Camena was past doing any such thing. And there was nothing Tell could do but make her as comfortable as possible until the pain wore out. 'Help me get her up,' she said curtly to Gerhardt. 'Can you carry her into the shade?'

Gerhardt lifted Camena, and gently laid her on the leaf-litter some metres up from the beach. Tell knelt beside her, making a pillow from some wild cherry twigs. 'It's okay, Cam,' she said softly. 'Someone will come soon.'

Camena moaned.

'It's come on awfully fast this time,' said Tell. There was no response, and she realised Gerhardt had gone back to the beach to pick up the shirt she had dropped when she stopped to tend to Camena. She moved down after him. 'Better leave that there, don't you reckon?'

Gerhardt jumped. 'Tell. You startled me.'

That was pretty obvious. 'Better still,' said Tell, eyeing him narrowly, 'I'll put it over Cammie and we can use hers.'

'For what?'

'For a signal, dillbrain. It's red.'

Gerhardt made an instinctive movement of denial.

'Watchman, are you thick or something?' asked Tell. 'If we're up in the trees, they won't see us, comprehendez vous? And if they're far off-shore we mightn't hear *them*. So we leave something on the beach they *will* see, so they know we're here.'

'They?'

'The rescuers, Watchman. Whoever Blenny's got looking for us.'

Gerhardt looked blank, but Tell could tell his mind was anything but quiet. 'What is it?' she asked curiously. 'What are you panicking about? We won't starve or freeze, even if we do have to stay out all night. And surely you're not afraid.' That was an angry joke, but she felt the disquiet was growing. 'You *are* afraid, aren't you?' she said in astonishment. 'What of? The dark?'

'Have you forgotten the danger so soon?'

'Your kidnappers? They won't come after Camena here. If they even exist outside your overactive mind.'

'Where could be better than here and now?' asked Gerhardt simply. 'We are a long way from help, and here they need not be unobtrusive. They could send five operatives. Ten. Who would see them? How could you and I stand against so many?'

'We're not that far from home,' said Tell. 'Even if we've been walking in the wrong direction we can't be *very* far from the marina. A couple of hours, tops. And Blenny must have the troops out by now.'

'RI-P may find us first.'

'Who the hell are Rye-Pee? Your mythical Middle East extremists? And what's it stand for, anyway? Rival Ignorance Party?'

'It stands for Rest in Peace, among other things,' said Gerhardt. 'You would not have heard of them.'

'They don't sound much like terrorists to me. More like grave diggers.'

'You might call them that, too. Certainly they are *very* interested in death.'

Gerhardt sounded quite dispassionate, but a shiver walked down Tell's spine, increasing the discomfort of her damp, salty clothes. She wriggled her shoulders, wondering if Gerhardt's incredible story could be true. If these RI-Ps were real, and if they really were after Camena, she'd be a sitting duck if they happened along. They all would. As Gerhardt had said, there would be no need for stealth. Unless she had lost her mind a week ago and this was all a piece of paranoid delusion.

She looked uneasily up and down the beach, half-expecting a squad of terrorists armed with bazookas or sub-machine guns, but there were only the pebbles, the sea-wrack and the trees. And the pebbles seemed very solid for a delusion.

'Would you know them if you saw them?' she asked curiously.

'Not necessarily.'

'Fat lot of good *you* are as a hero. You don't even know the enemy.'

'Mea culpa,' said Gerhardt quietly.

'Latin, now? I'm sick of your fun and games, Watchman. I think you're probably bad news for me *and* Cammie. And if her real dad's the type who attracts these grave-digging types as enemies, I reckon he's got to be bad news too. Cam's better off without him, and she's probably better off without you. Why don't you just go back to him — or to whoever really sent you — and get these RI-Ps off Cammie's case? How can she be a hostage for someone she's never met?' She glowered at him for a moment, but Gerhardt didn't react. 'All right!' said Tell coldly. 'You can hang around waiting for the troops to invade — I'm going on to stir up Mr Blenning. You hide out with Camena. Make compresses and keep putting them on her forehead — and don't get her too wet. One drowning per day's enough for anyone. I'll be as quick as I can.'

She turned and ran off along the beach.

For a second Gerhardt was tempted to let her go. Soon enough her presence in the Wild Zone would be reported by some outraged citizen. She would then be rounded up and dealt with by either RI-P or Hub HI-Q or even the Global Trust Council. Somewhere in the course of this she might learn the truth, but belief would come too late to be of any benefit to her. By the time she believed, someone would have acted to send her back where she belonged. Hub HI-Q and RI-P agreed on very little, but both would agree that Estelle Clancy had no business in the Wild Zone.

He had to get word to Moss as quickly as possible, and not only because of Tell. This affliction of Camena's was an unexpected complication, something Moss must have overlooked while researching her records. Gerhardt, too, had overlooked it while on the spot at St Saviours. And no wonder. Camena appeared to enjoy excellent health, so who would have suspected this flaw? Moss must be given a chance to consider this before word got back to Sib. Or even to Hub HI-Q. Perhaps Jens would help — but no. Jens had let him down badly once, and once was once too often.

Gerhardt had few illusions about Hub HI-Q. He believed in its general philosophy but then he had to. He owed his life and his continued existence to Moss and Hub HI-Q. He knew they could be every bit as ruthless as RI-P when it suited their purpose. They wouldn't want Tell, but would they even accept Camena as a part of the Programme now? He didn't know, but before he faced Moss and Hub HI-Q he must learn more about her condition, about its cause and its treatment. With Camena temporarily out of action, there was only one person with the necessary information, Tell, and he must fetch her back.

Gerhardt sent a powerful mental message after Tell. He had no idea whether she would receive it, for she was already out of sight and telepathy was usually accurate only while the practitioners were physically close. This factor, coupled with its unreliability and rarity, meant that Hub HI-Q had never bothered to try to isolate the gene responsible. Most people regarded telepathy as no more than a parlour trick; interesting, but without practical use. Even Moss disregarded it — but his own lack of facility might have had something to do with that. Nevertheless, Gerhardt reached out mentally for Tell. *Tell! Tell Clancy! Wait — I need to talk with you.*

I don't need to talk with you, Watchman. Her reply came clearly, as if she had spoken aloud. Probably she had. He had the impression she still didn't realise what she was doing.

Please. It is necessary.

Get stuffed, Watchman!

Gerhardt considered and rejected a more personal appeal. His status and desires cut no ice with Tell Clancy. *For Camena?* he thought instead. *It might be vital to Camena's safety.*

Really?

She seemed uncertain, so he began to jog along the beach in her wake, his feet crunching the pebbles, his heartbeat steady. If he had not been so worried, it would have been a luxury to be able to run with his normal free stride. He had had to be so very careful at St Saviours.

As usual when in the grip of one of her migraines, Camena was aware of nothing but her wretchedness and the terrible pain in her head.

Susan de Courcey had always seemed helpless when confronted by her adopted daughter's pain, practically wringing her hands when the migraine struck and taking Camena to doctor after doctor in an effort to find a cure. In the end she had been persuaded to accept the attacks as a debilitating but essentially harmless fact of life. It might have been a coincidence, but after her mother had reluctantly given up her search for the Holy Grail of the cure, Camena's headaches had become less frequent. Since entering her teens, she had suffered no more than two or three each year.

The worst thing about the migraines, apart from the pain, was the helplessness. Now she lay on the leaf-mould, a sea-soaked handkerchief over her eyes. To her distorted senses the sound of the waves was one with the regular throb of her head. She was drifting, but she whimpered protestingly when she was lifted again. She wanted to tell Gerhardt to leave her alone, but the words would not form. They were there in her mind, but if she opened her mouth she would be sick.

She was swinging through the air, the handkerchief sliding awry. Her head pounded, her eyes blurred and she was helpless as she retched.

A voice exclaimed angrily, and it was not Gerhardt but someone else. Tell? But Tell understood how things were. Tell would never blame her, not with the sea so close for clean-up operations.

If only Gerhardt would put her down.

Gerhardt caught up with Tell eight hundred metres along the beach. He was surprised she had gone so far, and annoyed that she had evidently continued after he had asked her to stop. 'I asked you to wait for me!' he said.

'Asked, nothing!' snarled Tell. 'You told. I don't take orders from you. Not when Cammie needs help.'

'*I* need your help,' said Gerhardt.

'Sure.' She took a deep breath. 'To fight off armed kidnappers. Safety in numbers, Watchman. We need the cavalry.'

'Camena seems very ill,' he said carefully, hiding his impatience.

'She is,' said Tell. 'But it's strictly self-limiting. There's nothing anyone but a doctor can do for her. She just has to get over it in her own good time.'

'Which might be ten hours.'

'Or more. Mostly these things come on in the afternoon and once she gets to bed she sleeps them off and wakes up fine in the morning. There's no way of telling whether they go off at midnight or at three a.m.'

'How often do they happen?'

'Couple of times a year. Why? Afraid you'll catch something?'

'No.'

'You're afraid of something, Watchman. I can feel it. Is it the kidnappers?'

He took a deep breath. This situation was badly out of hand. Perhaps a risk taken now would solve at least one of the complications.

Do you ever think it odd that we communicate, you and I? He sent the thought carefully in her direction.

'Of course I do.' She snapped it back without considering. 'I think it's odd you can communicate with anyone, the way you twist the truth. Why are you changing the subject? And why the inquisition?'

'I need to know,' said Gerhardt. 'I need to explain some things, but not just here. Come back to Camena. We should stay together and hide ourselves in the trees.'

'*You* hide,' said Tell. 'I'm going for help.'

'It's not safe. Remember, you've already been blown up and half drowned.'

'Geez, I'd quite forgotten.' She was being sarcastic, and he was prepared to knock her out and carry her if necessary, but she seemed to be thinking hard. 'Hey —' she said slowly. 'That explosion. Are you saying it wasn't an accident?'

'What do *you* think?'

'But you said these RI-Ps wanted to kidnap Cam, not kill her. What use would she be to them if she were dead? Particularly if there were witnesses.'

'Perhaps the explosion was an accident, but it seems unlikely. I am sure the *Kismet* was a RI-P vessel.'

'Hmm,' she said doubtfully, but she turned and followed him back along the beach to where they had left Camena.

Camena was not there.

At first Gerhardt thought they had come to the wrong place, but Tell unemotionally pointed out the leafy pillow and a small patch of vomit.

'She must have wandered away — come in search of us, ja?' he said.

'Get real. She can't even see straight! She can't even lift her head without throwing up.' They exchanged appalled glances. 'God, Watchman,' said Tell slowly. 'Maybe you weren't talking out your ear after all! Maybe they *have* snatched Cammie.'

It was no triumph to be proved right. 'I should not have followed you,' said Gerhardt. 'I should have let you go.'

'But how could they have got her so quickly? No-one else knows where we are and we didn't hear a thing! We should have heard. I heard you when you were yelling after me.'

'Someone knew. I have handled this badly.'

'She might still be somewhere about,' said Tell. 'She might have felt better suddenly. Her migraines don't *all* last so long. She might have gone looking for us.'

'An hour, only, these pains can last?'

'Well, I've never known of her having one that short,' admitted Tell. 'But I'm no doctor. And we don't live in the same house. Let's look round — call out to her.'

Do not call.

'Then how do we find her?'

'We search,' he said softly. 'We search in silence.'

Silence was hardly necessary. If RI-P *had* taken Camena they would be far away by now. But with no transport and no way of contacting Moss or Hub HI-Q, Gerhardt knew he and Tell had to take every precaution against being found themselves. RI-P would not harm him, not here, not now, but they might harm Tell.

In silence, they cast around the patch of bush, and up and down the beach. The shadows lengthened, and Tell was alarmed to realise how quickly evening was coming on. Quite soon, she could scarcely see the ground in front of her, and had begun to blunder into low branches.

She was exhausted by worry as well as physical effort. Added to her misery was the discomfort of goose pimples on her arms, the itch of her salted skin and the sullen ache in her thigh. She was cold, and thirsty, and frightened for Camena. She was also very angry.

'Why the *hell* hasn't someone come to get us?' she snapped at Gerhardt, hugging herself in an effort to keep warm. 'It's not as if we were lost in the back of beyond. D'you reckon they found Camena and thought she was the only survivor?'

'Perhaps,' said Gerhardt.

'But we would have heard them!' said Tell. 'Or seen them. They would have sung out.' Her voice went high. 'For God's sake, the *Kismet* went down in plain sight of land. They must have known there was a good chance we'd manage to swim for it — you and me, if not Cammie. They couldn't have known the life jackets were duds.'

He was silent, so she went on; 'We're not that far from the marina, remember. You hear about people dying a hundred metres from civilisation, sometimes, but this isn't a winter blizzard, it's the middle of March!' She shivered. 'I've had this, Watchman. Camena obviously isn't here. Oh — don't look like that! I'd do *anything* to help Camena, you know I would! If she *has* been snatched we should have gone straight back to the marina and raised the alarm. They could have taken her anywhere by now. Let's go and do it now, and hope to God it's not too late.'

'We must rest first. We have a long way to go.'

'Rubbish! The marina —'

'We cannot go to the marina, Tell.'

'*Why* not?'

'Because that is what they will expect us to do. Rest a while, and then we shall move on.'

'Where to?'

'A safe place. A place where I can summon help. Sit down. We have things to clarify.'

His voice was quite gentle, but when Tell made a move to turn away he reached out and put a hand on her arm, lightly, gently, but his fingers closed right around. Tell was reminded of the way Pris had grabbed her on the *Kismet*. 'Okay, okay,' she said agreeably, and forced herself to sit down and start untying her shoes. Their water-stiffened laces refused to give, so she gave up and jacked them off, heels against toes. 'Ugh. My feet are all toadstooly.'

Silence.

'I don't suppose you were ever a scout?' she said after a moment. 'A fire would be nice, if we have to sit here.'

He shook his head in the dimness. 'No fire, Tell.'

'Sit down, do,' said Tell irritably. 'Stop looming! I'm not going to run. God — Cammie must be freezing! Why the hell did I leave my jacket on the boat?' She paused, then said, 'There might have been an explosion, but surely I should have touched up my lipstick and fetched along my jacket before abandoning ship.'

Gerhardt sat down beside her and put his arm around her shoulders. Whether he was supplying comfort or restraint, she didn't know, but warmth began to steal over Tell and she wanted to move closer to its source. Despite her unease she was sorry for Gerhardt. He was a paid bodyguard who had lost his client's daughter — she had to accept that now. He had had a job to do, and he had failed. She wondered what he was thinking.

'I'm cold,' she said.

Gerhardt moved closer, but she knew his mind was on much more serious matters than her gawky self. Now she had an odd sense of thoughts skittering about like oil on a hot pan. 'Watchman?' she said after a while.

'Yes?'

'You said we had things to clarify.'

'We have.'

'You realise this is like a bad film,' she said. 'B-grade stuff. We're stuck in the sort of bad thriller they show late on Saturday nights.'

He was silent.

'Don't wallow. It's at least as much my fault Cammie got snatched, because I didn't believe it could happen. Watchman, why didn't you *make* me believe it? You could have, if you hadn't always acted so superior.' She paused. 'Admit it, you loved pulling the wool over my eyes, didn't you? You really wound me up.'

Gerhardt removed his arm. 'You were never meant to be a part of the operation, Estelle. I tried to discourage you.'

'Don't I know it!' said Tell viciously. 'You were going to let me drown. You even said goodbye to me — I think. Unless I imagined that bit? Anyway *that's* what I call discouraging! How cold-blooded can you get?' She meant to sound derisive, but her eyes grew hot and her voice thickened. 'I would have died, if it had been left up to you,' she muttered.

Tears slid down her cheeks, hardly more salty than her lips, reminding her of her thirst. The paradox of drinking her own tears struck her and she found herself smiling wryly in the dark. 'You know what they drink in space, Watchman?' she said. 'You know what they're going to *eat* soon, in space? Recycled human waste — gross! They feed it round a recycling plant and grow things that produce oxygen as well as food. Looks like shit. Probably tastes like shit. Reckon I'll stay on Earth. Adventures suck.' She paused. 'If you went on recycling sweat, piss and tears, you'd have enough to last you forever. Is that perpetual motion, or what? But if you were a bit thirsty in the first place, when they put you up in space, you'd always be that same bit thirsty, because there'd never be quite enough water.'

There was more silence.

'Come on — tell me the rest,' she said impatiently.

The side against Gerhardt was comfortably warm, the other was lonely and cold. It reminded Tell of the way she had sat in the bus, wedged between Camena and the window — was it six hours ago? Seven? Even eight? She wished it was Camena with her now, so that they could have curled up together for warmth. She wondered what Maureen would say if she knew Tell was snuggling up in the dark with Camena's 'pretty yummy' companion. Would she mind? David would.

'Talk!' she said, to escape her own uneasy thoughts.

'I'm trying to decide on the words,' said Gerhardt. 'What to say and what not.'

'Afraid of giving away some secrets?'

'Perhaps.'

'Yours or Cammie's dad's?'

He didn't answer that.

Tell was shivering now. Although one side was still warm, the goose pimples were blossoming on her arms and legs and her jaw was aching. She forced herself to relax. Tension would only make her colder.

'Let's start with you, then,' she said, hugging her drawn-up knees. 'Where do you come from? You sound Australian, but sometimes you use foreign words.'

'So do you.'

'I do not!'

'Comprehendez vous? Tres mal a la tete? And you understand Latin, a little.'

'Oh, that,' she said. 'That's just — well — talk. You pick that sort of thing up without meaning to, like slang. English is cluttered with foreign bits and pieces, and I got some of it from Cammie. She doesn't mean to show off, but sometimes it sort of bubbles over.'

'Ach, so!'

'Bits and pieces,' said Tell. 'A thing of shreds and tatters. Who said that?'

'Shakespeare,' said Gerhardt.

'You're only guessing. God, this is surreal! You're supposed to be giving me the good oil on you and Camena's dad. Why *did* he hire you? Are you his son?'

Gerhardt hesitated. 'No. And to tell the truth he did not hire me.'

'So it was all lies. *God*, Watchman. To think I was starting to trust you a bit! I actually believed the bodyguard bit!'

'Not all lies. Not even most. Camena's father *was* a scientist. Her mother *was* a young woman who did not rear her child. There really *are* people from whom I guarded Camena — and who have now succeeded in taking her away. All that is true.'

'Her real parents —' said Tell. 'Are they still alive?'

'They both died many years ago. Shall we begin with them?'

'Why not? Just don't *lie*.'

'Camena's father was born in 1950, the only child of two only children,' said Gerhardt, as if reading from a script. 'His name was Hadley Brand, and he had an IQ which was several points above the national average. He could have succeeded in any of a number of professions, but chose to become a marine biologist. He married, but his wife was infertile. He had a brief liaison with a female associate at a conference. This union produced a child — Camena — but the mother died shortly afterwards and a relative placed Camena for adoption. She was Hadley Brand's only descendant, but he never knew of her existence.'

'Then how the *devil* can you know she's his daughter? And don't tell me she's got a crown-shaped strawberry mark on her arm, because I know damned well she hasn't.'

'He is named as her father on her birth certificate,' said Gerhardt eventually. 'The documentation is clear, but because he and the mother had no further contact he was never told.'

'And how does this fit in with your kidnapper story? If Hadley Brand is dead, nobody can blackmail him into paying a ransom. He didn't leave her a fortune, so there's no possible reason for anyone to kidnap Camena . . .' Her voice faded, because it was hard to refute the fact that someone evidently *had*.

Gerhardt began to laugh, but he didn't sound amused. 'Ah, teur Estellita, but you're wrong! Her father left Camena something infinitely precious. He left her his genes.'

'I take it we're not talking Levis here?' joked Tell cautiously. 'Of course we're not. So — that's why Camena's a genius; just because of her old man. When did the guy die?'

Gerhardt's arm came casually around her shoulders again, and she felt his hand slide down her bare arm to close above her elbow, as it had once before. 'What now?' she said apprehensively. 'You — didn't kill him, did you, Watchman?'

'Hadley Brand,' said Gerhardt, 'died in the year 2010.'

Camena felt so ill that when she was laid on a soft, flat surface and covered with a blanket her only emotion was a vague thankfulness. There was a faint humming in her skull bones, a mild vibration, and then, incredibly, a gathering, lifting sensation.

Helicopter said the small, lucid part of her brain, but helicopters were noisy things, beating the air as Lindall beat eggs to make a cake.

Balloon, then. Hot air balloon.

Ridiculous.

It was dark when she woke. Her head throbbed warningly, but she knew from experience that her eyes would focus now. The fearful, one-sided blindness had passed, but for all she could see when she opened her eyes, the blindness might as well have become total.

'Tell?' she mumbled. 'Tell? Linnie?'

She felt uncomfortable, salt-stiffened and clammy, and she clearly remembered the accident. The disbelief as she had been tossed in the air, the sting of water in her nose, the pressure of the depths. Her legs trailing above her like the tail of a diving kestrel.

Blacking out, and waking to see Tell and Gerhardt bending over her.

The trek along the beach, the disorientation, the first hint of the approaching migraine, her collapse. Gerhardt carrying her into the shade, sickness, pain, Tell giving her comfort and advice.

Gerhardt lifting her again — but it hadn't been Gerhardt that time, because she had thrown up and been cursed in quite a different voice.

And then she had been transported in some kind of vehicle, and was now resting on a . . . bed? Certainly not her own bed, and not in her own house. Her room was always faintly lit by a street light when it was dark, and it always smelt faintly of cloves from the pomander balls in the cupboard.

She could not be in Tell's house, either, because Maureen had no spare room and this was not the creaking camp bed she had slept in so often. And it wasn't the sick bay at St Saviours. That was cool and pale and antiseptic, not dark and silent.

She reached out sideways, and encountered smooth walls, one on either side. Her scalp prickled and her heart began to pound in rhythm with her headache. Her exploring hands reached upwards, and her elbows were still bent as her fingertips brushed another smooth surface. A ceiling. Reaching down, she touched an equally smooth floor. *No wonder it was dark*!

Camena's breath came faster and panic welled in her mind. Where the hell was she?

Answers came reluctantly, and she could have cursed her clear intelligence. *Much* nicer to have been able to believe she was in a hospital bed, or even a stationary ambulance. Oh, *much* nicer to have been dumb enough for that.

She was in a prison. A cell. A hold, a tomb or a coffin.

The synonyms rolled grimly through her mind, and it was the last that almost broke her resolve. Prison doors could open, hatches could lift from holds, tombs had doors, but coffins were buried in the ground.

She had read too much. The hero imprisoned in the hold of a yacht. The man in the blacked-out van. The classic Poe horror tale of being buried alive. And, most frightening of all, the real-life experience of a kidnap victim who had been buried alive. Sensory deprivation. Solitary confinement. Passive tortures, designed to punish, to break the will — or to hide the victim of a crime. The kidnappers then, had found her.

Gerhardt felt Tell stiffen. 'You don't believe me.'

'You're nuts,' said Tell flatly. 'Mad. Pardon me — the polite term is *mentally disturbed*. Or perhaps you think I'm simple?'

'Teur Estellita,' said Gerhardt, 'you are anything *but* simple. And, being *so*, you can no doubt see my problem in trying to explain the unbelievable to you.'

'You're hurting my arm.'

Her respiration was fast, her heartbeat picking up. Fight or flight? Gerhardt didn't dare to relax his grip.

'I have proof of this fact,' he said.

'You had proof for Cammie. Letters from her ever-loving father, nein?' said Tell nastily.

Gerhardt winced. 'This is always difficult for Recoverees to accept.'

'*Always*? You've pulled this stunt before?'

'Not I,' said Gerhardt, 'but others have done so.'

'Oh, nice. So there are more out there like you! Well — I suppose it would have been a waste to have fired up the oven for just the one fruitcake.'

He shifted his grip and took hold of her other arm, twisting her to face him. 'Stop it, Tell! Stop making smart remarks and listen to me! Camena is in danger and so are you. You must accept what I say.'

Her face was a darker shadow in the night. 'So we're back to the B-grade films,' she said. 'Big hero comes over all macho and stupid heroine stops resisting and sees the light. Or else she slaps his face and he shakes her and then kisses her silly. Or maybe she runs, catches her foot and falls flat on her face. Oh, and twists her ankle. Pick a card. Any card! Now let me go!'

Gerhardt retained his grip. 'Then don't listen,' he said cuttingly. 'Keep your prejudices. Believe whatever you want, but *don't* go running off. Your life is your own, but you have no right to endanger Camena — or me.'

'And *you've* no right to keep me here against my will!'

'I'm not a violent person, Tell,' he said truthfully, 'but if you won't calm down I'll knock you out. You can't get away from me. I'm faster than you and much stronger, and I know where I am. Which is more than you do, whatever you choose to believe.'

'We're on the beach, somewhere between Penguin Point and the marina, and that water out there's Kestrel Bay,' said Tell. Her voice was shaking.

'There is no marina now, Tell. And Penguin Point eroded into the sea during a freak earthquake in 2460. The place we are now is called the Wild Zone, and has been for a century or more, since the island was declared a Global Trust.'

'Yeah, right.' Her voice was mocking, but there was an undertone of despair. She was afraid. She thought him insane and dangerous, as if her fear would shield her from belief. Like clenching a jaw against toothache.

'Think, Tell.'

'I'm thinking,' she said grimly, and tugged experimentally at her arm.

Think. In your place, in your time, how many telepaths have you met?

'None!' she snapped. 'Not in any place or time.'

Accept it, Estellita. You know what I am.

'Stop it!' Her free arm curved protectively about her head, as if she could shut out his directed thoughts.

You know, because you are one as well.

'Stop it! You're hurting me!'

He should have stopped right there. It was very dangerous to force telepathic communication with a subject who was unwilling. At best it was the height of bad manners. At worst, it could bring about a catatonic state. He had already pushed the boundaries way past the acceptable limit, but he had pushed so many boundaries through so many limits by now that it made him cold to consider the probable consequences. And he *must* convince Tell of the truth. Either that or knock her out. Otherwise, she would run.

He wished he could take his time and be gentle — but perhaps there would be no time. He must push on and take the risks for himself as well as for her.

We are telepathic together, you and I. It is not so common in my time, nor yet so rare. He tried to convey a mental shrug at the concept, as if it were not so very important.

'But it still d-doesn't mean this is a different time . . .' Her voice was shaking, and high. 'Just because you think you can get into my head . . .'

If we are still in your time, why is there no rescue for us from Blenning?

Why was there no debris from the Kismet *in sight when we came ashore?*

Where is the track and why have we not reached the marina or the point?

He tossed the thoughts to her deliberately, one at a time, giving her a second to consider each, but not time to respond. He felt the tension in her muscles, just as he felt the tension in her mind as she fought to dredge up logical answers to his questions. As she fought also to pretend this communication was of the normal, verbal kind. She seemed very much afraid.

This is normal too, he told her. *I learned it as I learned voice speech, from Jens.*

Normal! Her thought hit him with a wave of protest and he almost reeled from its intensity. She didn't accept it yet. He admired her courage and her strength, and feared it too. He should have sent her back. He waited for the space of thirty breaths, sensing the turmoil of her thoughts, aware of her on every level. The awareness built into almost unbearable tension. If she hit him again with a mental blow his mind could be in danger. He had felt this pain only once before, from Jens . . .

'Tell,' he said, in protest and entreaty.

He felt her shudder, and then she took another breath and spoke aloud.

'You're saying you're from the future? You're saying we're *in* the future. You're saying you can put your thoughts into my mind, and pick up my thoughts back. Is that it?'

'We are in your future, Tell. My present. As for the telepathy, it isn't quite so simple, but it isn't abnormal either.'

She made a jerky motion with her hand, and he let go of her.

'Why?' she said. '*How?* When? Not the mind thing — the other. What are you?'

'I am an operative with Hub HI-Q's Strategic Recovery Programme.'

'More lies...'

'I think,' he said tiredly, 'it would be better if I begin at the beginning, nicht wahr? And better that you listen and understand.'

'That's what you said before! And what about Camena?'

'We can do nothing for Camena until we reach the disclosure unit.'

'Oh.' She sounded fretful, and he wasn't surprised. 'Can you read my mind right now?' she ventured.

He sensed her deep unease and answered with a half truth. 'Nein. I can read nothing unless you send it to me.'

'I don't believe you.'

Then read my mind, if you can. He sent the challenge in her direction, then leaned back and looked deliberately at the moon. *You see?* he added after a while. *You read nothing unless I send to you. It is a closed book.*

'Good,' she said.

'You know a book has much to say, but unless you open the covers, you cannot read it,' he added.

Lucky for you.

The rejoinder stung like hail. He glanced at her warily. She was a much stronger telepath than any other he had met. She could be very dangerous.

'It is not such an uncommon gift,' he said again.

That was true, but it was *very* uncommon for an untutored natural telepath to function as well as she did.

He glanced at the sky. They had been resting for a quarter of an hour; perhaps they should move on. 'Come,' he said. 'Put your shoes on. We should go on to the disclosure unit, and I will tell you as we go. Take my arm so you won't get lost.'

The thought she shot at him was so rude he blinked, but it seemed to be the last bullet in her armoury, for she shrugged and did as he suggested.

Camena forced her mind to work logically. Without sitting up, she felt round in every direction, an exercise which confirmed her fears. The coffin-shaped space in which she lay was two metres long and less than a metre wide, and, she judged, a little over a metre high. There seemed to be no doors, and it was empty except for herself and the couch. That was the bad news.

The good news, if she could consider it that, was that the temperature was pleasant and the air was so fresh as to suggest good ventilation — or air conditioning. She couldn't hear any fans, so presumably the cell connected somehow with the open air.

The lack of amenities in her prison — she must think of it as a prison rather than a tomb — might also be construed as an encouraging sign. The kidnappers had provided ventilation, but not food, water or toilet facilities. This seemed to suggest that, unless they intended her to die slowly of thirst and starvation, they meant her no immediate harm and would shortly pay her a visit.

The kidnappers. Gerhardt had warned her, and had tried to protect her, but they had snatched her after all, taking advantage of the confusion when the *Kismet* went down. Perhaps they had even engineered that sinking, although the failure of her life jacket could easily have robbed them of their prize. Someone would be in trouble for that, if they needed her alive.

Had they also snatched Gerhardt and Tell? She had no idea, but she must be quick and clever, and hope her father would act decisively to pay the ransom or have her rescued. He *must* care, for he had provided Gerhardt as a guardian.

Protective custody would have been safer, said her mind, but she pushed the thought away and began to plan. After all, protective custody might have lasted for months. At least now the enemy had been drawn to make a move, and she had been forewarned. She knew who they were and that they wanted something her father could be forced to provide. Money? Information? A commitment?

When they came she would face them with composure. She would persuade them that she neither knew nor cared anything for her father; would plead ignorance of the entire affair. Better yet, she would deny her own identity. She would try to convince them that she was someone else — Lindall, perhaps, or one of the other girls on the boat, or even Tell.

She supposed Pris and Red were involved in this and tried to remember if they had ever addressed her by name. She thought they had not, so, unless they had a clear, recent photograph or a record of her retinal pattern or fingerprints, there was no way they could be one hundred per cent certain of her identity. She bore no birthmarks, had no particular distinguishing characteristics. Medium height, medium build, dark hair and olive complexion. She was very ordinary, except for her analytical brain.

Just as they might not identify her, she would take care that she could not identify them . . . her safety might depend on it, after the ransom had been paid. Perhaps she could blindfold herself, or suggest they did so — her head thumped and Camena closed her eyes in gratitude. Her migraine. It had always been a burden and a curse, but now it might become a blessing.

The symptoms of a classical migraine sometimes lasted two or three days and no-one could hope to interview a person who was all but unconscious with pain. Think helpless. Think pain. Think disturbed vision and disorientation.

Breathing deeply, Camena folded her hands and tried to sleep.

'Hub HI-Q,' said Gerhardt, 'is an organisation dedicated to improving the human race.'

Tell snorted. 'So was Nazism.'

'Nazism was based on the myth of racial superiority,' said Gerhardt patiently. 'Hub HI-Q deals in fact, not myth, and mercy, not extermination. Hub HI-Q believes our species future depends on building our intelligence, on producing better minds, and by preventing further degradation.'

'The Aryan race,' said Tell distastefully. 'Hitler, again.' She was needling him, and it might have been a stupid thing to do, but she couldn't seem to stop. Fear seemed to give her a bad case of the smart alecs. She had to accept the telepathy thing, and now it was in the open she realised that part of her mind had suspected it all along. Did that make her nuts? Not necessarily. But the fact of telepathy proved nothing about this preposterous idea that they were wandering around in the future. That was *really* impossible, yet Gerhardt seemed to believe it. So for now, the best hypothesis was that he was mad.

Too late, she realised she should have found a way of staying put. Right now she had no idea where he was taking her — except that it was a 'safe' place. It didn't sound very safe to her.

'Hitler believed in racial purity,' agreed Gerhardt. 'Which he tried to get by selective breeding and by killing those who didn't fit his theory.'

'And was he the founding father of this Hub HI-Q?'

'Hub HI-Q's intentions are quite different from Hitler's. They — we — don't advocate killing. We only try to improve human intelligence through —'

'Selective breeding for genius. *Ugh*. That's totally disgusting.' Tell shuffled away a little. Breeding genius! *That* was where Camena came into the picture. *Ugh*, she thought again.

'*Not* selective breeding!' said Gerhardt. He sounded exasperated and Tell wondered whether that was a good or bad sign. 'Hub HI-Q simply encourages HI-Qs to have more children.'

'*More* kids? That's a turnaround!' She tried to sound interested, and convinced.

'Until the early days of *your* century, health and intelligence were balanced by natural selection. The healthiest children survived to pass on their healthy genes, and the more intelligent found ways to avoid avoidable risks.'

'Survival of the fittest, ' said Tell. 'We did that in Blood-and-Guts, yonks ago.'

'Right. But the balance became unstable. Until the twentieth century, HI-Qs and IQ-normals alike tended to have big families. Some of the children in each family nearly always died, and it was usually the weaker ones. Immunisation and other medical improvements meant that suddenly, more and more of these children began to survive.'

'So people stopped having so many kids,' said Tell. 'In Australia, anyway.'

'The trend certainly started in the western world,' said Gerhardt, 'but by the end of the twenty-first century it had spread all over the globe. It all began with HI-Qs. People whose intelligence was of a high order. HI-Qs understood that smaller families brought great financial advantages to the children they *did* produce. Since HI-Qs have also tended to be ambitious, and to choose demanding careers, improved contraception and better health care meant that they could plan to produce their few children later in life. At a time when IQ-normals were still producing three or four children, HI-Q couples, or couples where one partner was HI-Q, often had none.'

'Maybe they had the sense not to bring more kids into an overcrowded world. Maybe they had more interesting things to do than change nappies,' Tell replied.

'No doubt the HI-Qs of that time would have argued that having few or no children meant they could arrange their lives to maximise their time and talents, but this surge of productivity had a payoff.'

'Hasn't it always,' murmured Tell.

'The payoff was that more and more HI-Qs failed to pass on their superior genetic heritage. From comprising something like two per cent of the general population their numbers gradually fell until they added up to something like half of one per cent. Not only that, but the effect spread downwards, via HI-Qs who had IQ-normal partners. The average intelligence of the human race began to fall. Intelligence tests and requirements had to be gradually re-calibrated — downwards, and school curriculums simplified. Only a little, but once that sort of trend is established, it's hard to reverse.'

'Genetics is only part of it,' argued Tell. 'We did that in Blood-and-Guts too — nature versus nurture. Education has a lot to do with how people turn out. So has environment. We have to learn a lot of stuff our parents never did, and we still have to learn most of the stuff *they* learned as well. We do it. That doesn't sound unintelligent to me.'

'The effect had hardly begun in your time,' said Gerhardt. 'Even in the next century the change was very gradual. First, the average IQ dropped a fraction of a point, and then another fraction. At the same time, the standard of health declined a little. Immune systems became a little less competent, but medical science bolstered the victims, and helped them produce children — who often inherited the genetic tendencies to poor health.'

'I can see what you're getting at,' said Tell reluctantly, 'but who are you to say which children should, and shouldn't, be born?'

'I might ask the same question of *your* society, Tell,' said Gerhardt. 'Do you not have a vocal majority calling for exactly the same power?'

'Abortion on demand,' said Tell uneasily. She didn't like the way this conversation was going. It was all very well to discuss moral issues with Sister Pat, but she didn't care to discuss this one while stumbling through the dark with Gerhardt Watchman. His touch on her arm was distracting her, but if she pulled away she would probably fall. And, he might think she was trying to escape.

'Abortion is not the issue here,' said Gerhardt. 'I just mentioned it as an example of an attitude that has changed between your time and mine. To me it seems a peculiar paradox that babies with a poor genetic make-up were often saved at enormous expense while others, whose genetic heritage was superior, were never allowed to be born.'

'Abortion is a choice, though,' argued Tell. 'You're talking about telling people to have, or not to have, children. Surely that decision is the right of the people concerned.'

'But the burden of that decision often falls on others,' said Gerhardt softly. 'For example, even in your time, Tell, there was a lot said about the ageing population. A great many people, having retired from work, were living on for two or even three decades more, burdening the health and welfare systems. To alleviate the problem they were encouraged to make provision for themselves before they reached retirement age, but by the end of the twenty-fourth century it was not age that was the problem, but general ill-health and reduced intellectual ability. Population growth was down all over the world, but the enormous majority of those remaining were increasingly dependent on the expertise of the few.'

'I take it you *are* a HI-Q? So what did you HI-Qs do about it? Kill off the sick ones? Make people sit exams before they could have kids?'

'Hub HI-Q has never harmed or coerced anyone. It has certainly never taken a life without the consent of the person concerned. It is simply doing what it has done since its inception; finding strategies to restore the health/intellectual balance to what it once was.'

'By getting healthy geniuses to have more kids than the others. Or at least as many. Well — it all sounds very enlightened, but if everyone's so sweet and reasonable, what's the problem? And where do your grave-diggers come in?' She bit her lip nervously in the darkness, because once more she had forgotten her resolve to pander to Gerhardt's delusions. 'I mean — it's very complicated, and I'm not feeling my brilliant best. Couldn't you tell me the rest of this at a café or something? I could really murder for a hot chocolate.'

At a café there would be a telephone. And lots of other people.

Gerhardt knew Tell still didn't believe him. That was the trouble with making disclosure here, in the Wild Zone. He had noticed while still aboard the *Kismet* that the bush along the shoreline closely resembled that of his own time. If he had been able to make the Recovery from Trinity Street, as intended, he and Camena would have come through the veil on the site of a disclosure unit. The units were equipped with enough proof to convince any but the most pigheaded Recoveree of reality, but here, in the Wild Zone, no such proof was available. And Tell was getting impatient.

She was obviously cold, and although he had no trouble in regulating his body temperature he knew he couldn't remove his clothes and offer them to her. She'd probably be shocked, and besides — the shorts and shirt wouldn't provide much extra warmth. She stumbled again, and he used that as an excuse to bring her closer to his side, holding her lightly, absorbing the chill into his own body. With one level of his mind he was conscious that, despite the danger, he was enjoying the physical contact. He was tempted to probe a little and find out if she enjoyed it too, but that was against the code. It was true enough that he could not lift thoughts directly from her mind, but he could pick up a general impression of her emotions.

At one time, Gerhardt would have discussed situations like this with Jens. Throughout his childhood, Jens had always provided Gerhardt with both a standard and a sounding board. Jens had been ready to answer any question, to discuss any subject. He had seldom sat in judgement, but he had always been transparently truthful, never leaving anyone in any doubt about his personal opinions. Or so Gerhardt had always believed until that last disastrous encounter.

He had trusted Jens implicitly, but the last time they had met he had realised that Jens, like his own natural-born contemporaries, must have always seen Gerhardt as something a little less than human; a quasi person who was required to use the codes of courtesy, but not entitled to expect them. A non-person who could be subjected to a mental and social abuse that would have brought instant retribution if the victim had been a natural-born.

But there had been retribution, of a sort. Moss had seen to that.

'Well?' prompted Tell. 'What about that hot chockie?'

Gerhardt came back from his painful memory of the past into the uncomfortable present. 'Forget the hot chocolate,' he said seriously. 'I have to tell you about RI-P.'

'We could drink and talk . . .' she offered.

'That's not possible, just now. RI-P,' he said, 'are a group of people who don't like what we're doing. They believe the human race has a right to decline if that's its destiny.'

'They're entitled to their opinion,' said Tell coolly.

'Of course,' said Gerhardt. 'But does that mean they're also entitled to try drowning you?'

Tell thought about that. 'Not really,' she said. 'No. So. We've got the good guys and the bad guys. The good guys are geniuses who want all things bright and beautiful and the bad guys are dummos who want us back in the Stone Age. Right?'

'Simplistic,' said Gerhardt. 'Hub HI-Q was originally a social club whose members represented the intellectual cream of society.'

'Like Mensa?'

'They were a little like Mensa, but they included people who wouldn't have been eligible for Mensa membership. Hub HI-Q was always more flexible. It encouraged members who were talented in all sorts of ways, and after a while they became devoted to a common goal, that of restoring worldwide intelligence to twentieth-century levels and, if possible, raising it still more. With this in mind, Hub HI-Q members were encouraged to have children together. The membership of the group doubled over three generations, but they didn't reach their goal. The gene pool was too small for safety. And the rest of the community —'

'Got their tights in a twist?' suggested Tell.

'Yes,' said Gerhardt sombrely. 'They certainly did.'

He crunched along the pebbles for a time and Tell wondered if he had finished the lecture. She began to lag a little, hoping to slip free and make for the marina, but Gerhardt simply slowed his pace to match her own. His grasp on her arm was light and gentle, but she had no doubt that would change if she tried to get away.

'So what happened next?' she asked. Her legs were getting tired, and her eyes burned from trying to pick out landmarks in the darkness.

'Reverse snobbery went mad,' continued Gerhardt. 'The Hub HI-Qs had expected their third and fourth generation descendants would choose partners from outside the group. That would have widened the gene pool and spread the rising IQs through the community by the ripple effect, but when the time came, it proved very difficult to find IQ-normals who would even consider socialising with HI-Qs, let alone accept them as partners.'

'I'm not surprised,' said Tell dryly. 'Who wants to feel inferior? And what if you got stuck with bringing up a kid that ran rings round you? So what happened next?'

'After two more generations had tried and failed to find outside partners, Hub HI-Q tried to trace descendants of the original members of Mensa,' said Gerhardt. 'They didn't have much luck, because it turned out that a huge percentage of twenty-first century Mensa members had no descendants at all.'

'So that was that,' said Tell. 'Are you going to give up? Or take to cloning yourselves? If you inbreed, you'll lose everything you've gained.'

'After that,' said Gerhardt, 'came the Recovery Programme. Hub HI-Q decided to go fishing where the fish were. In the past.'

At last, Tell began to see where the story was leading, and what it had to do with her own current situation. 'I suppose,' she said after a few seconds, 'this is where Camena and I come in? Your Hub HI-Q fished for us, or rather for Cammie — using you as the bait?'

Gerhardt wondered if she really understood, or if she was merely pretending to accept his story. This disclosure was more than ever like a game of cat and mouse — or perhaps like a fencing match. He was telling the truth — well, most of the truth — to cut down her defences, she was parrying and riposting with words, while waiting for him to drop his guard.

I'll not do it, you know, he thought. He was almost proud of her.

He felt her start of surprise. 'Not do what?'

I'll not play your game, Estellita.

'Game? The only *game* is yours,' she said. 'Get out of my head, Watchman. I didn't invite you in.'

That was true, but her emotions were shifting and she didn't seem as angry as she should have been. 'And, since you're making the rules of this game,' she added, 'tell me if I'm right.'

'Half right,' he said. 'That is where Camena comes in, ja, but I was not bait. How could I be bait?'

'You *know* how,' she said impatiently. 'You must have looked in the mirror. You must have seen the other guys at the pool.'

Gerhardt was startled. He knew his general type had been a consideration while Moss had been grooming him to befriend Camena, but his physical aspect had never seemed particularly appealing to him. He had always felt that his pale skin and blue eyes acted like a tattoo to advertise his origin. He blinked and recovered in an instant. 'Nevertheless,' he said, 'I was not bait, but the operative assigned to the Recovery. To be her friend and reassure her once we were through the veil.'

'Recovery from what? Camena's not sick! Except for her migraines she's as strong as a horse.'

'It's a figure of speech,' he said hurriedly. 'But yes, Camena was chosen as the prospect for . . . for . . .'

'For your captive breeding programme!' snapped Tell, and once more Gerhardt felt her furious distaste. 'God — I've heard some lines, Watchman, but that one takes the fruitcake!' Tell continued. 'You brainwashed Cammie into thinking you were going to protect her, but *you're* the only one she needs protecting from. You and your bloody Hub HI-Q. What were you planning? To be more than her *friend*?

Were you going to breed a litter of little Watchpeople? Well I reckon you've backed the wrong horse, Watchman. Camena would never want you.'

That comment hurt, and he lashed out in response. 'I suppose you think I'm not a fit leman for any natural-born!'

Huh? She seemed honestly taken aback.

'Camena would be offered her choice of partner,' he said more calmly. Moss had always been a trifle vague about the exact mechanics by which Recoverees were integrated into society, so he had had to depend on old reports for information. 'She probably would not choose me. Neither would I choose her, unless she wanted me. And she would not be allowed to make any commitment until she had been thoroughly —'

Brainwashed!

The thought hit him squarely, and once again he was amazed at how strong her mind was — strong and potentially dangerous. Strong telepaths could kill by overloading the minds of their victims. The corollary of this fact was that the victims had to be strongly telepathic themselves for the jolt to have an effect ... He must warn her before she did some damage; possibly to him since they were mentally synchronised! She probably had a limited focus, but he wouldn't be sure until she'd been tested by Hub HI-Q. But Hub HI-Q, he recalled wryly, would never test her at all. Instead, they'd send her back ...

'Not brainwashed,' he said evenly, resisting the impulse to rub his temples. 'Debriefed. Camena will be given the chance to live in our society for some months before making her decision, and after that she may wait longer before taking a partner. A partner of *her choice.*'

'Let's get this straight,' said Tell. 'You say Camena gets to pick some HI-Q guy and have kids with him?'

'Not necessarily. Her choice might equally well fall on an IQ-normal plus — or even on a fellow Recoveree.' If she could find one.

'So Cammie picks a guy and has kids. Or else they pick one another.'

'Right,' said Gerhardt. 'With every support and encouragement from Hub HI-Q.'

'And she stays on here — in your time — for the rest of her life.'

'She could, if she chose, donate ova to the gene banks and return to her own time within weeks. Or days.'

'Or stay and have her kids the usual way and *then* go back?'

'That is not a viable option.'

'Why not?'

'Camena could not return to your own time after spending much time with us, because she would be physically older and people who know her would recognise that and wonder how it had come about. Paradox.'

'I guess they'd ask her, and decide she was nuts when she told them. Yeah.'

Gerhardt knew that would never happen, but he held his peace. No point in alarming Tell about something that he devoutly hoped would never come about.

'I thought time-travel was supposed to send you back to the time you left?' said Tell sceptically. 'That's what happened in all the stories *I've* ever read. You leave 1999 on the last Wednesday in May. You spend a year in the past, or the future, then you hop in your time machine and go back to the same Wednesday in time for tea.'

Gerhardt sighed. 'That kind of time-travel is a myth, Tell. Time is linear. We could return Camena to the moment she left your time, however long she stayed with us. She would find herself in the sea, after the explosion, at the point from which she was Recovered. She would be older. Although we can manipulate linear time enough to perform Recoveries, we can't manipulate genetic time.

'You are fifteen years old. If you stay here and now for ten years, you will be twenty-five years old when you return through the veil. Do you understand? It's the opposite to what happens to astronauts who go beyond the speed of light. They quite often come home to find their children genetically older than they are themselves.'

'So she can't stay on too long at the fair, or someone will wonder why she's still in Year Ten when she looks about twenty-five. And when she gets to be ninety, her birth certificate will say she's eighty.'

Gerhardt paused. He was treading shaky ground here, stepping from solid truth to half truth and back again. 'That's the theory,' he said. He knew the theory wasn't at all the same as the practical effect, but — who was to say it mightn't work that way this time? Since RI-P had interfered to such a degree anything was possible.

'Then why bring her here at all? Why didn't you explain this at home and ask if she wanted to come? What you've done is practically kidnapping! No, it *is* kidnapping! You snatched her after the accident, but you snatched her all the same.'

More shaky ground, but at least he had one explanation to offer. 'I could have done as you suggest, but would she ever have believed me?'

'Of course she wouldn't. But she might have agreed in theory. You could have done your telepathy act.'

'Camena is not telepathic in the slightest degree,' he said.

'Did you ever bother to try? No! You filled her mind with rubbish about kidnaps and bodyguards and her ever-loving daddy, and then you kidnapped her yourself. And then you dumped her — us — in the sea. Why didn't you arrange to end up on land?'

'The Recovery was *meant* to happen later in the day when we *would* have been on land,' said Gerhardt. 'But since Camena seemed to be in danger of drowning, my hand was forced. If everything had gone as planned, we'd have arrived close to the disclosure unit and we wouldn't have been walking a long way now.'

'And I wouldn't have been walking at all,' said Tell darkly. 'I'd have been at home, having tea. Or no — I'd have been with David. Having tea, in any case.'

Gerhardt felt suddenly weary, and relieved that they *were* walking. If things had gone as planned — Tell would not have been having her tea. 'I should be at the disclosure unit with Camena by now,' he said.

'And you've lost her, so you're dragging me along instead.'

It was very dark, and there was only a slip of a moon. Tell trudged along, stumbling more frequently as she tired, becoming numb with the cold. Away to her left was the faint heaving gleam of the sea, to the right was the density of the trees. That orientation meant they were heading in the right direction; towards the marina. There would be no-one there at this hour, but there was an all-night pharmacy at the shopping centre. She could persuade Gerhardt she needed to make a purchase and take it from there. Ask for help, ring Maureen or David. Find out what the hell was going on.

She stumbled again, and this time Gerhardt took her hand. She'd not linked hands with anyone in a long time — and now here she was, walking hand in hand with a telepathic psychotic.

Unless his story was true.

The walk back to the marina seemed to be taking a very long time. Tell glanced at the luminous dial of her watch several times. Amazingly, it seemed to have survived both explosion and immersion, although the time it stated seemed to make little sense. Nevertheless, it was going, and as the minutes flicked over and added up to become an hour, she began to feel a cold ball of fright building in her chest. They should have seen the shopping centre lights long ago.

If she could have believed they were lost, and walking in circles, she would have felt better, but logic said they couldn't be lost. Just as a computer will match information while searching for a file or a function, so Tell's mind matched pieces of data, again and again.

No two pieces seemed to fit together, but if she laid out the facts as Camena did when composing syllogisms, she might be able to reason out a conclusion.

Fact; the *Kismet* had only *just* rounded the shoulder of the bay when the engines blew. It had not yet reached Penguin Point.

Fact; she and Gerhardt had swum ashore from that point. The shape of Kestrel Bay being what it was, they must have swum to either the north shore or the south.

Fact; the north shore had been much closer.

Fact; she doubted she could ever have swum to the south shore. She was a speed swimmer; she didn't do marathons.

Fact; *if* they had reached the north shore and turned left, they would have walked to the dead end of Penguin Point.

While walking in that direction, the sea would have been on their right, the bush on their left.

Fact; they had turned right, therefore the sea was on their left and the bush on their right.

Fact; to have walked straight on, or north, would have taken them inland, away from the sea. Yet the sea was right *there*, a couple of metres away.

Conclusion; if all the above were true, then they should have reached the marina by now. In fact, when she really thought about it, it became obvious that they should have reached the marina before Camena's migraine had taken hold.

So; where the hell were they?

Logic had no answers, so Tell began to sift through the possibilities.

Fact; Gerhardt was telepathic, and so was she.

Therefore . . .

Therefore, what? Was it all a delusion? She'd never suffered delusions before, but she'd never been telepathic before, either. Perhaps it was some sort of trick. Perhaps Gerhardt had, somehow, sometime, hypnotised her. Brainwashed her into believing she was telepathic, and that she was walking through the night on the strangest journey she had ever taken.

Only — that sort of brainwashing was pretty major stuff, and if Gerhardt were *that* good at it, he'd have had no trouble in going that little bit further and convincing her his impenetrable rigmarole was true.

He hadn't done that, so it appeared, in the manner of Camena's syllogisms, that the tale *was* true.

Tell had reasoned herself neatly round into a circle. Which way to the padded cell?

While she was still contemplating this, swallowing panic and almost choking on it, Gerhardt did turn inland. Now her watch informed her that they had been walking for three hours and her feet were hurting fiercely. 'I've got blisters,' she said huskily.

'I'm sorry, Tell,' said Gerhardt. 'There's no other way of getting to the unit. We have to keep on walking.'

'At least let me get my shoes off again.' She removed her hand from his. 'Don't worry. I won't run away. I'm convinced. I think. God! I wish I wasn't.'

They should have been walking through cleared ground, along a tarmac road, but the ground under Tell's sore feet seemed to be grass, or leaf-mould. She still had no idea where they were. She wondered if Gerhardt knew, for he stopped every so often as if to correct their course.

Sometimes, the lie of the land seemed tauntingly familiar, but it wasn't until another half hour had passed that Tell's sick suspicion became a certainty. There was the stark tip of Silicon Peak, and that meant the gently rising ground ahead was, incredibly, the site of Cockatoo, her own home town.

She gave a whimper of panic.

'You recognise this place, Tell?' asked Gerhardt. His voice was quite gentle.

'Yes,' she said shortly. 'It's where I live. Lived.'

'The syntax *is* awkward,' said Gerhardt. 'I find it simpler to look on the two times as two places, each with its own now and its own then.'

'That's impossible.'

'Langsam! You have had to consider time zones before, haven't you? For telephoning?'

'Yes, but —'

'Did you trouble over your syntax then? Did you say "it will be midnight in Perth an hour ago"? No, you said; "It is one a.m., WA time", and you corrected automatically.'

'It's all very well for you,' she said. 'No doubt you're just as happy in tomorrow as you are in today. *God*, Watchman! I feel sick!'

'I have never been to tomorrow,' he said sharply. 'Nor has anyone else.'

'Why wait? If you can zip around the perpetual calendar the way you obviously can, why not pop into tomorrow for a sneak preview? Afraid of meeting yourself?'

'That's one problem, yes. But Hub HI-Q would never countenance any attempt to visit the future. To move ahead in my own time-line would risk changing my present. I would know what was to come and might take steps in my own present to pervert my future. It is forbidden.'

'You don't seem to mind risking Cammie's and *my* present. So. What happens when you take us back home, if Cam decides not to stay on here? I mean, now? She and I will know what's going to happen. Hub HI-Q and all. And the longer we stay, the more we'll learn. Or are you planning to wipe our memories before we leave?'

There was a pause, and she knew he was choosing his words. His mind was closed to her probing, but she had the impression he was stepping through a mental minefield. 'That will not be necessary,' he said at last. 'I trust — I hope Camena will choose to stay.'

Tell's thoughts flinched away from the implications of that one. If Camena stayed, that meant she would be going home alone. Everyone would want to what had happened to Camena, and there would be an inquiry. She would be questioned, and she would have to be careful what she said.

If she told the truth, they'd think she was lying, or send her to the funny farm. *That* would change her life all right. Well — if it was going to happen it was going to happen. Correction. It had *already* happened, from where she stood now. Tell felt like crying. She was so cold, scared and exhausted that she didn't know what to do.

'Watchman,' she said.

'Tell?'

'You said this fishing business is where *Camena* comes in. Your Hub HI-Q sent you to fetch her so she could have children here. Now, I mean. To pass on her genius genes.'

'Ja,' he said. 'That is correct.'

'So — where do I come into the picture? Nobody fished for me . . .'

Gerhardt had been hoping she wouldn't ask that, but he supposed it had been inevitable. She might be worried about her friend, but she wouldn't be human if she were not also worried about herself. The truth was that he didn't know what would happen to her now. He had a good idea what *would* have happened if Recovery had gone according to plan, but since RI-P had changed the script the situation was fluid. Tell would never know it, but it was possible that RI-P had done her a very big favour in the short term. He hoped it would be allowed to stand. He'd have to ask Moss about that.

They had almost reached their destination, and he was able to use this as an excuse to avoid answering her directly. 'Wait — I must locate the entrance of the disclosure unit,' he said with relief.

'Don't you know where it is?'

'It's difficult to see without a search key and I don't have one with me.'

'Of course not,' she said dryly. 'You didn't have a chance to bring much luggage.' She shivered. 'Neither did I.'

Gerhardt moved a few metres to the west, and bent to tug open the roof hatch of the disclosure unit which, like most of the buildings in this area, was built below ground level.

The place that had once been the town of Cockatoo was still a town, of sorts, but now it provided temporary housing for people who needed privacy for creative or scientific purposes. Since the entire island of Tasmania was now designated a Global Trust, visible human intrusion was held to a minimum.

'Come on in,' said Gerhardt, lifting aside the hinged hatch. 'Sit down and slide.'

Tell seemed to be looking apprehensively at the darker aperture, so he added; 'The light will come on when you pass the sensor.'

Obediently, Tell slid feet-first into the unit. The light came up, and Gerhardt allowed her enough time to move away from the hatch before he followed, drawing it closed above him. As it sealed, he felt the tension draining out through his fingertips. While he and Tell were inside, no-one could find them. Except Hub HI-Q, and he'd worry about that later.

He was struck by the pleasant ambient temperature. Building underground had a number of advantages, economic, environmental, and aesthetic, but Gerhardt reckoned the conservation of energy was one of the greatest. 'You'll soon feel better in here,' he said to Tell.

Like hell! Tell moved distrustfully across to sit on the low couch. She was rubbing her arms, and, although she looked a long way from comfortable, he could see her slowly relaxing in the warmth. 'Now what?' she said. 'Do I get something to eat, or would that mean I was stuck here forever like Persephone in Pluto's court?'

'Certainly you can eat,' said Gerhardt. 'I ate in your time.'

'Hmm.' She sounded doubtful. 'What, then? Do you have food pills, or what?'

'Freeze-dried,' said Gerhardt. 'At least, it is here.'

He began to prepare a meal, moving slowly, allowing Tell time to become acclimatised. At first, she sat like a visitor, but after a while she was looking around with interest.

The unit was small, with curved walls and ceiling of sealed natural earth, cloaked outside in half a metre of soil and vegetation. Inside, it was self-contained, with a good supply of food, washing facilities, simple clothing and an information terminal.

'It doesn't look very high-tech for the twenty-fifth century,' said Tell.

'Twenty-seventh,' said Gerhardt. 'What did you expect? Anti-gravity? Three-hundred-storey buildings? An empty planet?'

'I don't know. I never thought. I never expected I'd have to *expect* anything. I never expected to be here.'

He handed her a bowl with a portion of reconstituted vegetables and rice; a standard high-carbohydrate meal. 'HI-Qs have learnt not to appear high-tech, as you put it,' he said wryly. 'If we keep a low social profile, we stand a better chance of eventually integrating ourselves with the rest of the population — of convincing them we are normal human beings.'

'Yeah,' said Tell. 'Like — it's so *normal* to start importing people from the past.' She tasted the food, pulled a face and then began to eat.

'You said I was never meant to be a part of the operation,' she said after a while. 'So why did you bring me? Why didn't you leave me in the water? Maybe I would have swum ashore.'

'I didn't *bring* you,' he said, bending forward to take her bowl. 'You came of your own accord. In fact, I tried to leave you behind — remember?'

'Leaving me to drown.' She shivered. 'I thought I was imagining things, but you really *did* say it, didn't you? You really told me goodbye. Or you put it into my mind. How sweet.'

'You can't have it both ways, Estelle. Either you had to stay alone and take your chance in *your* time or you had to come with me and take your chance in mine.'

'You left one option out,' she said sourly. 'How about the one where *you* keep your long nose out of our business and neither Cammie nor I has to go anywhere?'

Gerhardt sighed. 'You mightn't have liked that option as much as you think, Tell. Correction. You wouldn't have liked that at all.'

Tell stared at him wordlessly. She obviously wasn't ready to challenge that and perhaps he should have said nothing. He knew now he would fight to prevent her going back. One abandonment was enough. He was committed, and surely Moss would help. If Tell *had* to go back it must be to the point of departure, and not to Trinity Street. And RI-P must be forced to leave it at that.

He knew he should contact Moss immediately, but he told himself he wanted to wait until his mind was clear. He was *not* afraid of what Moss might say, because Moss was bound to decide for the best. *Think of it as a rescue* ... Fair enough, for the Recoveree, but where did that leave the peripherals? The answer to that was simple; the peripherals were not part of the programme and could not be considered at all.

He half-wished he could contact Jens instead, but that was a child's wish, a desire to go back to the comfort of childhood. He could not go back, and after that last confrontation he couldn't trust Jens anyway.

'To get back to the choice you *did* have,' he said quickly, 'it seems that for some reason you chose to come mit moi. Or perhaps it was Camena you wanted to follow?'

He had wondered about that. The bond of long, complementary friendship *might* have been enough for Tell to have followed Camena, but it was highly unlikely. It seemed more probable that the telepathic bond she shared with *him* was to blame for her passage through the veil. She had not been consciously aware of it at the time, and by all the rules it should not have existed at all, but it seemed just possible that she had somehow linked with his mind as he made the Recovery. If so, the implications opened all sorts of possibilities for himself and Tell. He must discuss them with Moss.

'Think,' he said, suddenly feeling much more cheerful. 'When I made the Recovery, how and when did you decide to follow?'

'I didn't.'

No?

No. At least — I don't think I did. I was drowning . . . Damn you, Watchman! You said goodbye to me!

What did you do then? Whom did you follow?

'I didn't,' she said aloud. 'I didn't follow anyone. It was purely an accident. And now we're here — what next? Can we help Camena?'

Gerhardt pushed his hands into the pockets of his shorts. They were stiff with salt, and he wanted to get clean. 'We can't do anything for Camena just now,' he said. 'I have to contact someone first. He'll know what to do, both for Camena and about you.'

'Do it now then.'

'Tomorrow,' he said.

'Can't you do it now?'

Of course he could. Moss never seemed to need much sleep. But he needed to be alert to deal with the complicated report he must make, and he needed to think about the best way to get Moss's approval for his new idea. It would not be easy, but it was the only chance for Tell. He must have all his wits about him, though, or the chance would be nothing at all. Even on his best days Moss could make him feel dull and foolish. It must be left until morning.

'I'm scheduled to report tomorrow,' he said truthfully. 'This evening was supposed to be spent making disclosure to the Recoveree.'

'But you made it to me instead,' said Tell. 'Watchman, who *has* got Camena? Is it Hub HI-Q?'

'It could be,' he said reluctantly, 'but they have no reason to interfere in an authorised Recovery, although it did not go to plan. I'm afraid it's much more likely to be RI-P, as I told you before. They disapprove of the whole Recovery Programme and of Donor HI-Q, so they interfere with it whenever they can. They would do a great deal to prevent Hub HI-Q from making more Recoveries — and it seems that they may well succeed. The Programme is much less dynamic than it was — in fact Camena is the first successfully retrieved Recoveree for some years.' And how confident he had been of that success.

'The grave-diggers,' she said soberly.

'They believe the decline in mental ability is part of the destiny of the human race,' said Gerhardt.

'So they want to let us all go to hell in our own way?'

Gerhardt nodded. 'They also uphold the right of the individual to die in his or her own time and in his or her appointed fashion.'

For a moment he thought he had said too much, but perhaps not, for Tell yawned. 'They sound pretty sensible to me, but I reckon it was a bit excessive to risk drowning us just to keep you from Recovering Camena. They won't hurt Cammie now, will they?'

Gerhardt turned to face her, for on this point, at least, he could truthfully reassure her. *Believe me, teur Estellita, Camena will not be hurt in this time.*

Tell gazed at him for a few seconds and then nodded slowly. *If you say so. I believe you this time. God knows why!*

'Because I am telling the truth,' he said. 'There is a shower over there, if you wish, and spare clothes in the basket.'

Tell gave him an ironic glance, seemed about to say something, then shook her head wearily and went into the opaque cubicle.

Since the water controls had been overlaid by twentieth century taps, in readiness for Camena, Gerhardt left Tell to it. He prowled around the unit for a while, then clambered out through the hatch. It was unwise to expose himself again, but he needed to think about choice and truth and the burden of knowledge. If Camena were still in the present, she would be unharmed. She should be permanently safe once she was under the protection of Moss or Hub HI-Q — if only she could be brought to make the sensible choice. Tell was another matter, and she might never be safe at all.

Gerhardt was very tired. Camena was his responsibility, and would be until she had undergone disclosure. Tell was his responsibility too, now, because he had elected not to take her back through the veil to where she belonged. *Take* her? he thought derisively. It might have proved impossible after all.

The cool air touched his arms and legs, and he looked thoughtfully at the moon. The mist on the surface was surely an illusion, but it looked as if it would cling to his face like cobwebs. The strands of time were like cobwebs, he thought, tough, yet easily torn.

It was possible that Camena had already been returned to her own time. If so, a second Recovery *might* be planned, but it would be horribly complicated. Already two parallel time-lines existed where there should have been one. A third could cause wide-spread changes, maybe even disasters that would echo through to the present. It would be very difficult to Recover her again, and Hub HI-Q might decide to cut its losses — and Gerhardt's place in its secretive world.

For Camena's sake, as well as for his own, he had better hope Sib was holding her in the present. As long as they did so, the RI-Ps would treat Camena very well. They would certainly *never* hurt her, although they wanted her dead.

Tell was lying on the couch when Gerhardt returned. The lights had adjusted when she lay down, but brightened again as he entered. Through half-closed eyes she saw him wave a hand towards a wall-mounted control and watched the lights subside. Well, that was nothing miraculous. There were dimming touch-switches in David's spare room. There were underground houses in Coober Pedy, and solar power all over the world ... but she no longer doubted she was in another time, because nothing else could explain the total disappearance of the marina and Cockatoo. Nothing could explain an identical twin of Silicon Peak.

In the morning Tell would have a good look round the site — there might be something familiar left. After all, the outlines of Iron Age forts could still be seen in the grain fields of Great Britain, and she might make a fortune as an archaeologist here ... what was she thinking? The people of

Gerhardt's time could go anywhere and who knew how many of them were prowling the past, 'Recovering' anyone they chose?

How many so-called 'mysterious disappearances' were the result of interference from roving HI-Qs? People snatched out of time, out of their lives, hauled into the future willy-nilly. Although they did have the choice of going back if they wanted to . . .

She supposed that made it better, but why should the HI-Qs stop with Recoveries? Why not progress to strategic assassination? All in a good cause, of course, but she'd bet her life the authorities in this century had a 'better-dead' list locked in a vault somewhere. Presumably under time-delay, which meant one of *them* could get it whenever he wanted.

Gerhardt was in the shower, trying to be quiet. Being alone with him in the wilderness was one thing. Being alone with him in this unit felt like quite another. Treat it like school camp, Tell thought resignedly, but at every school camp she had ever attended she had roomed with three other girls and the boys had been not only in a different room, but across the compound in another building, with strict teachers on guard. And none of those boys had had Gerhardt's potential for time-travelling mayhem. He might slide through the veil and reappear *any* time, in the middle of the night, perhaps, in the girls' dormitory. But that kind of behaviour didn't seem to be Gerhardt's style, so she wouldn't worry now. She trusted him in some ways, and that was strange, considering his performance so far.

She felt herself drifting, clinging to Gerhardt's assurance that Camena would not be hurt.

Believe me, Estellita, Camena will not be hurt.

Gerhardt Watchman was a pain, and she wished she'd never met him. She wished Camena had never listened to his lying story, but somehow she did believe he cared what happened to Camena. Although if he thought he could soft-soap her by using cutesy nick-names he had another think coming. Gerhardt had called her *Estellita* more than once, and his mental tone had made it clear that he thought of it as an endearment.

The first time he had used it was when she was drowning under Camena's weight, while they struggled together to remove the weighted life jacket — and, in the light of what she knew now, it seemed increasingly less likely that those death-traps had been accidental — *Estellita ma amata* ... that was what he had said, and if it meant what she thought it meant — well, it wasn't the sort of thing any boy should say to a girl he was leaving to drown. *Goodbye* had been implicit in that piece of mangled Latin, and she hadn't been ready for goodbye. Not from him, not then, and perhaps not ever.

The blood surged in Tell's cheeks, because here in the dark she understood precisely whom she had followed into the twenty-seventh century. And why.

PART THREE

PLATEAU

Children born of Donor HI-Q Recovery stock are to be regarded as fully human in every aspect. Nevertheless, since it has been ensured that they will not suffer the burden of ill-health or inadequate intellectual potential, it is their responsibility to repay in some order the effort and expertise which has been employed on their behalf. To this end selected DHQ offspring are to be trained by HI-Q alpha individuals to continue the work of Hub HI-Q.

Camena woke to a faint high buzzing noise, and to daylight filtering through the window.

Window? There had been no window! Or had she missed it, in the dark?

She began to sit up, then remembered her resolution. Play possum. Play dead. In the sweet light of morning, that seemed a little unnecessary. Still, she would be cautious.

She sat up very slowly, rubbing her temples as if she was still suffering. And that wasn't so very far wrong. The migraine had passed, but the after-effects lingered. It was like the after-pain in a cramped muscle where the fierce agony of a nocturnal cramp faded as soon as the muscle could be persuaded to relax, but often there was a moderate ache for a day or two afterwards.

Camena kept her hands over her eyes as if shielding them from the light, peering through the lattice of her fingers, rocking slightly as if from continued pain. The rhythmic motion allowed her to inspect a semi-circle of her surroundings.

She had been moved in the night.

Not only was her current cell day-lit, but it was spacious as well. The bed was a couch, and she was covered with a light cellular blanket. There was a small table with a chair, an armchair, a chess board, and a pack of cards. The high buzzing came from a cat which was curled on the armchair, blinking mildly and purring in the sun.

It was a very big cat, but otherwise appeared quite normal.

There were no obvious peepholes or surveillance cameras in the room, but that didn't mean much. Strides in the science of miniaturisation meant a camera could be the size of a credit card — or the size of a twenty cent piece. It seemed quite likely that someone was watching and recording every move, but also quite likely that someone wasn't.

If she really *had* been kidnapped, would they have put her in such a pleasant room?

Perhaps — if they wanted to lull her suspicions. Perhaps — if they wanted her to be sympathetic to their aims. Kidnap victims often became quite friendly with their captors, provided they were decently treated. If she knew that, presumably the kidnappers did too, and they might have decided to capitalise on that theory. *She* would have, if she'd been a kidnapper.

Well, she was all in favour of good treatment, especially for herself. And if anyone *was* monitoring this room, he (or she) would now know that the prisoner was awake.

'Is there anyone there?' she called softly, but the only answer came from the cat, which mewed sleepily, rose to its paws and yawned, the stubby tail stiff with the effort. It sprang down from the chair and skittered across to rub confidingly against her hand for a moment before rolling over to play-fight her fingers.

The play-fighting hurt, so Camena withdrew her hand, staring thoughtfully at the cat. It wasn't a cat, it was a kitten, and quite young at that. *Kittens* had stubby tails, *kittens* play-fought, and skittered about like fluff-balls, and purred with that curious high buzz. And if this one was less than half-grown, it was an even bigger specimen than she had thought.

Gerhardt woke to a brusque summons from Hub HI-Q. It startled him, and he realised he had overslept. The viewscreen had already appeared and Jens was watching him. Gerhardt forced down his instinctive feeling of pleasure. A garment once out-grown can never fit again, he reminded himself. And just as well, since Jens had let him down. His first reaction was superseded by a strong desire to disable the viewscreen, but to give in to such violence would be to descend to Jens's own level. He forced himself to face his old mentor with composure. Jens belonged to his past, and was nothing to him beyond one more Hub HI-Q Communicator. A telepath who mouthed the codes but broke them when he chose.

'Response,' he said coolly.

'Recovery success.' It wasn't a question. Jens's expression was dour, but a curious ripple seemed to pass over his face as his bright eyes found the sleeping Tell. Just for a moment, he looked like the Jens whom Gerhardt remembered from his early days. 'L'advent?'

'Ja,' said Gerhardt. 'Complicae.'

That was putting it mildly, perhaps too mildly, for Jens frowned, leaning forward. 'Daichcue —'

'RI-P interference,' broke in Gerhardt.

Jens nodded sharply. 'Expected, Daichcue Forn. Come. Leave Recoveree.'

Gerhardt swore under his breath. It was difficult to bluff Jens, who was HI-Q beta, telepathic and highly empathic, and who had once known him inside out. And until quite recently, Gerhardt would have sworn he knew Jens as well. But then had come the disillusion, the complete turn around.

Eight years before, Jens's various skills had qualified him to become a permanent resident communicator at Hub HI-Q while others of his generation had been filtered into the community. As an expert on both technical and telepathic connections, Jens had always been a stickler for the codes of courtesy, and he had impressed these codes on Gerhardt.

'Strength/talent, Daichcue Forn. Match strength/integ.' That was what Jens had said so often. What it meant, of course, was that those who were capable of high-quality telepathy must never use it to coerce an unwilling subject. *Whatever* the temptation. Just as those skilled in hypnosis must never use it for their own advantage.

A high-minded attitude, but one without which twenty-seventh century HI-Q society would have been a highly dangerous place.

After Moss had taken over his training, Gerhardt had continued to see Jens, but the visits had dwindled, and relations between the two fostermen, never especially cordial, had become strained. Gerhardt had found his sense of loyalty equally strained. They had such different attitudes to so many things. And finally, it had seemed easier not to associate with Jens at all.

That distancing had come about quite naturally, for Jens's field of interest, aside from his communications duties, embraced twenty-second century western culture. For this reason he had never been concerned with the research on Camena de Courcey. The burden of that task had been wholly borne by Moss, who, though officially retired from active HI-Q Recovery work, nevertheless kept his position as Head of the Recovery Programme.

'Time,' Moss had said succinctly when Gerhardt had tried to assume what should, properly speaking, have been his own research responsibility. A short answer which covered everything. Moss knew Time. Moss *had* Time. Gerhardt thought that, if it had been possible, Moss would have taken on the Recovery as well. Only Camena de Courcey's age and circumstance had prevented him. Moss agreed that, in general, a new student would be easier than a teacher to graft onto a late twentieth century school, and would have a lesser effect on the host community. *No* effect would have been the best option, but that was impossible. So Gerhardt's appointment had been confirmed. To Gerhardt's surprise, Jens had suddenly renewed contact and been furious, claiming Gerhardt was quite unsuitable for the job. He had invaded Moss's unit and tried to take Gerhardt back to Hub HI-Q for what he termed 'spec. brief'. Pretty strange for a man who had virtually ignored his ex-foster-son's existence for the past three years! Moss had seemed to agree.

'*I* brief my fostern!' he had snapped.

And then Jens had done the unforgivable, unleashing a forced telepathic order with callous disregard for either the proprieties or for Gerhardt's mental health. This, from Jens, who had always pretended such disgust at such misuses! Gerhardt had recoiled, both bewildered and sickened. It had not taken Moss long to realise what had happened. Apparently one look at Gerhardt's face had been enough. He had thrown Jens out of the unit.

'Beta/omega!' Moss had spat, locking the hatch. 'Is it any wonder he cannot get a partner? No IQ-normal would stomach him and all his beta genes will not outweigh such arrogance, such a disregard for the codes and for my rights.'

Gerhardt had been badly shaken, and Moss had touched his shoulder in a rare gesture of comfort. 'Forget Jens, Fostern,' he had said more gently. 'He lies in your past. I am your present, and I have every confidence in your suitability for this role.'

And for a while that confidence had seemed justified. Everything had gone well until, through very little fault of his, RI-P had managed to prejudice the Recovery.

And now here was Jens, giving orders again, just as if he still had a right to Gerhardt's respect. At least, at this distance, he could use nothing but screen-boosted verbal mode.

'Recoveree leave nein,' said Gerhardt firmly. 'Code Hub HI-Q.'

This was quite true, and even if the girl on the couch had been Camena, he would still have refused to leave her. Since she was Tell, it was doubly important for him to stay. He moved forward to screen her from Jens's view. That was discourteous, and for a second he gloried in the subtle insult. But he must be cautious. Jens was still his technical superior.

'Orders?' he asked, allowing mockery to ring through his voice. Reminding Jens of an order he had tried to force home, an order he had had no right to give, least of all in that mode. 'Strength/talent, Beta Jens. Match strength/integ,' he added, driving home the reminder.

But it seemed Jens remembered well enough.

'Untime/ code,' he said sadly. 'Advice, only. Leave her, Daichcue Forn.'

'Nyet,' said Gerhardt, and dismissed the screen. His hands were shaking a little. He had remembered that he was just as guilty as Jens when it came to forcing communications on the unwilling. Tell had been *very* unwilling.

But I had to! he thought defensively. *There was no time — no other way. I would never have risked harming her if there had only been time to take it slowly . . .*

He had had no time to observe the code — but wasn't that just the excuse Jens had offered for breaking code with *him*? And perhaps with more justification, for Gerhardt understood better than Tell how to face such violation without coming to harm. But what had been so important to Jens that he could not have left it until there *was* time to spare?

For a moment, he was tempted to contact Jens again and offer him a chance to explain, but Tell was stirring, so he turned back towards the couch.

Watchman . . . Oh God . . .

Her thought was unfocused, uncertain, and he realised it wasn't meant for him.

'Hello, Tell,' he said in what he hoped was a neutral tone.

She blinked at him hazily, then got up. 'Was that your boss on that screen? He looked nice.' Her voice sounded uncertain too, and she cleared her throat before continuing more strongly. 'Have you talked to him about getting Cammie back?'

'That was Jens. Listen. We have to locate Camena before Jens finds out who you are.'

'Why? Who is he? What will he do if he does find out?'

'Perhaps send you back.'

Oh. 'And how do we locate Camena?'

'Moss will know what to do.'

'Who the hell's Moss?'

'HI-Q Alpha Moss. My fosterman. Foster-father, you might say.'

'Haven't you got a real one?' She was forcing a jaunty tone, and it made him uncomfortable. So did the subject under discussion.

'No,' he said shortly. 'My genetic parents were Donor HI-Qs.'

'Does that mean you were a test-tube baby? Far out! That explains a few things, I reckon,' she said. 'This Moss — didn't he have any kids himself?'

'Ja, many. They were grown before he fostered me.'

'Which was when?'

He shrugged. 'Eight years ago. Before then I was with — another fosterman.'

Tell shook her head slowly. 'Weird, Watchman, weird. Haven't you got *any* relatives?'

'I told you,' he said, 'my parents were Donor HI-Q.'

She looked blank, and he began to prepare another meal. 'Donor HI-Q Recoverees,' he said, over his shoulder.

'*What*? Like — like Camena is going to be, you mean?'

'Yes. My genetic parents were Recovered, as I have Recovered Camena. They chose the option of donating sperm and ova before being returned to their own times.'

There was silence, and he turned to see Tell staring at him as if he had sprouted green hair.

'Es macht mir nichts aus,' he said irritably.

'What?'

'It's all the same to me. Has no-one told you it is rude to stare at the socially unfortunate?'

You, socially unfortunate? 'And I thought my parents were weird! Did you ever meet them? Did they meet one another?'

'Maybe they met at Hub HI-Q. I don't know. I have their DNA charts so there will be no danger of inbreeding. Incest is still taboo, even in our time.'

'I see.' She was still staring, and he wasn't sure what to make of her expression. Her thoughts were coloured with some kind of shock — he wasn't sure of the exact source of her discomfort, but it didn't seem to be the prejudice he had met in others. 'Have you any children yourself, Watchman?' she asked abruptly.

'Not yet.' He could have had, if he had chosen to insist on his rights. In theory, no HI-Q operatives could be asked to risk their lives before they had had offspring, but Moss had advised him to wait a while. Donor HI-Q offspring were treated with caution by HI-Q natural-borns and with even more by the IQ-normals. He could have taken the precaution of becoming a Donor HI-Q himself, but he'd hoped to find a partner willing to have him act as practical co-parent, eventually. He'd known it might take a good while, and the time for the Recovery had come before he had achieved his goal.

'Brothers or sisters?' asked Tell.

At least he knew the answer to that. 'I have ten half siblings whom I have never met. Donor HI-Q children are placed at wide geographic intervals, to disperse the gene pool.'

'And do the lucky adopting parents know what they're getting?'

That really stung, and he felt himself paling with anger. A strange sensation, since he usually kept his circulation well under control. '*What* they are getting, Estelle Clancy, is human beings. Like you. Genetically, there is no difference between a child of Donor HI-Q stock and a natural-born of the same parentage. It may be made superior through genetic manipulation, but it will never be less.'

By many people (as he had cause to know) the child *was* considered less, but Gerhardt pushed the thought aside.

'I didn't mean it that way,' said Tell.

'My fostermen knew. They are both HI-Q operatives themselves. The other fosters, all IQ-normals, did not.' He paused and added, 'Moss was the operative who Recovered my genetic parents, and when I had completed my first decade he chose me to train as a Recovery Operative.'

Tell looked uncomfortable. 'It seems a bit strange — but who am I to say so? Maureen and David aren't exactly a shining example for . . .'

God!

Her horror echoed directly from her mind to his, and Gerhardt creased his forehead in sudden pain. *Estellita?*

'Maureen and David. They're *dead*. *I'm* dead. Cammie's dead — we're all *dead*!'

She was pale, and actually swaying, and Gerhardt reached out to steady her. 'Don't!' she snapped, avoiding him. She collapsed on the couch and dropped her head to her knees.

'Estellita mia,' he said, touching her shoulder. 'Don't think of it. Remember what I told you —'

Abruptly, Tell sat up and slapped him across the cheek. Not very hard, but it stung. The shock silenced him.

There was a strained pause, and then Tell looked up. She still looked sick. 'You were saying?' she said politely.

'I was reminding you of the time zones. You are obviously not dead, since you are here slapping me. Your parents in their time are not dead. Don't think too much, Tell, and try to appreciate the irony.' He laughed. 'One of *my* parents died in the late twenty-first century and the other was born ninety years afterwards and died in 2196. Had it not been for Moss and those two successful Recoveries I would never have existed. I know that but I don't think about it. What's the point?'

'Yeah,' she said hollowly, 'what's the point?'

Tell had had a trying day, but it seemed a pretty feeble excuse for turning on Gerhardt like that. After her realisation the night before, she could no longer blame him for dragging her into the twenty-seventh century because she had finally admitted to herself that it wasn't his fault. She had followed him of her own accord. She had not been drawn to Camena, nor to some mythical concept of safety, but to *him*. Gerhardt Watchman. That was frightening, and she refused to dwell on it. For one thing she didn't want him picking up the knowledge, and for another, she had far too many other things on her mind.

She had followed a boy — a man — across the veil of time. She accepted that fact, but she still didn't know how she had done it. Come to that, she didn't know how Gerhardt did it either. It was all very well of him to talk blithely about manipulating time and Recovering people to improve the gene pool, but *how* was it done? It couldn't be teleportation, because they hadn't moved in space.

She wondered about the other Recoverees, the ones who had been hoicked without a by-your-leave into the future and had decided not to stay. Why did none of them talk about their experiences after returning home? Surely they weren't *all* afraid that no-one would believe them, because it would have been quite simple for them to have fetched back proof of their stories. Clothes travelled through time — and it was just as well they did. Presumably other solid objects could do the same.

Maybe most of the Recoverees came from a later period than her own, or decided to stay in this present. It would be a sacrifice to lose touch with their friends and families, but exceptional people often had to make sacrifices to their talents. Maybe some HI-Qs defected quite cheerfully, trading their predictable lives for a chance to explore the future.

'I wonder if I've got any descendants here — or if Camena has?' she said to Gerhardt. 'We might be going to have — I mean we might have had — children. You could be my great-great-great-great grandson!'

'Impossible,' said Gerhardt curtly, and Tell felt snubbed. Of course it was impossible. Hub HI-Q had bred Gerhardt from Recovered genius stock and unless one of her own descendants had married a genius there was no way she could be connected with him. *And don't forget it!* she admonished herself.

'What about Camena then?' she persisted. 'Maybe some of your HI-Qs are descended from her. *She* qualifies, even if I'm not good enough.'

Gerhardt shook his head. 'Recoverees are chosen from among HI-Qs who never had children. Otherwise Hadley Brand would have been the preferred candidate, since males are able to produce more offspring than females. Under Hub HI-Q-registered partnerships current male HI-Qs average ten descendants in the first generation while current females average three.'

'I see,' said Tell faintly. Her distaste at the idea of controlled human breeding programmes stirred again. Gerhardt had said he had no children, but she couldn't help wondering what his attitude might be if a girl of suitable pedigree came by.

'The situation is a little different with Donor-HI-Qs who choose the ova/sperm option,' continued Gerhardt. 'Their genetic donation is tested for bad recessives then dispersed as widely as possible. Since the donor females don't actually bear the children themselves more ova can be implanted.' He moved over to the terminal.

Tell shivered. 'Do many pick doing it that way?' she asked. 'It sounds pretty horrible.'

Gerhardt frowned. 'A lot do. I can never understand why, when you consider what they have to . . .'

'Yes, yes, yes, I get the picture,' said Tell hastily. 'Why don't you clone yourselves instead?'

'The incidence of lethal mutation is unacceptably high among cloned genetic tissue.'

'Oh,' she said.

Gerhardt touched some buttons, making what Tell thought must be the twenty-seventh century version of a phone call or a fax message. 'Moss will come soon,' he said.

'And what are you going to tell this Moss about *me*?'

'The truth,' said Gerhardt shortly. 'He has made several Recoveries, and he may be able to solve the problems with this one.'

'Won't he be mad at you for stuffing up and at me for muscling in?'

Gerhardt didn't answer, but by now Tell was becoming used to his silences. It was only when recounting the history and habits of Hub HI-Q that he seemed to have a lot to say.

Watchman? She tossed a cautious thought in his direction, and he jumped.

Not so loud... There seemed to be a breath of exasperation in his mental comment.

Loud?

Doucement ... softly. Let the thought float on its own momentum. Don't hurl it like a ...

Fast bowler?

Gerhardt nodded. 'Ja, a fast bowler. It hurts my head.' He moved away from the communicator, shutting himself off from her thoughts. Presumably he had nothing more to add.

Tell sighed, and wondered what Moss would look like. Were the races still separate in this time, or had they all inter-married to produce a nice milk-coffee blend? Gerhardt's colouring could hardly be a typical sample. He might have been born into the current century, but his parents had not.

If she had thought of visiting the future at all, she would have expected to find Australia as one huge city with the northern suburbs of Melbourne mingling with the lower reaches of Canberra. She would have expected swarming billions of people, or perhaps everyone dead of AIDS or nuclear attack. Well — AIDS or nuclear attack could have played their parts in reducing the world population to whatever it was now. So could those interminable wars that boiled over into the nightly news. With thousands dying daily of disease and injury, Tell had never quite grasped how the population could keep on growing at all.

What would the people of this time look like? Would they recognise her immediately as different? And how would *she* appear to Moss? An inferior specimen from a long-distant past? She looked down at herself. She had dressed from the selection in Gerhardt's unit in a daze the night before, but the garments didn't look too strange. The cut was odd, and the colour seemed to be a sort of camouflage design, but apart from that the clothing of the twenty-seventh century was simply a pull-on shirt worn with floppy knee-length shorts. One size would fit most people, so it seemed fashion was out of vogue. What a pity. It would have been interesting to have stepped out in something weird and iridescent — thigh-high boots would have been fun . . .

'Shoes?' she said. Her own were past wearing.

'In the basket,' said Gerhardt. 'Take any pair — they mould to fit.'

Tell slid her feet into moccasin-like shoes. The interior was spongy and almost gooey, and she recoiled.

'Walk across the room,' directed Gerhardt.

Tell stood up, and felt the soles and uppers squishing. *Ugh!* 'Oops — sorry.'

Gerhardt grinned suddenly. 'That's what I thought when I had to wear *your* sort. Only it was more, *ouch!*'

Tell shuffled forward, trying to walk normally. The squishiness was dying away. 'Is this a HI-Q invention?' she asked.

'The substance was developed by a team of IQ-normals for industrial purposes,' said Gerhardt. 'It was a HI-Q designer who applied it to domestic footwear.'

The shoes had firmed by now, and she had to admit they were comfortable. Such moccasins would never slip or chafe or give their wearers blisters. No wonder Gerhardt had objected to twentieth-century shoes. They must have felt like strait-jackets. 'Now what?' she asked.

'Now we leave,' said Gerhardt. 'Moss is waiting for us above.'

Tell hadn't heard any vehicle, but she followed Gerhardt out of the unit. She looked eagerly about, but, although the contours of the land were familiar, there was nothing left of Cockatoo. Perhaps some of the saplings she had known lived on as geriatric trees — but every person who had walked the streets and swum in the pool was gone. Only Silicon Peak remained unchanged. Only Silicon Peak, herself and, somewhere, Camena.

If there are ghosts . . . She couldn't finish the thought.

There are no ghosts. Gerhardt's mental tone was firm and reassuring.

A vehicle was waiting under the trees. 'Well, it isn't a flying saucer,' said Tell.

'Sol-plane,' said Gerhardt.

'Plane' seemed to be about right, for the vehicle was flat and broad, just tall enough to provide head room as Tell scrambled in to be greeted by the driver. 'Camena de Courcey! How delightful to meet you at last.'

Tell shot a mystified look at Gerhardt. *I'm not —*

Later. Gerhardt's thought was unmistakably an order.

'Thank you,' she said lamely. 'Mr —?'

'My name is simply Moss. We no longer use the formal modes of address with which you are familiar. We rejoice in equality while upholding the exceptional.'

'I see,' said Tell, although she didn't, quite. The seat seemed as gooey as her shoes, but firmed almost immediately to fit her contours.

The vehicle rose to skim above the trees. There was no sound, no vibration, no sense of movement at all, and even as she gazed through the windows they were becoming opaque. Polarisation? Well, she supposed Maureen's old Ford would have seemed equally mysterious to a visitor from the thirteenth century. At least she wasn't freaking out and babbling about witchcraft. She wondered how a thirteenth century Recoveree would cope. He or she would probably be reduced to a screaming heap by now. Or was that sort of thinking just prejudice? If Hub HI-Q's theory was correct, the folk of the thirteenth century might have been more intelligent than the folk of the twenty-first.

She shook her head. It seemed that one could get used to anything, even being hijacked into the future.

Gerhardt was beside her, and she thought he seemed unusually tense. Perhaps this Moss wouldn't be as forgiving as she'd been led to believe. She looked doubtfully at Moss, but he seemed very ordinary. He might have been any age from fifty to seventy, and looked nothing like Gerhardt at all. But why should he? They weren't related. Knowing nothing of her parents had always seemed to make Camena feel incomplete; how must Gerhardt feel, knowing his own had returned to their own times without waiting to see him born? She wondered if they had been paid for their 'donations', and if so, in what currency. Twenty-seventh century money surely wouldn't be legal tender in their times, and sudden wealth would certainly have changed their destinies.

Gerhardt must have decided not to waste time, for he cleared his throat. 'Recovery complicae. To Hub HI-Q?'

Tell found herself holding her breath. Would Moss blast Gerhardt here and now? But it seemed he would not. Instead, he said casually; 'Really? How unfortunate. We must see what we can do to mend matters.'

The rest of the trip was silent, but brief. After five minutes Tell became aware that the craft had landed. The windows cleared, the door opened and they climbed out. Moss tugged briskly on a lever, causing the vehicle to buckle, concertina, and fold down to a package about the size of a grocery carton.

Oh well, thought Tell. We have folding baby strollers, folding bikes and sewing boxes and beds — why not a folding plane?

The inventions she had seen so far all seemed to be developments of ideas dating from her own time ... Even the television series about Dr Who and the Tardis were represented, in a fictional sort of way.

She looked about. The sparse, rocky surroundings seemed familiar and the air was cooler than it had been when she entered the sol-plane. 'Where are we?'

'Plateau Lake,' said Gerhardt.

That explained the familiarity. She and Maureen had spent a night here at the Plateau Guesthouse a few weeks — a few centuries ago! No matter what Gerhardt said, Tell found it impossible not to boggle at that. Rock weathered slowly, so perhaps she had sat on one of these outcrops before. The thought should have been reassuring, but it was not. She was a long, long way from home.

As briskly as he had dealt with the plane, Moss lifted a hatch in the ground. He slid inside, and Tell and Gerhardt followed.

They were in another disclosure unit.

'Haven't we just come from here?' asked Tell plaintively. 'I thought we were going to Hub HI-Q.'

Moss smiled. 'Later, we may visit Hub HI-Q. I prefer to hold private discussions in my own home, Camena. It contains fewer ... distractions, and has a number of useful features.'

'Moss designed the disclosure units,' said Gerhardt. 'He used the same design for his own base.'

'I never waste good material,' said Moss, and smiled again, as if he had made a joke. His teeth were strong and white, like false ones, but Tell thought they were probably real. The twenty-seventh century must have sorted out tooth decay and gum disease. Besides, if Moss were a HI-Q, he would have come from excellent genetic stock. She wondered how old he was. His springy white hair gleamed with health and his skin was unweathered. Not a chicken pox scar in sight. A nasty thought hit her then, and she passed it on to Gerhardt as she sat down on the couch.

Watchman — what if I'm carrying disease germs? Your — Moss — hasn't been immunised. I'd hate to set off another wave of Black Death.

Have no concern, Estellita, thought Gerhardt back, *our natural immunity is excellent.*

Don't call me that!

That comment went home, just as her slap had done, and Tell saw his eyes widen, then narrow in pain. So, apparently, did Moss. His gaze sharpened and he looked very thoughtfully from Gerhardt to Tell and back again.

Telepathic, Camena? The surprise was evident, but the signal seemed fuzzy and far away.

Tell was suddenly cautious.

After a moment, Moss turned to Gerhardt. 'Sit, Fostern, and tell me what happened. I trust the experience has not been too much of a shock to our Recoveree?'

'Well, I wasn't expecting to swim across seven centuries,' said Tell honestly as the couch adjusted to accommodate Gerhardt as well.

Moss chuckled, and the indulgent sound set Tell's teeth on edge. 'Who does? My fostern would have failed in his duties if you *had*. But where did you swim? The sensation is more like falling, to most.'

Tell glanced at Gerhardt. He looked uncertain — somehow diminished. He had seemed eager to lay their problems in Moss's lap, but now they had the chance to do so, he was obviously having second thoughts.

Well, she could sympathise with that. Gerhardt might be three years her senior but he obviously had the same problems in his relationship with Moss as Tell had in hers with Maureen.

'Wrong?' asked Moss. He was sitting back in a relaxed fashion, but his eyes were watchful.

Gerhardt swallowed. 'Recovery pre-intended.'

'Viel?' Moss's gaze had been on Gerhardt, now it swivelled to rest on Tell.

'Intended zero minus twenty sec,' said Gerhardt.

'Error of caution.'

'Necessity. Attack.'

'Aggressor?'

'RI-P.'

'Def-identity?'

'Nyet. Prob. ninety. Inex-ops.'

It was as if they had shifted into a verbal high gear, thought Tell. They were speaking English — mostly — but a lot of words seemed to be truncated or missing. Was this some sort of shorthand code, or the language of this time? In greeting her, Moss had used normal syntax —

Courtesy to you, shot Gerhardt without taking his gaze from Moss.

The shorthand conversation bounced back and forth like a table tennis ball. Tell identified some French, German, Russian words — if this were the way Gerhardt usually spoke he'd done a wonderful job adjusting at St Saviours. It must have been like wading through treacle, or listening to a tape played back at the wrong speed, for him to speak and understand the idiom of her time . . . and not only to speak it, but to send it directly from his mind to hers. She tried to focus her own mind. If she had been *reading* this conversation, she thought she'd have understood most of it, but the high-speed delivery was beyond her. And then she caught her own name, and Camena's, the syllables sounding formal and familiar — and was that a reference to migraine? No doubt Gerhardt was trying to explain how Camena had come to be snatched.

The discussion ended, Moss blinked and turned back to Tell, visibly adjusting himself to her level. Tell swallowed. She'd seen Camena do that, but Camena had never made her feel like a moron.

'You are Estelle Clancy, my fostern tells me,' Moss said affably, 'and not Camena de Courcey. My apologies for mis-calling you!'

'It isn't Watchman's fault,' said Tell. 'He brought Cammie along just the way he was supposed to. I sort of — brought myself. I think.'

'Watchman?'

'Gerhardt. Your —'

Moss nodded. 'So you helped — Watchman — Recover the prospect and were then caught up in the Recovery yourself.'

'That's it,' said Tell.

'Most curious. In fact — unique.' Moss shifted verbal gear again and snapped something at Gerhardt. This time, Tell caught none of it, but Gerhardt frowned and nodded. He seemed very uncomfortable.

After a moment he said; 'Return RI-P sceno?' He sounded hopeful, almost pleading.

'Condoning?' Moss's tone was carefully surprised, but Tell had the feeling he was enjoying the situation and she saw Gerhardt actually bite his lip as if to keep back a retort.

What's wrong? asked Tell, but Moss was claiming her attention.

'My dear Estelle,' he said, 'I apologise unreservedly to you, on behalf of both my fostern and of Hub HI-Q. It was unpardonable of us to embroil you in our activities. It was even more unpardonable of RI-P.'

'I think I involved myself,' said Tell awkwardly. She had decided she didn't care for Moss, or for his tone. Having him apologise to her didn't ring true. Especially after the way he treated Gerhardt.

'Nevertheless,' said Moss, 'you have been put to some pain and inconvenience. You should have been Returned immediately, but perhaps my fostern had other matters on his mind.'

'Yes, I expect he had,' said Tell. She felt a flicker of protest from Gerhardt, but when she glanced at him in surprise, he was looking wooden. Well — so would she if someone made her look small. 'He was worried about Camena, and —'

'And no doubt he enjoys your charming company, my dear,' said Moss.

Tell resented that, but there were more important things at stake than an old man being arch. '*Can* you send us back?' she asked. She'd gained the impression that a return trip might be a problem.

'Surely, surely. You may go whenever you please — although the less time you spend with us the easier the transition will be. The diversion, rather, since we have a uniquely complicated situation.'

'Camena will come with me, as soon as we find her.' Tell stuck out her jaw.

'Camena de Courcey. We have gone to some — trouble — to Recover Camena de Courcey,' said Moss thoughtfully.

'She never asked you to.'

'True.'

'Neither of us ever asked for any of it,' said Tell. 'It was your idea.'

Moss seemed to make up his mind. 'Expense, time — pouf! Camena de Courcey will be leaving us as well. Perhaps sooner than intended.'

Gerhardt made an appealing gesture. 'Surely Camena will choose to remain, once disclosure has been made? She is . . .'

'Hush,' said Moss, and smiled at Tell. 'My fostern seems somewhat attached to his Recoveree. It happens, occasionally. I repeat, Camena de Courcey will probably leave us. With reservations, of course. We shall, of course, be sorry to see her go, but it is the only way.'

'Of course it is,' said Tell crossly, and frowned at Gerhardt. *What d'you think you're playing at, Watchman?*

'The Recovery was made from the sea, so any return should be made to the same venue to avoid paradox,' said Gerhardt.

'In general we try to avoid temporal paradox, in order to placate RI-P,' said Moss placidly. 'Yet, Fostern, it appears that RI-P itself worked to produce the — incident — which caused our Recoveree and this young lady such discomfort. Really, I am surprised at their lack of finesse. Yes. RI-P must learn to accept compromise, just as we have done at Hub HI-Q. We shall unravel their — incident — you and I.'

'No,' said Gerhardt softly, and Tell felt tension in the arm that brushed hers. There was also tension in his mind, although she couldn't reach his thoughts.

'Yes indeed,' said Moss. 'And now — to practicalities. Has Estelle interacted with anyone else since her arrival?'

'Nyet.'

'Good. Fostern, leave us now. I wish to interview Estelle. She at least must leave us *very* soon — make no mistake — but I cannot forego a unique opportunity.' He sighed. 'I fear — I very much fear — you and Sib's foolish team have gone some way to proving the point of those who denigrate the Recovery Programme.' He cleared his throat. 'However! The game is not over yet. Off you go. Estelle will remain with me.'

Gerhardt looked mutinous, but under Moss's gaze he shrugged and left the unit without another word.

Tell felt cold. While Gerhardt was near, she had felt *some* contact with her own time, but now she was truly alone. She braced herself for probing questions about her century.

'What do you want to know?' she said. 'I'm not an expert or anything.' *Blast you, Watchman! Why did you go and leave me?*

'Relax, Estelle,' said Moss. 'You may think me sentimental, but I am eager to right my fostern's mistakes.'

Tell blinked. Moss seemed to her to be as sentimental as a hanging judge, and she wished he'd stop talking about mistakes in connection with herself and Gerhardt. It left a nasty mental taste.

'Is there something you wish to ask, Estelle?' suggested Moss.

This too was unexpected. Her mind was buzzing with unasked questions, and a nice safe test-case came to hand. 'Are there Recoverees from before my time? You Recovered Camena. Have you tried to Recover — I don't know — Leonardo da Vinci? Or Emily Brontë? Neither of them had children and they were geniuses, weren't they? They were geniuses who *did* things. Camena is my best friend, but she doesn't *do* things. Not if she can help it.'

'Camena de Courcey is very young,' said Moss. 'It is possible she would never, as you put it, have *done things*, but the potential is there and what lies passively in her may well become active in her children. As to your other query — in theory it would be possible to Recover the subjects you mentioned. However; at least one of them would have been excluded from the Donor HI-Q Programme by a defective constitution.'

'You can cure TB now, can't you?' asked Tell. 'I think even we can do that.'

'No doubt,' said Moss, 'but the genetic tendency would remain. We could possibly remove it by manipulating the genes but we are loath to interfere too much. The other subject would have been equally unsuitable, although for other reasons.'

'What reasons?'

Moss paused, and Tell wondered if he were censoring his reply.

'Records — accurate, computerised records — are unavailable for any period prior to the mid-twentieth century,' said Moss at last. 'Even the birth and death dates of possible Recoverees may not have been accurately recorded, so it would be difficult to trace their exact whereabouts in any given time.

'There is also the fact that most HI-Qs in earlier times *did* produce descendants at much the same rate as did the IQ-normals. Those who did not were usually handicapped by ill-health or other defects rendering them unsuitable for use as Donor HI-Q stock. Is there anything else?'

There were plenty of other things she wanted to know, but Moss's pragmatic tone made her shiver. Suitable, unsuitable — it probably wouldn't be healthy to know too much about this world of the future. 'Computerised records', Moss had said. No doubt he had used them to research Camena. Birth certificate, adoption certificate, school reports, Mensa membership, driver's licence, marriage certificate, university records, electoral roll, credit history — Camena would have collected a mass of documentation during her lifetime and so would Tell.

There would also be death certificates, so there was no way Tell was going near any such records, even if Moss would allow it. If the information were right *there* she'd never be able to resist reading it, and that would be suicidal.

For instance — what if she discovered that she had married someone and then divorced him later on? If she knew ahead of time that the marriage would fail, she probably wouldn't marry at all. Then her future would be changed. The kids she would have had wouldn't be born and goodness knew how many current people would suddenly cease to exist. Moss wouldn't like that. Neither would RI-P. Either or both might take steps to force her to conform. And *she* wouldn't like that. Better not to know. If you knew — how could you go on living?

'All I want is to find and go home with Camena,' she said mildly. 'Watchman said RI-P wouldn't hurt her, but she must hate being kidnapped. Can you help us, Moss?'

'Naturally.' Moss smiled. 'Fostern has given me a succinct account of the — incident — Estelle. Perhaps you would care to do the same?'

'Is there time for that?'

'Oh yes, I think so, don't you?'

Which probably meant she'd better make time. Or else.

She wasn't too sure what Moss could do to her if she refused. Not too much, she trusted, for if she returned to her own time with injuries or mental trauma *that* would change her future too.

'I don't know much,' she said. 'Things are moving too fast for me. I mean — I only just found out — last night — that time-travel even existed — how does it work, anyway — no, don't tell me. I might go and invent it too early, or something, and change history and I wouldn't want to do that for anything.'

Her answer was disjointed, but it was the best she could do. While she gabbled on to Moss, she was sending frantic mental messages to Gerhardt, uncertain whether he was in range or would answer her if he could. Uncertain that she was even doing it properly.

'Let the thought float on its own momentum,' he had directed. But she hadn't time to try that now. She had to deliver it in her own personal fashion, hard and fast.

Watchman! Watchman! He wants me to tell him what happened.

Gerhardt's answer came back reassuringly. *Do as he asks, but take care, Estellita mia. If he asks you what you want to do, do not make any commitment.*

Well, she wouldn't. It was up to Moss to make the commitment. Preferably one to send herself and Camena home as soon as possible . . . and preferably *not* back into the sea. She blinked, realising that Moss was watching her. It gave her the creeps, but now she knew Gerhardt was only a thought away and took some strength from that. 'Sorry,' she said. 'I was sorting things out in my mind.'

'And did you succeed?'

'I think so. I hope so. Where do you want me to start?'

'Begin with the events of the day of your inadvertent Recovery.'

Yesterday. Seven centuries ago. Tell sucked in her lip. 'You don't want to know what I did at home?'

'Every detail. Quite apart from the present problem, I am a student of the twentieth century, and I welcome this chance to become privy to the lifestyle of a young IQ-normal. So far all of our first-hand information has come from past HI-Qs who approach my own level of intelligence.'

Ouch. Dubiously, Tell described the breakfast, the frantic packing of two bags; one for school and the Activity Day, another for her evening with David. 'I took one bag on the bus, and left the other in Maureen's car boot. That's the . . .'

Moss held up a hand. 'I am familiar with the terminology, Estelle.'

Of course he was. Just as Gerhardt's English was too perfect, Moss's was pedantic, but neither of them was ever less than fluent.

'Was this a break in your usual pattern, Estelle?' asked Moss.

'It was Wednesday,' said Tell. 'I always go to my father's place on Wednesday, and Maureen — that's my mother — always forgets to bring my stuff to school if I don't make sure it's packed.'

'So this day, this Wednesday, began in just such a way as any other.'

'More or less. The particular activity was the only thing different. We have Activity Day every other Wednesday, but usually it's lectures and stuff at school. About one time in four it's an excursion, but never to anything very exciting, because we have to go there and back in an afternoon. The *Kismet* excursion was different, because it was a special offer. I think in the beginning Mr Blenning was just going to take us to the Sail Museum — he loves ships — he's got a thing about the *Endeavour* — but then the offer came in.'

'The *Kismet* was the vessel from which you fell?'

That was one way of putting it. Tell nodded.

'Was there anything unusual about this vessel?'

'Yeah. The life jackets,' said Tell. 'At least three of them were lemons. Some of the others' were okay, but I don't know about Red's and Pris's. Pris was on the life-raft, but I think Red might have been killed in the explosion . . . he was right near the engine when it blew.'

'Possible, but unlikely,' said Moss. 'RI-P operatives are well trained to take care of themselves. This explosion was a clumsy trick, but an audacious one and almost successful. To try to kill the Recoveree — yes, that was not so strange for RI-P — but to risk death of the others, and to risk drowning *you*, Estelle —' He shook his head. 'Had any of you drowned as a result of the incident it would have made a paradox far greater than any minor temporal flurry my fostern's activities may have caused.'

'Watchman could have drowned too,' reminded Tell. 'If he had, that would have made a much bigger difference to you.'

'Not so. Fostern is not a constant of your time. He has never moved forward along his lifeline. So, had he died in that explosion, his death would not have altered his own future which, by definition, would never have existed. His future does not exist until he reaches it, at which time it ceases to be his future and becomes his present. Do you understand? He was never part of the fabric of your century, simply —'

'An appliqué?' suggested Tell.

Moss beamed at her. 'An apt metaphor, Estelle. You have an interesting mind, although you are not HI-Q. It seems a pity that we cannot offer *you* the same elite status we planned to offer your friend.'

'To stay here forever?' said Tell. 'Thanks — but no thanks, even if you *did* offer. I want to get on with my life in the usual way, in the usual time. And I *don't* want to know what's coming. Besides — staying on would *really* muck up my future because I'd be having it here instead of there.'

'Quite,' said Moss. 'You are wise, Estelle — perhaps wiser than you understand. I am glad that you do not seek this knowledge, for if you did, I would be forced to take steps to prevent your gaining it. And now — continue.'

Obediently, Tell continued, describing the time in the museum, the two crew-members of the *Kismet*. She wondered if Moss recognised Pris and Red from her description, and what would happen to them, if they were from this time. If they were still alive. Had their activities been illegal, or simply reprehensible? Were they criminals and terrorists, or had RI-P the status of a political party in opposition? Her mind worried the problem as she described the way Pris had pushed herself and Camena over to the rail just before the explosion.

'I think Red might have started the engine before he was supposed to, because it certainly seemed to give Pris a shock when it blew. She didn't have much time to get out of the way.' She realised she was clenching her hands at the memory, and consciously tried to relax. 'Watchman tried to stop her, but it all happened so damned *fast*. It was in no way his fault.'

'And your safety device was sabotaged,' mused Moss. 'Curious. It almost seems . . . a moment, Estelle — you will excuse me?' He touched the arm of his chair and a keyboard swung out. At least, Tell thought it was a keyboard, but it was wafer-thin and the keys — if they were keys — were evidently not tactile. A holographic screen ghosted into being, but since she was sitting at an angle from Moss she could not see the information displayed.

Moss was evidently a speed-scanner, for his perusal of the screen lasted mere seconds. He dismissed the keyboard, and returned his attention to Tell.

'What was that about?' she asked.

'Nothing of importance, Estelle. I merely verified a minor point with the record, which seems to indicate a greater perversion of history than we expected. Continue.'

'Do you reckon — maybe — these RI-Ps didn't know which one of us Camena *was*?' asked Tell. 'Since they tried to drown me, too?'

'An intriguing surmise,' said Moss. 'The story, Estelle.'

'We hit the water,' continued Tell glumly. 'Camena got the worst of the explosion, I think — I was only thrown overboard, but she was knocked unconscious. I expected the life jacket to make me bob round like a cork and float on my back — usually they do — but it just got waterlogged straight away. It dragged me down. I thought I was going to drown.'

'But you did not.'

'No. But I've got a horrible feeling we still might. If — when — you send Cammie and me back home, do we *have* to be sent back into the water? Cammie's not much of a swimmer and even with Watchman to help I'd have trouble getting her to the beach. I could swim back by myself, I think, but not with Cammie. So maybe you could send us back before we get — got — on the *Kismet*. Or after we get back to shore. Is that possible?'

'Many things are possible,' said Moss. 'Your request is duly noted. Continue.'

'Thanks — I think. Well — I managed to get the thing off. It sank. I could see the others and they were bobbing along all right — there was a life-raft close to them and Pris was on it. I never did see Red again, but of course I was looking for Camena. I couldn't see her — or Watchman — then I saw him dive — he'd got out of his jacket and he was diving to find Camena.' She drew a shaky breath. 'He saved her life,' she said in a rush. 'There was no *way* she could have swum up, even if the thing hadn't been dragging her down, because she'd been knocked out in the blast. And I didn't even know where she was. Watchman saved her, and he could have drowned himself.'

'It was his function and his duty to preserve the Recoveree,' said Moss.

'Even if it killed *him*?'

'My fostern is of valuable stock, but his genetic code exists in no fewer than seventeen other current HI-Qs. Within a decade, as the bearers mature, the concentration will increase exponentially. If all goes well, the end of the decade will see no fewer than sixty-five HI-Qs, IQ-normals and normal-pluses carrying that same genetic code. Three decades more will see a further three hundred and seventy.'

'But they wouldn't be Watchman any more than I'm Maureen. Genetic code is only part of the picture. A *small* part. You don't love someone for his genes and his IQ!' She caught herself up. 'Wouldn't you mind if he had drowned?' she added numbly. 'Oh — hold on — you could have Recovered him, couldn't you?'

'Oh no,' said Moss. 'Recovery would not have been possible in my fostern's case. He is valuable, but not irreplaceable. His training has made an interesting challenge since I retired from the life of an active operative — I would regret his passing on that account. I dislike wasting time, effort or material, although his performance in this matter has been rather poor. You find this attitude unacceptable, Estelle?'

'Yes,' said Tell frankly. 'And it wasn't his fault . . .'

'If it had been, he might have been re-trainable,' said Moss with a sigh. 'As to my attitude; consider this. All of us must pass. Our physical selves are finite, it is our genetic heritage that should and must be preserved. I myself have fathered fifteen healthy children, and my descendants now number more than one hundred and thirty.'

Tell gulped. She had once called Gerhardt cold-blooded, and had believed it, then.

Camena waited. There was no longer any point in pretending illness. Her captors obviously intended her to be comfortable and contented. They had supplied familiar surroundings, light and warmth, amusement, and even company. She had never been overwhelmingly fond of cats, but she appreciated them aesthetically, and she knew stroking a pet was supposed to have a normalising effect on the human blood pressure and nervous system.

She moved cautiously across the room and crouched to test her theory. Her head throbbed dully, but compared with the agony of the night before, the pain was laughable. Her hair flopped forward around her face as she reached for the kitten, giving it plenty of time to avoid her if it wished. She pushed her hair behind her ears with her free hand, not liking to flick it back as she usually did while her head still ached. Something was wrong with her hair.

Her hair was clean. Subconsciously, she had expected it to be heavy and stiff with salt. And not only her hair was clean. She licked her lips, touched the back of her hand and then her own shoulder with her tongue. Not a trace of salt. And her clothes — they *were* her own clothes, the crimson and silver shirt, the faded denim shorts. They, too, were clean and fresh. Someone had cleaned her, and her clothes, while she slept.

Illogical, thought Camena. Perhaps — *just* perhaps — someone might have sponged her face and hands without waking her. But to undress her and wash her hair; that should have been impossible. Dressing her again would have been especially difficult. The shorts had been last summer's jeans, and fitted very snugly.

Camena's forgiving thoughts soured. She had been blown up, half drowned, had suffered a migraine, been kidnapped and now, it appeared, she had also been drugged. No wonder her head was still aching.

'Kittens!' she said crossly. 'Huh!'

Leaving the kitten, she moved across the room, but though the sunlight poured through the window like clover honey, all she could see was her own face and the room behind her reflected in the glass. No wonder she had not detected spy-holes or cameras. The window was a one-way mirror.

Gerhardt walked away from his fosterman's unit. Moss was wealthy, and, although retired from active operative status, he enjoyed an excellent constitution. He was eight decades old, and there seemed no reason why he should not live for half as much again. Hub HI-Q policy was to spread desirable genetic patterns as widely as possible, but in the early days, when IQ-normals had turned their backs on the chance of bearing exceptional children, many of the HI-Q youth had consoled themselves by choosing partners whose genes reinforced rather than complemented their own. Instead of the all-round high-grade competence Hub HI-Q had hoped to achieve, strains of reinforced mental ability had appeared. Many were HI-Q alpha or beta, and longevity had been an occasional side-effect.

Moss was an excellent example of this trend, and although he paid lip-service to the tenets of Hub HI-Q, Gerhardt had always suspected his fosterman enjoyed his HI-Q alpha status for its own sake. Certainly he had a strong sense of self admiration — or vainglory as it might once have been termed.

Tell Clancy was a long way from HI-Q, let alone HI-Q alpha, perfection, but she intrigued him. Now Gerhardt considered it, he realised that she always had. Right from the start, when she had challenged his right to befriend Camena. It was more than physical attraction, although that was a part of it. It was something she had, something she might have offered him without diminishing herself. If only things had been different.

Gerhardt sighed. It was obvious that Moss intended to return Tell to her own time whatever he said and, by the tenets of Hub HI-Q, Moss was right. There was no shadow of a claim for keeping her here and now. *Camena* was the Recoveree, *Camena* the one whose precious DNA must not be lost to the human race. Keeping Tell here for more than a few weeks was plainly out of the question. She must go home, despite his strong desire to keep her safe; Hub HI-Q would send her back to the site of the Recovery, to swim for her life — and perhaps to drown. At least she would have the advantage of being rested, and she would not be weighed down by RI-P's cruel device ... Would that be a paradox? Perhaps not, for she had removed the life jacket herself. Perhaps she would swim to shore, and what happened to her after that would be in a fluid state.

He wondered if the whole affair of the *Kismet* had changed things greatly for the peripherals. Apart from Tell and Camena, the lives of at least three others from St Saviours would have been quite strongly influenced. RI-P Base must be losing its grip if it was condoning interference on this scale. Or perhaps their fanaticism was finally out of control.

Fanaticism was a cancer. In its early stages, it often masqueraded as virtues such as faith and commitment, but eventually it would become perverted and grow to a monstrous thing. Fanaticism knew no boundaries, and fanatics would do anything to further their cause. They would kill innocents to prevent the death of a murderer, they would bomb a school to express their disapproval of some governmental decision. Fanatics were irrational; and terrifyingly thorough.

Yes, RI-P's attempted murder of himself, Camena and Tell had all the hallmarks of fanaticism. Hub HI-Q had never harmed anyone in pursuit of *its* goals, but since the *Kismet* incident, RI-P Base couldn't say the same. He wondered how Moss would deal with it. Strictly speaking, it was a matter for Hub HI-Q Central, but in this case, that would boil down to Moss. And so would the question of Tell's future.

He wandered towards a rocky outcrop and sat down, linking his arms around his knees in unconscious imitation of the way Tell often sat. A pose that was bad for his circulation. He straightened his legs and removed a pack of cards from his pouch. It was his old familiar pack, and he had missed it while working in Tell's time. He had missed playing the game of solitaire in the way it should be played.

Gerhardt shuffled the century of cards and split it into two unequal piles. HI-Q, IQ-normal. He cut the pack and began to turn up options. HI-Q alpha — IQ-normal; supposedly a poor match. He laid it aside and tried again. HI-Q gamma —

IQ-normal-plus. That was better — the children of that match would be borderline HI-Q, and if matched with HI-Q in the next generation, the resulting offspring should be HI-Q to a high probability. If he were matched first with an IQ-normal, his offspring would . . .

. . . probably be IQ-normal. No matter how he cut the pack his probabilities were bound to be poor unless he matched with another HI-Q whose attributes reinforced his own. His parents had been born too early for reinforcement to have taken place in his generation.

Hub HI-Q *never* harmed Recoverees. Hub HI-Q offered Recoverees a unique chance of life and fulfilment. But Tell was not a Recoveree. The cards seemed to shimmer, and it took Gerhardt a moment to realise that his eyes were blurring. It had to be the cold wind of the plateau.

Abruptly, he swept the cards together and began to lay out solitaire. Alpha, Beta, Gamma, Delta — Kings, Queens, Jacks, Maids — Fire, Earth, Air, Water. But the Water Maid was missing, trapped under the pile to the right.

He was frowning over the game, wondering whether the traditional Queen-snatch might be properly performed to Recover the Maid, when one of Tell's vigorous thoughts touched down in his mind. More often than not, he noticed, she used her telepathy to insult him, but this time her mental tone was worried — almost panicky. *Watchman! Watchman! He wants me to tell him what happened.*

Gerhardt steadied himself. *Do as he asks,* he thought, *but take care, Estellita mia. If he asks you what you want to do, do not make any commitment.*

An unwelcome and unfamiliar tightness gripped his throat and he swallowed, hard, and went back to his game. Almost furtively, he Recovered the Maid.

Moss didn't give Tell long to dwell on his attitude to his unsatisfactory foster son. Instead, he reminded her, quite gently, that there was more to recount.

'After Watchman dived for Camena, I helped him get her life jacket off. That is, I tried to help. I couldn't manage the catch so I supported Cammie while he got it undone. I was tired, so I handed Camena over to him.'

Actually, she thought Gerhardt had taken Camena, and had swum away with her, leaving Tell to fend for herself. Fair enough, he couldn't have helped them both, but it still made her feel hollow to remember it.

'The story?' Moss was prompting her — again. To someone of his intellectual calibre, her pauses and ramblings must be maddening. *Tough*, she directed her thought to him, but he didn't react. And probably just as well.

'Watchman swam off with Camena,' she said obediently. 'I expect he thought I'd swim to the others — or be picked up by a rescue team. I could have gone to the life-raft, I expect but somehow — I didn't think of it then. And Watchman had gone. Well, I wasn't his problem, was I?' Not by Moss's standards, she wasn't. Not by Gerhardt's standards, either.

'I started swimming too, but it was choppy and I couldn't see where I was going. I must have swum after Watchman and Cammie, because the water got warmer all of a sudden. I thought that meant I was getting hypothermia, so I just kept on going. I hit some rock and then I was washed up on the beach. I couldn't see the *Kismet* or the life-raft or anyone else, so I started yelling out. After a bit I found Watchman and Camena. She was unconscious.'

'At what point did you realise that you had been inadvertently Recovered?' asked Moss.

'I don't really know,' she said honestly. 'I didn't know Recovery existed. I didn't know time-travel existed. I didn't believe in it, at first. Not until I had to.'

'We prefer not to use that specific term,' said Moss. 'It implies that the journey through the veil is itself the purpose; that one may go visiting the centuries from no better motive than curiosity.'

'Don't you?' asked Tell.

'Certainly not! We of Hub HI-Q are fully aware of the dangers and we take care to use the technique responsibly. Only selected operatives understand the procedure, and we impress upon all of them that this knowledge is a privilege and a responsibility. We employ it only on rare occasions, and only when the quality of the prospect seems to warrant the risks of Recovery.'

'Has it made any difference?' interrupted Tell. 'These Donor HI-Qs you've fished up from the past — have they done what you wanted? Produced the kids for your project?'

'The Recovery Programme has been operational for less than half a century,' said Moss reproachfully. 'How can you expect adequate data in so short a time?'

Tell shrugged. She couldn't, of course. Camena was the one who could calculate data and probabilities.

Moss leaned back. 'Exactly. Would you believe there are fools who are trying to close us down? But — to return to your own experience. When did you begin to suspect the truth, Estelle?'

'I think I knew something weird was going on quite soon,' she said. 'I just didn't know what it was. I thought the explosion might have addled me a bit. I would have wondered sooner, if it hadn't been for Cammie's headache. I knew *something* was wrong, but I didn't know what until

Watchman explained. Even then I thought he was a bit crazy. And then — he made me understand.'

'And how did he contrive that?' asked Moss.

'He made me understand by taking me to the disclosure unit,' she said firmly. 'I recognised the general lay of the land, but Cockatoo — my home — wasn't there any more.' She swallowed. 'I might just have hoped I was in the wrong area, but for Silicon Peak. It's there, and it hasn't changed.'

Moss held up a hand. 'We seem to have moved rather rapidly through the events which took place *after* Recovery. One point which remains a little unclear is how my fostern, having effected a safe Recovery under less than ideal conditions, allowed RI-P to steal Camena de Courcey. I understand that she was unconscious at the time?'

'She was unconscious when we first hit the beach,' said Tell, 'but she soon came round. We started walking along the beach. I — Camena and I — thought we were walking back to the marina, and we both wondered why no-one came to meet us. We were pretty thrown by it all, and Camena got a migraine and had to lie down. I ran on ahead to get help and Watchman called after me to stop. I'm afraid I didn't, so he came to fetch me back. He had to, you see, because I thought the marina was just along the beach and it wasn't.'

'And then — while my fostern was fetching you back — Camena was taken.'

'I suppose so,' muttered Tell. 'I shouldn't have left her, but I thought I could go for help. Watchman knew better, but I didn't listen until it was too late.'

'This migraine,' said Moss slowly. 'Does Camena suffer it often?'

'Only a couple of times a year,' said Tell. 'Why?'

Moss sighed. 'I did the initial research on Camena de Courcey — the research designed to assess her suitability for our purpose. I examined her records and was agreeably impressed, not only by her scholastic achievements and general intellectual capability, but by her physical condition. She appeared little short of perfection. Nowhere did I find any mention of chronic ill-health.'

Tell was about to come to Camena's defence because, after all, biannual migraines could scarcely be construed as 'chronic ill-health', but then she thought of something.

If her migraines made Camena somehow unsuitable for the Donor HI-Q Programme, that might improve their chance of going home together. So far, it seemed that Moss intended to send Tell back almost immediately, while keeping Camena — once he got her back from the RI-P — until she made up her mind.

If Camena decided not to participate in the programme, or to participate only by donating ova, she would probably be sent back to arrive at the same time as Tell. This would make little difference to Tell, but Camena would be alone in this strange time for ages. If Gerhardt had been in charge of her, it mightn't have been so bad, but Moss seemed certain to take over and Tell knew Camena would never be able to stand up to Moss. He might have believed he was behaving with old world courtesy, but his patronising manner set Tell's teeth on edge.

Camena, for all her intellectual brilliance, could sometimes be suggestible, and if Moss implied that it was her duty to stay on, then Camena might just do it, particularly if she were offered an extra inducement, such as the chance to mix freely with other HI-Qs. Camena had so few ties to bind her to her life at home — casual friends, an elder, adopted sister — and Tell.

But if Camena were to be found unsuitable for Donor HI-Q, it followed that she and Tell would be sent home together, as soon as Camena was found. There was no way Hub HI-Q would want to keep an unsuitable prospect cluttering up their brave new world, any more than they'd want to keep Tell.

If Camena *wanted* to stay it would be selfish to deny her the chance, but what about Tell, going home alone, forced to pretend grief for a drowned friend whom only she knew had not drowned at all?

Tell chewed her lip. She didn't know what to do for the best.

Camena faced the one-way mirror. 'Hello, through there,' she said. 'I think it's time we met.' She sat down in the chair with the kitten by her feet and after a few minutes a door opened behind her. The woman who came in was small and spare, with cropped grey hair and surprisingly warm brown eyes. She was wearing a nondescript skirt with low-heeled shoes and a cardigan over a pin-tucked blouse. A brooch was pinned to the cardigan. Celtic silver? No, thought Camena. That's a double helix.

She raised her eyebrows very slightly and waited.

'A curious situation, isn't it, Camena?' said the woman.

'Very,' said Camena dryly. It was obvious that she had been accurately identified.

'I never know quite what to say.'

'You make a habit of kidnapping people?'

The woman looked amused. 'Hardly.'

'But you've kidnapped me. I presume that means my father has something you want, and that you believe that by holding me hostage you can persuade him to give it up. It won't work, you know. My father doesn't know me. Our only contact has been two short letters and a bodyguard. And why did you keep me in that dark place?'

The woman shook her head decisively. 'That was an unfortunate incident, wasn't it? I'm afraid my young friends — the ones who found you — thought you would be safer if no-one knew where you were. Fortunately, that no longer applies. As for your father; this matter has nothing — or almost nothing — to do with him.'

'No-one else will pay you. Linnie and Justin aren't rich and as far as I know I have no other relatives. I certainly haven't got any political associations.'

'I am not interested in payment of any kind,' said the woman. 'I am interested in moral principles. May I sit down?'

'Be my guest,' said Camena. She was dismayed to find her hands shaking slightly, and clasped them in her lap. The kitten looked up, saucer-eyed. Camena knew there was a breed of cat known as the Maine Coon. It was much larger than a usual domestic tabby and she wondered if this kitten might be one. 'If you don't want payment,' she said as the woman took her place in the other chair, 'why bother to kidnap me?'

Another tight smile. 'We did not. Rather, we have removed you from the clutches of those who *did* make an attempt.'

'Nonsense,' said Camena curtly. 'I was shipwrecked after an explosion. Gerhardt saved me.' She may have sounded calm but in the back of her mind the emotive words were decking themselves with exclamation marks. *Kidnapping!!! Shipwreck!!! Explosion!!! He saved me!!!*

'In the short term, perhaps,' said the woman. 'I presume you're referring to the young man who has recently pushed his way into your life?'

'Gerhardt Watchman is my bodyguard.' There was another one; *bodyguard!!!*

'Gerhardt Watchman, as you call him,' said the woman coolly, 'is an unfortunate boy who has been duped into believing himself an agent for a politico/scientific group known as Hub HI-Q. I'm afraid he has been badly misled — but we can't consider him entirely blameless. No doubt he told you a very plausible story?'

Camena felt a tiny cold worm of unease. 'He said I was in danger,' she said cautiously.

'Don't feel bad about being taken in, Camena. He is a clever young man, although quite unstable, and his mentor is both brilliant and thoroughly unscrupulous. This Watchman, as you call him, has won your trust by lying to you. He has misdirected you at every turn, and, if our people hadn't stepped in to prevent it, he would have delivered you to his employers.'

'Why? What for?' asked Camena. 'I'm not saying I buy your story. For a start, you haven't even told me your name. And Gerhardt has saved my life, whereas you have not only shut me in a dark cell, but probably drugged me as well.'

'Concealment was considered necessary while we investigated the exact circumstances of your situation; as for drugs — you have been given no more than a mild sedative, which was to save you undue stress. As for names; surely you can see that "Watchman" is a pseudonym? And a very obvious one, if I may say so.'

'It is,' said Camena. 'But there are people whose names coincidentally fit their occupations.'

'That may be so. My name, however, is not so apt! I am simply Dr Sib. Would you care to see some identification?'

'That's all right,' said Camena. If the woman were telling the truth there was no need for identification. If she were lying, no doubt she would have some fake ID. 'I told you, there's no-one to pay a ransom for me,' she said. 'So why would anyone go to so much trouble to take me *or* to get me back?'

'You have certain personal attributes, Camena, which certain people find interesting,' said Dr Sib.

'Sure. A high IQ. I don't know anything that would be any use to anyone though.'

'To put it bluntly, Camena, there are any number of reasons why an unscrupulous man might want you in his power.' Dr Sib shook her head. 'If you had been taken as intended, you might have found yourself participating in scientific experiments, none of which you would have enjoyed. That sounds very melodramatic, doesn't it? But not all my colleagues in the world of science are as scrupulous as I would like.'

Camena nodded. 'It *all* sounds very melodramatic. Okay, this unscrupulous person had me grabbed, and you rescued me. What's in it for you?'

'Satisfaction,' said Dr Sib with a grin. 'Satisfaction in righting a wrong, and, I'm afraid, a certain satisfaction in putting one over my — opponent.'

'What about my father? Is he connected to this opponent? Or to you?'

'I'm sorry to have to tell you this, Camena, but your father has been dead for quite some years.'

'Oh.' The blow was unexpectedly bitter. 'I had letters . . .'

'Fakes, I'm afraid. I told you the young man was clever.'

Camena looked down at the kitten's wide flat skull. The fur grew in a quaintly marked M-shape and the ears were still youthfully soft. 'What about Tell?' she asked at last. 'Is she here?'

'Tell?'

'My friend. Estelle Clancy. She was with us — me — on the yacht and later, on the beach.'

'Really?' Dr Sib's eyebrows rose. 'Strange. My young friends didn't mention a second girl. Was this Estelle sitting with you?'

'I don't really remember,' said Camena. 'I don't notice much — outside — when I have a migraine.'

'I can quite understand that. Hmm. I assume your friend is still with the young man. Don't worry — she won't have come to any harm.'

'How do you know?' asked Camena sharply.

'My dear, our opponents will be quite well aware of your whereabouts by now, so it won't profit them at all to hurt your friend.'

'Won't they use her instead of me?'

'I doubt it. I really do. She would be quite unsuitable for their purpose.'

'Oh,' said Camena. 'You keep talking about opponents. Can't you be more specific?'

Dr Sib grinned again, giving an unexpectedly youthful aspect to her face. 'It's all to do with politics; you might call it the politics of scientific research. Otherwise known as the policies of intervention. But politics is a boring subject, don't you think? So much talk and so little action. And half the time the action that *is* taken is counter-productive or downright harmful. Have I set your mind at rest?'

'No,' said Camena. 'I want to find Tell and go home.'

'Of course you do! And of course you shall. But how are you feeling? Not too much the worse for your experiences, I hope?'

'I've got a few bruises and my ears are still ringing,' said Camena. 'But at least my migraine is gone.'

'Migraine. Yes indeed, a most unpleasant affliction, or so I'm told.'

'Very,' said Camena.

Dr Sib nodded sympathetically and got up. 'I expect you'd welcome being rid of it for good.'

'Not much chance of that,' said Camena.

'Oh — you never know your luck! After today you might never have a migraine again! Now don't worry. We'll soon have you back where you belong.'

'Can't I go now?'

'I could drop you off now, but wouldn't it be better if we find your friend first?'

'How long will that take?' asked Camena suspiciously. 'My sister Linnie must think I've drowned.'

'It won't take long. And don't worry about your sister. You may be sure the police have already notified her of your whereabouts. Now — I'm quite confident that we will find your friend easily and then either I or my brother will take you back to Cockatoo at — oh, a few minutes after four?'

Camena let out a long breath. 'That will be fine,' she said.

Gerhardt was laying out a new game when he became aware of a shadow across his cheek. A presence, to which he reacted with an instinctive feeling of pleasure. *Tell?* He glanced up. It was not Tell, but Jens, who should not be there. He should still have been on duty at Hub HI-Q.

Gerhardt shook his head to clear his confusion. Why had he thought it would be Tell?

'Busy?' suggested Jens.

An idle question, for he must be perfectly well aware of the answer. Furthermore, he obviously wanted to know why Gerhardt was playing solitaire on the plateau instead of attending to his Recoveree.

'Yet contra me?' he added. Direct as always. Jens never skirted an issue he wanted to address.

'Contra code, sie,' said Gerhardt, and reinforced the accusation with a mental jolt.

Jens turned out his hands in apology. 'D'accord. Verzeihen sie.'

He said no more and Gerhardt, the wind knocked from his sails, looked up to meet his old friend's gaze.

Necessity, said Jens. *Time nyet.*

Mea culpa also, admitted Gerhardt, and gestured resigned acceptance of the apology. After all, he had broken code with Tell.

Ja? With?

Recoveree — time, nyet for code . . . said Gerhardt pensively. *Time.*

There was irony in Jens's mental tone, an irony which Gerhardt was only just coming to appreciate. With inborn talent and careful training, he and Jens could cross the veil of time, yet still they could not take time as their tool in times of sudden need. The realisation was humbling, but it went a long way to restoring the old bond between them.

'Moss mit Recoveree,' said Jens aloud.

'Recovery complicae,' said Gerhardt, in explanation and excuse.

'Ja.' Jens's dark eyes seemed to be reading his face, and he gestured at the rock. *You permit?*

Gerhardt nodded, and Jens sat down, economically, as he did everything. His complexion was much darker than

Gerhardt's, and with his high-bridged nose and wide slit of a mouth he could not be considered handsome. His eyes were tired, but Gerhardt knew he had not yet completed his fourth decade. It came as a slight shock, as always, to reflect that Jens must have become his fosterman when he was little older than Gerhardt was now.

Jens clasped his hands in his lap and gazed out over the barren plateau towards the lake. Bathed in quiet, which was the way he used to be.

Gerhardt moved uneasily, but Jens took his time before speaking and for once he didn't come straight to the point. 'Moss mit Recoveree?' This time, it was phrased as a question.

'Ja.'

'Complicae?'

'In hand,' said Gerhardt.

They sat in silence for a little longer and then Jens sighed. 'Recovery ich one,' he said.

That was news to Gerhardt. 'Recoveree?'

'Belaria Lane. Latwenty-one.'

Jens's voice was as precise as always, but Gerhardt felt as if a colder wind were blowing. Whatever Jens was about to say, it was nothing he wanted to hear. 'Option?' he asked.

Jens shook his head and tilted his hand a little so that Gerhardt understood that the Recoveree had been returned through the veil. Another one who had elected not to stay.

'Why?' he asked. '*Why* that option? Are they all mad?'

Jens looked at him gravely. 'No options, Daichcue Forn, ever, now. Options one time, ja — none these many years.'

'The tenets of Hub HI-Q state that the options will be given!' he protested. 'I accessed the original records.'

'Mounting paradox, Daichcue Forn. Options withdrawn.'

'You mean there's no choice now? I didn't know!' In his agitation, Gerhardt found himself slipping into the idiom he had been using with Tell and Camena.

'Spec brief,' said Jens. 'Gave pain — to save more.' He shook his head.

'If you'd explained properly, I would have listened,' said Gerhardt.

'Moss,' reminded Jens, and Gerhardt nodded. Moss had made very sure they'd had no privacy for explanations or discussion.

'But — how can Hub HI-Q condone harm to Recoverees?'

Jens looked sad. 'Truth can lie.'

Yes, thought Gerhardt distractedly. Moss had taught him how that technique worked. He had become fairly proficient at remoulding the truth, but he had never learned to delight in it as Moss did. 'Then — what happens?' he asked. 'If the options don't really exist?'

'Options ... mist on the moon. There, but not there. Now, there is only the death. *The* death as was fated.'

Gerhardt swallowed. 'Your Recoveree — Offspring?' If there had been none, then the Recovery would have been wasted, the Recoveree diverted from her life-line for nothing. And if it were all for nothing, perhaps RI-P was right to try to close the programme down.

Jens shrugged and got up, laying his hand briefly on Gerhardt's shoulder. 'Camena de Courcey, Daichcue Forn,' he said slowly. 'She too is mist on the moon. Forget her.' He turned and began to walk away.

Gerhardt stared after him. The cold wind was blowing all around him now, battering his life to its foundations. Jens *had* tried to warn him, before. Jens had believed so violently in Gerhardt's right to know the truth about Recovery that he had violated his own rigid codes. '*Pain, to save more*'. He had thought it kinder to inflict a temporary mind pain on Gerhardt than to leave him to learn the truth *after* the Recovery. He had tried to warn him his briefing was incomplete, that he had not been told all the facts.

And Gerhardt, Daichcue Forn, protégée of Alpha Moss, had reacted with sanctimonious horror, and had never stopped to ask himself why Jens would have broken code. It had taken his own need to do so and now this meeting with Jens to make him see the truth. And the knowledge had come too late.

Jens was almost out of sight, away across the rocky terrain. It was too late to catch him physically but perhaps he was still just in telepathic range. Camena was lost, but Gerhardt's mind was not on Camena just then. *Jens? A moment?*

Reluctantly, it seemed, Jens stopped walking and looked back, his face a swarthy blur.

Estelle Clancy — Peripheral to de Courcey subject, said Gerhardt. *Records, bitte?*

Jens raised a hand in acknowledgment, and walked on and Gerhardt sat down to wait. The sun warmed the rocks and the sparse vegetation was unshaken, but the cold wind still blew in Gerhardt's mind, scoring away his thoughts until they were barren as stone.

'Estelle,' said Moss softly. 'I can see you are troubled. Since the subject of your friend's health seems a delicate one, perhaps you would care to continue your tale from the time you noticed Camena's disappearance?'

'Oh. Sure. Well, we didn't see who took her or how,' said Tell. 'When we got back — and we weren't gone long — we couldn't find her. We looked until it was dark, and then

Watchman told me where — and when — I was. I thought he was mad, so he took me to the disclosure unit and I was convinced. We crashed — went to sleep, I mean — there. Then this morning Watchman called you, and you came to fetch us and here we are.'

'A most enlightening story,' said Moss. 'We must now, of course, locate your friend — although, to set your mind at rest, I can tell you I have a very good idea of her current whereabouts.'

'Good. We can get her back, then, and then she can decide when she wants to come home,' said Tell.

'I think you may rest assured that Camena de Courcey will be going home with you, Estelle. I believe — I am practically certain — that the tests I intend to make will uphold my conviction that the only solution is to return you both almost immediately to your own time to rejoin your lives as if none of this had ever happened. And — to avoid further complications with RI-P, and to prevent any other problems that may have resulted from this affair, I shall have your return finetuned.'

'How?' asked Tell.

'The method is not your concern. Suffice it to say that you will arrive at a somewhat later period of the same day — shall we say at around 16:10 rather than 13:38? That way you will avoid any renewed risk of drowning and arrive on dry ground — in fact, in the midst of civilisation! Drowning, after all, was never your destiny.'

'I'm glad to hear that! But what about the time gap?' said Tell suspiciously. 'Won't people wonder where we've been if we disappear from the excursion? Won't they think we *have* drowned? And ask questions when we suddenly pop up at home?'

'The explanation will be simply made. It will be assumed that you swam ashore and set out to walk. You turned inland and were collected by a passing motorist who then deposited you in Trinity Street and drove on. Will that suffice?'

'Trinity Street is a bit out of our way ... I live at Leadbeater Court and Camena at ...'

'Will it suffice?'

Again the implication was clear. It had better suffice, or else. And after all, it was a far better scenario than the one involving more salt water.

'Okay,' said Tell.

'Then that will be all,' said Moss affably. He turned away, and spent some time working with the view-screen she had seen before. Tell fidgeted, but eventually Moss turned to her again and said smoothly, 'Perhaps you will have the goodness to summon my fostern? You will be spending the remainder of your time here in seclusion, for obvious reasons.'

On the point of sending a mental summons to Gerhardt, Tell decided to play it safe. The situation seemed to be under control, but it always paid to have an ace left to play, and Tell's ace was her telepathy. Moss might know it existed, but he could not know its extent. If Gerhardt had told her the truth, her telepathic power was well above the average. 'I'll call him in,' she said casually, and walked towards the hatch. Gerhardt had left it unsealed, so Tell stuck her head out and called. 'Watchman! Your — Moss wants you!'

Her voice rang out through the bleakness, and she saw Gerhardt raise his head. He was sitting on a rock, and from his posture she deduced he was playing cards. Again.

Talk about fiddling while Rome burns! she commented lightly. It wasn't over yet, but if it hadn't been for Gerhardt, she would have been feeling positively lighthearted. Moss was tricky, but she'd talked him round into doing almost exactly what she wanted. She hoped he wouldn't turn on Gerhardt after she and Camena had gone. The stuff-up hadn't been Gerhardt's fault and it looked as if the worst could be tidied up.

Breathing the crisp air of the plateau, she watched as Gerhardt swept up his cards and came towards her. She caught his eye as he neared the hatch, and gave him a crooked smile. *It's going to be okay for Cammie and me, Watchman. I hope it's going to be okay for you.*

There was no response. *S'pose you can't come back with us?* she thought wistfully.

But Gerhardt's response was cold and short.

Impossible.

She ducked out of the way, trying not to feel hurt; after spending two hours in Moss's company, she had a great deal of sympathy for Gerhardt's silence. David and Maureen might be worth no better than C plus as parents went, but she wouldn't have given Moss any more than an F. No, an F minus. Maureen had joked about infanticide, but Moss would probably commit it without a second thought. No wonder Gerhardt had some gaping holes in his personality.

But Moss hadn't murdered anyone yet, so far as she knew. It wasn't against the law to be a cold fish, and Moss certainly seemed to believe in his own weird code of conduct. He'd apologised for her inconvenience, and had even agreed with her that Camena would be better employed attending St Saviours in the twentieth century than producing HI-Q babies in the twenty-seventh.

If she did choose to go home with Tell, Camena would never have babies at all. Tell wondered why not, and whether Camena would mind. There could be many reasons. Perhaps she'd be so busy achieving that she'd simply never find the time to be a mother. And why should she, if it wasn't a high priority?

It was all very well for Gerhardt and his colleagues to talk about Camena's duty to pass on her genes, but they were looking at it from a twenty-seventh century point of view. That was about as valid as applying twentieth century perspectives to Bloody Mary or the Spanish Inquisition. It simply didn't work.

Tell wondered if she should warn Camena that she'd never have any children at home, but decided to hold her tongue. In fact, she'd better forget it all, if she could. Forget Moss and sol-planes. Forget self-fitting shoes. Forget about Gerhardt Watchman, who wouldn't exist in her time any more.

That thought hurt quite a lot, but Tell knew she'd get over the pain. She'd have to. It was no use crying for the moon and impossible was impossible. She'd put him out of her mind and perhaps, in a few months or years, this whole weird experience would seem like a dream or a product of her imagination.

One thing was certain; there was no way she was going to blurt out to anyone that she'd been time-travelling to the future! Even if they believed her story... what good could it do? It would probably start a panic with sensationalists claiming the Martians had landed, or that the evil future people were playing chess with human lives. So they were, but she couldn't stop them and they didn't seem to do much harm.

Maybe she and Camena could start a secret society, hold annual meetings for returned Recoverees. Advertise cryptically in the newspaper Personals... *Calling all HI-Qs and Donor HI-Qs...*

Maybe they would laugh over it when they were fifty. Or maybe they'd avoid one another's eyes and never mention it at all.

She wondered what Mr Blenning would say when the two of them came safely home after vanishing in the bay. She wondered if there'd be a Missing Persons report on Gerhardt, or if he'd be pronounced legally dead. Legally dead for a person who wouldn't be born for seven hundred years! She shook her head in perplexity, but concluded that Moss would have it covered. She didn't like Moss but she couldn't deny his intelligence. No doubt some clue would be discovered that would imply that Gerhardt had simply swum ashore and left the district. Or perhaps there'd be an official letter transferring him to a 'new school'.

She smiled at Gerhardt as he sat down beside her on the couch.

Fostern. Is that your real name? Sounds more like a bottle of beer!

The term is a contraction of 'foster son'.

What's your real name then?

I am known as Daichcue Forn. An elision of DHQ number 49.

God! A number-plate! Trust you for that!

Tell seemed amused and slightly shocked when he told her his registered appellation. It had always seemed good enough to him, and no-one but Jens had ever used it much anyway. Moss always called him Fostern, while HI-Qs of his generation, when they addressed him at all, generally did so as Forn, his number name. All forms of his name sounded strange to him now, but he supposed he would soon get used to them again. Odd, to have to get used to his own name, but during the past few weeks he had immersed himself deeply in his Gerhardt Watchman identity.

He must displace that persona as quickly as he could. He must, or Jens's final prediction would come true.

Forget her, Daichcue Forn, or lose your mind.

Jens had actually clasped his hand, offering hypnotic assistance, but how could he forget what he had learned? How could he bear to forget, and continue as if his world were still a stable place?

Forget her, Daichcue Forn, or lose your mind.
But if I forget her, my mind will be a lie.

The amusement was dying in Tell's eyes, and Gerhardt looked away, not wanting to see what replaced it, not wanting her to read the emotion in his own. A Donor HI-Q child had no right to true emotion any more than he had a right to a normal name.

'Moss?' he said abruptly to his fosterman. His voice control was adequate; Moss scarcely accorded him a glance. Too busy summoning the viewscreen, contacting Sib at RI-P Base. Sib and Moss, Hub HI-Q and RI-P Base — they were a pair — forever opposed, forever symbiotic. They seemed to need one another.

Out of the corner of her eye, Tell saw the holographic screen shimmer back into being. She edged around a little to get a better view. This time it didn't display an information grid, but the head and shoulders of an elderly woman. Television? Video? But the woman's eyes moved, seeming to focus on Moss. A telephone, twenty-seventh century style. Not so different from a satellite hook-up, or real-time Internet conferencing, after all. She had seen a more basic version at the disclosure unit.

'Ja?' The woman did not seem overjoyed to see Moss, but neither did she seem dismayed.

Moss smiled benignly. 'Sib? Report Camena de Courcey, Iatwenty? Have?'

'Ja.'

'Ill-done, Sib,' said Moss, and actually clicked his tongue. 'Risking peripherals!'

What's he mean? asked Tell.

Gerhardt glanced at her and then away. His eyes were opaque.

What's a peripheral? Watchman!

There was a pause, then Gerhardt replied, as if reluctantly. *Folk ex Reco-frame. Blenning. You.*

Why are you talking shorthand? Why are you pissed off? Who's that on the screen?

Another pause. Then with more reluctance still — *Sib is the head of RI-P.*

The woman looked harmless, but so, thought Tell, had some of the most ruthless people in history. Her face held both humour and intelligence; she looked like a retired head teacher — or someone's aunt. She and Moss bandied unintelligible comments, but somehow there was much less urgency than Tell would have expected, and none of the sharp recriminations.

This woman — or some of her colleagues — had almost killed Camena and herself and, despite all that had been said, she still didn't really know *why*. Gerhardt had said RI-Ps disapproved of the Recovery Programme and disrupted it every chance they got. Well, she could go along with that. The Recovery Programme was high-handed at best and it had caused Camena and herself nothing but grief. Hub HI-Q might think they were doing the human race a favour with their Recovery of lost genius genes, but who wanted to breed a lot of little Mosses? A litter of lichen? Most historical geniuses were decidedly odd, anyway, so if RI-P wanted to short-circuit the Recovery Programme, that was fine with Tell.

But why did they have to use violence? RI-P obviously had time-travelling capabilities, so why had Pris and Red not simply dropped in at St Saviours and explained their position to Camena at the beginning of term?

'Hi Camena — if someone comes to you with a cock-and-bull story or an offer you can't refuse, spit in his eye, okay?'

The answer to that came pat. Camena wouldn't have believed them. She might have believed Gerhardt, but if he'd told her what he really meant to do she'd have laughed at him. And so would Tell.

No matter how she tried to swing it, Tell kept stubbing her mental toe against that fact. If Gerhardt or Pris had told Camena the truth at the outset, it would have got them nowhere. But that didn't excuse the violence, or the lies. Better if Hub HI-Q and RI-P had simply stayed out of Camena's life. Even though they were going home, it would take a while to recover from the various shocks they had received.

Camena would have to re-adjust to the fact that she had no living blood relations, and Tell would have to adjust to the idea that Gerhardt Watchman was — not dead, but not yet alive.

And here was Moss conversing with RI-P and giving the woman Sib no more than a verbal slap on the wrist.

What the hell's he playing at? she shot at Gerhardt. *Why doesn't he just kick her in the backside and tell her to hand over Camena so we can both go home? He think it's fun being drowned?*

He's arranging to meet Camena now, replied Gerhardt. His mental tone was terse.

What's wrong, Watchman?

I am tired.

She turned to look at him critically, but he turned away.

Moss and his opponent seemed to be closing the deal, and Tell didn't like the look on Moss's face. He seemed satisfied. Smug, almost, as if he had got his own way or put something over someone. The woman Sib also seemed satisfied, but well in control and at last she nodded briefly, and raised one hand.

Tell wondered what had been offered, or bartered, in exchange for Camena's release. It had to have been something RI-P valued more than Camena. Could Moss have told Sib the game was up and offered RI-P immunity from prosecution if she handed over Cammie pronto?

That would account for Sib's agreement, but not for her satisfaction.

'What's going on?' she asked nervously.

Moss dismissed the screen. 'The deal is struck, Estelle. Camena de Courcey will be released immediately into my custody.'

Tell sighed. 'Can we go and fetch her now?'

Moss shook his head. 'I have said already that you must stay in seclusion, Estelle. Apart from my fostern and myself, Sib is the only HI-Q who knows you are here.'

'When do I see Camena?' asked Tell.

'After her interview has been completed and certain tests have been run.'

'You said she could come home with me.'

For the first time since she had met him, Moss showed impatience. 'I have told you already that the most likely outcome of this botched Recovery is that Camena de Courcey will be leaving this time with you. If not, she will remain with us only as long she desires. No-one will force her or coerce her to stay longer and she will be dispatched through the veil when her duties, if any, have been performed. She may call a halt to any duty at any time, save only that she will not be permitted to depart during any trimester of active pregnancy. If she desires to leave while in that state, the pregnancy would naturally be dissolved or re-implanted. We cannot risk retrograde paradox. Do you understand what I am saying, Estelle?'

'Of course I do!' snapped Tell. 'If she wasn't pregnant Wednesday morning, she can't show up six months gone in the afternoon. I might not be HI-Q, but I'm not bloody stupid.'

'Then why do you constantly question what I have said already?' Moss sounded almost aggrieved.

'Do you blame me?' said Tell. 'Watchman couldn't lie straight in bed, and you're the one who's brought him up. He must have learned how to bend the truth from *someone*.'

'A Hub HI-Q operative must often present the truth creatively,' said Moss. 'My fostern appears to have overstepped the boundaries. His part in this operation is over.'

'It is my right to escort the Recoveree to Hub HI-Q for options briefing!' said Gerhardt.

'You forfeited that right, Fostern, when you allowed RI-P to win a hand,' said Moss. 'Fortunately Sib intervened or there is no knowing what might have happened.'

'This operation is my responsibility. I should be making the decisions. It is my prerogative to make sure Camena is offered . . .'

Moss looked at him coldly. 'Not any more. You abdicated that right when you came to me and asked my help.' He paused to let that sink in.

'I am the one Camena trusts.'

'I hardly think she trusts you now! You allowed her to be diverted by RI-P while you pursued your separate interests with her friend. I shall now go to RI-P Base to greet the

Recoveree and apologise for her quite unnecessary ordeal. You, Fostern, may remain here with Estelle until I contact you.'

'I must brief Camena —'

'No. It is evident that you favour Estelle's company so why not enjoy it while you may? You have heard how eager she is to leave us. Perhaps your charms are less than even I believed.'

They stared at one another, Moss relaxed and in control, Gerhardt with fists clenched. After a moment Moss nodded sharply, once, then turned away to lift the hatch. He drew himself up and out of sight and replaced the cover with a soft clunk. A strange sensation touched Tell's eardrums, as if the pressure in the unit had changed. She shivered.

'Is he really going to let us go home?' she said abruptly to the back of Gerhardt's head.

Something about the stiff set of Gerhardt's shoulders made her shiver again. Either he knew something that she did not, or he was more flayed by Moss's cruelty than she would have expected. And it *had* been cruelty, a swift cutting down to size that had been designed to humiliate rather than instruct. Why else had it been delivered in the pedantic brand of English Moss knew Tell would understand?

As much to gain reassurance as to give it, she reached out to touch his arm. It might have been wood for all the response he showed. 'Watchman?' she said uncertainly.

He flinched, but did not turn round.

Tell cleared her throat. 'If you stand there much longer rigor mortis will set in.' Tentatively, she flexed her fingers. 'Come on Watchman — worse things happen at sea — in fact worse things *did* happen at sea. To us. Remember?

'You got us out of that one,' she said, ignoring the fact that she had had to save herself. 'If it hadn't been for you,

Camena would be dead. So. Are you going to hand-deliver us home, or do we just step off a cliff into the blue and hope for the best?'

Gerhardt's shoulders shrugged, very slightly.

'You don't *know*!' said Tell. 'What do you mean, you don't *know*? You fetched us here, you take us back. Isn't that the deal? Isn't that what always happens?'

'My first Recovery,' said Gerhardt in a low voice. 'Meinen zuletzt.'

Relieved that he was talking, Tell pressed her advantage. 'Does that mean your last? I shouldn't wonder if it was! Moss is pretty pissed off, isn't he? Look on the bright side; you might find something else to do. Something you'll like better. If you ask me this whole Recovery idea stinks.' She paused, but Gerhardt didn't respond. 'Hasn't Moss ever told you the normal procedure? He's Recovered lots of HI-Qs, or so he says. How did he take them back? Did some of them decide to stay on here?'

'They were all Returned.' He jerked his head impatiently, and Tell heard the comment echo in his mind. *They were all Returned* . . . For some reason Gerhardt seemed to find that shocking.

'So maybe they didn't like the twenty-seventh century. Maybe Moss put them off. Still — I s'pose he's not all bad. He's sending us home this afternoon, and I suppose our lives will just take up about where they left off. Only we won't end up in the sea on Wednesday and you won't be there at St Sav's tomorrow . . . There, I finally sorted out the time thing! I hope you're proud. It *will* be tomorrow for Camena and me. And yesterday times a million over or so for you. You'll never have to do Blood-and-Guts again — but you won't forget us — quite. Will you?'

She was still standing with her arm outstretched, her hand resting on Gerhardt's upper arm. It was a silly sort of pose; she must look like one of the less tasteful plaster ornaments that used to decorate Victorian bird-baths. Or a shop-window mannequin gesturing gracefully at nothing. She dropped her hand and stood awkwardly, waiting for a response from him. Any response.

'What happens now?' she asked. 'Will Moss bring Camena here, or do we go to RI-P Base or the Recovery unit? That might be best. If you send us home from here, we'll wind up hours from home. If we go from *there*, we end up right on our doorsteps in Cockatoo. Right?'

'Trinity Street,' said Gerhardt. His voice sounded dry and empty. 'You return to Trinity Street.'

'Oh well, he seems to have it all worked out,' said Tell. 'We get home to Trinity Street at 16.10. That's ten past four, isn't it?'

His silent misery was getting to her.

'Don't be so morbid, Watchman,' she said. 'I know the Recovery got stuffed up, but that wasn't your fault. And there's no harm done. There's life beyond Recovery, you know. For all of us.'

Finally, Gerhardt turned to face her. He was smiling faintly, but his eyes looked blind. A shiver walked down Tell's spine.

'Watchman?' said Tell uncertainly. Could he be facing prison? Or worse? Just for being fooled by RI-P?

'I am not Watchman,' he said. 'Gerhardt Watchman was a myth. I invented him, nicht wahr? and now he's served his purpose. *I* am Daichcue number 49, nyet? Letters and numbers, Tell. A number-plate for a name and you were right. I am less than human. And it *was* my fault in the end.

I should have stayed focused on Camena in the Wild Zone. I should never have diverted my mind to you. I should never have brought you through the veil at all.'

'I brought myself,' said Tell. 'Remember?'

'Why?'

'I had to look after Camena, I guess. Or maybe I fancied a look at the future. Can I keep the shoes?'

Gerhardt shook his head. *You followed me, Estellita. You got yourself into my mind and you reproduced the alpha state in your own.*

'So? We all make mistakes! I *am* a mistake. If David and Maureen hadn't made the mistake of their lives, I wouldn't be here today.'

It was a bad mistake, Estellita, the one that brought you into my mind, but I'd not unmake it. I wouldn't forget you, though I could. Moss knows I left you behind in the sea. He knows I couldn't let you die again. He knows I can't keep you and I can't let you go. Moss knows everything. As I invented Gerhardt Watchman, Moss invented me.

She stared at him, wordlessly, struck by the bitter self-recrimination.

Jens was right, he continued. *Jens was right! I'm going to lose my mind, but I can't forget you. I can't let you go back to Trinity Street.*

PART FOUR

TRINITY STREET

Death is the end?

'What are you on about?' Tell asked, frightened. 'I don't understand. Of course you can let me go home. Me and Cammie, both. Watchman — don't you go cracking up on me now! We need your help to get us home! You might be as crooked as a Möbius strip but I trust you anyway. God knows why.'

Gerhardt put out both hands, blindly, as Camena sometimes did while in the grip of a migraine. Asking Tell for help, or comfort, or both.

This is a very bad idea, thought Tell distractedly. She longed for Maureen, who would have enfolded Gerhardt in a motherly embrace and sent Tell off to make him a coffee. What would David have done? He would have offered advice, but never his arms. It wasn't a thing men did. Or not for other men. It wasn't a thing Tell did, either, as a rule. Maureen would, but Maureen wasn't Tell.

Tell was *not* Maureen, but she couldn't turn away. Nor could she sit and do nothing, as if she didn't care.

Tell reached out.

As a motherly embrace it was a failure. For a start, Gerhardt was much taller than Tell, and she didn't have cushiony breasts or maternal hands, experienced in patting shoulders and smoothing foreheads. Even her shoulders were on the bony side and surely no comfort for weeping on. Not that he was weeping, exactly.

She had once wondered if holding Gerhardt would feel like holding a statue and she was dismayed to find that it did. It was crazy to cuddle a statue and she tried to withdraw, but Gerhardt abruptly came to life and was holding on. He had his face down somehow on her head and it was really very uncomfortable. Quite different from his warming or restraining grip out in the Wild Zone.

Disjointed phrases came into Tell's mind. 'He enfolded her in his embrace.' 'He took her in his arms.' 'He buried his face in her hair.' 'His lips found hers.'

All the romantic clichés. And that was the trouble. They never seemed to mention that faces were bony, or that it was physically impossible to bury anything bigger than a chopstick in a normal head of hair. And they certainly never confided that taller heroes were inclined to lean and that hands grasping at your shirt twisted it up and gave you a chill.

Her mouth was pressed against his shoulder, bruising her lips, and she couldn't say a word.

Watchman, she thought, *get off*.

Her neck creaked and she staggered a little. He might have been lost in a waking nightmare, but it wouldn't help him if they both fell down.

Let go! she scolded. *You're hurting me.*

His hold slackened and she managed to regain her balance and straighten her neck. 'Come and sit down,' she said, relieved. Her heart was thumping hard. She pushed him towards the couch and sat down beside him, reaching up to put her arm over his shoulders. That was probably another bad idea, but she couldn't offer him support and then take it away. Besides, she'd taken advantage of his warmth down on the beach, so the least she could do was offer the same to him. He wasn't cold in the body, but perhaps he was cold in the soul.

'Slide down a bit,' she suggested and after a moment he did so.

There was a long, fraught silence. Tell was right out of her depth with this one. How could you offer comfort or hope when there was none? She didn't really know *what* was giving Gerhardt the horrors, and until she found out, anything she said might make it worse.

Perhaps she could read it somehow from his mind? But she flinched away from that.

It's all right, she thought, trying to direct the feeling rather than the actual words. She paused, and then added helplessly; *I'm here.*

Again she longed for Maureen, or even Sister Pat. Nothing was sure but death and taxes, Maureen always said. And — love could move mountains, just like faith, said Sister Pat, but it had to be the right kind of love. The wrong kind made more mountains than it moved and lover and beloved could both be the losers. Loving-kindness. That was the kind to have. That was what moved the mountains. Not the kind that was stabbing at Tell right now.

'What is it, Watchman?' she asked. She couldn't bring herself to call him by his ridiculous number-plate name.

Gerhardt didn't answer, but she heard him draw a shuddering breath.

'You can tell me,' said Tell. 'I'm good at listening and you won't have to face me tomorrow. Your secrets will be safe as a grave. So come on, what was it that hit you so hard? Not all that rubbish Moss said?'

Gerhardt was slumped beside her, and Tell thought her arm might have been plastic for all the good it was doing. As a comforter she was a dead loss and he probably wished she'd butt out and leave him to his misery. She looked at his averted face, and saw the graze on his cheek, lightly scabbing over. That had happened in another century, but he still carried the marks, which meant her scraped thigh would still be sore when she went back home. Whatever part of her was snubbed and aching now would still be hurting too. 'I might as well make a cup of tea or something, since you don't feel like talking,' she said. 'Where do you keep the kettle?'

Gerhardt took another deep, shaken breath, and seemed to pull himself together. His shoulders straightened and his head came up. His eyes began to focus. 'Don't go, Tell.'

'I'm not doing much good here,' she said, withdrawing her arm. 'I would help you if I could, but I'm out of my depth.'

'Don't go.' His voice sounded strange and she remembered that he was — she couldn't quite formulate what he was. It was easier to remember what he wasn't. He wasn't a bodyguard, or Camena's boyfriend. He wasn't really Gerhardt Watchman and he sure as hell wasn't fifteen. He was a young man of the future and he was walking some private wilderness alone.

The valley of the shadow, she thought, with a superstitious shudder. The valley of the shadow of death. His death? Was execution the penalty for bungling a Recovery?

'Don't go,' he said again, and she wondered what it was he wanted her to do. Join him in his wilderness, or draw him to higher ground? Moving mountains?

I don't really know you, she thought, troubled.

Nor do I any more.

He shifted position so that she was leaning against him instead of the other way round. 'Tell,' he said slowly. 'What would you say if I asked you to stay?'

'Stay? Where? Sitting on this couch?'

'Stay in this here. In this now. Mit me.'

She squirmed round to stare at him in amazement. His eyes were still strained, but the blank horror had passed and his pupils were dilated, the darkness swallowing the blue. 'Me stay on *here*?' she said. 'In the twenty-seventh century? I can't. I'm not the Recoveree, nor even a HI-Q! I'm just a — a stowaway. I followed you blind, by accident, and now I have to go home.'

'You didn't follow by accident. You wanted to come with me. Couldn't you want to stay?'

'Since the alternative was death by drowning,' she said coldly, '*wanting* didn't come into it.'

'It does now. Remember, you are telepathic. Hub HI-Q might be interested in that.'

'I think it only works with you.' She bit her tongue, because that had been a careless thing to say. She wanted to calm him down, not encourage him in this fantasy.

'Perhaps you have a limited telepathic focus, but to be able to focus at all is rare. Some can receive, or broadcast at random, but to communicate as you do, untrained, is extraordinary. It took me a decade to learn it well.'

Tell thought about that. It was a novelty to think herself extraordinary.

'Wouldn't you like to stay?' He leaned his cheek against her head and she felt his breath in her hair and shivered.

'No. Come on Watchman, let me up.' His grasp tightened and she subsided, but she wasn't remotely at ease. His transition from despair to calm had seemed sudden and complete, but she didn't think it was genuine.

'You could stay.'

'You know what it is, Watchman?' said Tell carefully. 'Mad. I seriously mean that. You know perfectly well I can't stay here. Now. I've got a life at home.'

'You could have a life here and this could be your home. Why not?'

'You've been telling me *why not* all along. Remember the little paradox problem? I'm not supposed to be here. Moss doesn't want anyone to *know* I'm here. I've got to go home with Cammie. I *want* to go home with Cammie. You can come too, if you like. I told you that before.'

'I cannot come. I want you to stay.'

'As *what?*'

'Whatever you want. My partner, my leman, if you like.' He touched her cheek. *I would like that, and so would you. I never thought I could love, but now I know I can.*

But I'm not HI-Q . . . But Tell felt her mouth curve and an incredulous smile was dawning, as if she had been offered a present.

Then Gerhardt slid his arms around her back, kissing the side of her face. He was not in the least like a statue now.

Estellita, our children will be . . .

Suddenly Tell realised she'd been flung the oldest line in the B-grade movie compendium. 'For God's sake, Watchman, leave it off!' she said, struggling to sit up straight. 'No!' She turned her face away from his. 'This isn't fair. Talking love when you only want to . . . No, get your hands off me. Watchman, get *off*!' She was alarmed now, and exasperated. She knew that in theory any reasonably fit woman should be able to get out of a situation like this, but self-defence techniques seemed to depend on having room to manoeuvre. They also seemed to depend on the woman being willing to cause pain if not actual damage to the man. Well — she was willing.

She got one hand free and grabbed one of his, bending a finger back, hard. He let go with a curse and she scrambled away and retreated to the other side of the unit.

'Did that bloody Moss put you up to this?' she asked. Her hands were shaking and she clasped them together. 'Is that why he left us alone in here, so you could try to get round me to — how do you put it? *Fulfil my duty to Hub HI-Q?* I haven't *got* any duty to them — or you.'

'Moss has nothing to do with this. I want you to stay with me. Please, Estellita. I need you to be here.'

If he was acting, she reckoned he deserved a silver Logie.

You followed me, Estellita mia. You could have swum to the life-raft, but instead, you came to me.

'I was looking for Camena. I had to help you with her.'

After I had her safe, still you came with me.

'I wasn't thinking, okay? I was almost drowned! I didn't even know where the life-raft was! Don't you understand? I've got to go home where I belong.'

'Why?' He came towards her and Tell backed away. 'It's all right, Tell, I'm not going to touch you if you don't want it. I thought you were offering something to me. You did put out your arms.'

'I was offering a bit of a hug for moral support, because you seemed so suicidal. That's *all.*'

He looked at her steadily.

'Okay,' she conceded, 'so it wasn't quite *only* that, although I thought so then. I hated to see you hurting, but — yes, there's always been *something* there.'

'Then we have a foundation to build on . . .'

She shook her head, swallowing a lump which comprised far more pain than anger. 'It isn't enough. Oh, come on, Watchman. You must be able to see it's just not on. It wasn't on at home and it isn't on here. Not to breed you telepathic kids, but also not for any other reason.'

You loved me enough to follow. You loved me enough to offer your arms. Love me enough to stay.

Get out of my head! she snapped. 'Look at it from my side. What if I stayed for a while, and did as you suggested. I'd just keep on getting older, right, at the normal rate? My hair would grow. I might even have a baby. Many things would change. I'd have to go home eventually, and Maureen would notice if I looked different. She might notice if I had a few stretch-marks, too. And what about me?' She spread her hands appealingly. 'How could I ever go back to school if I'd lived with you for a while? How could I ever settle for something else? Or — okay — how could I settle for some*one* else, after you? You might not be much in the sensitive-new-age-guy stakes, Watchman, but you're sure as bloody hell unique. So the sooner I go the better. Before I get hooked any more.

'God — stop looking at me like that! I'm fifteen years old, Watchman! No *way* am I hopping into bed with the man from tomorrow then going home to find I'm twenty-one and feeling like a widow! This isn't *my* now, it's yours. It isn't my today or even my tomorrow. By rights, I've been dead for close to seven hundred years!'

'Stay forever, and make this your now,' said Gerhardt.

Tell laughed. 'And change about my history and God knows whose else! What about Maureen if I never came home? What about David — and Betz? What would they think and what would they do, if I never came home?'

'They would mourn you as drowned, then find they could go on living,' said Gerhardt.

'Well — I won't do that to them, and I won't lay that on myself.'

'What of me?'

'Come off it, Watchman! I'm not laying anything on you. If — if you want to be with me so much, you can come to *my* now with me.'

She saw him shake his head.

'There you are then,' she said. 'You can't or won't, and I can't or won't. And that's not all. Look. You say Cammie won't have any kids, but *I* might. Nice normal kids, with a nice normal dad. Not for a while, but maybe in twenty years, once I get over thinking of you. I might write a great book or take up wood-carving or sculpture or pottery. There are a lot of things I might do, and if I stayed on here they'd never be done.' She caught Gerhardt's eye and added hastily. 'And don't you tell me my future.'

You did not have children, Estellita.

That was a blow. 'Why not?' she said indignantly. 'What happ . . . no. I don't want to know. I'm going home to get on with my life. The life I had before *you* turned up at St Sav's and started putting things into my head!'

'You can't go home,' said Gerhardt.

Tell licked her lips. 'So now you're saying it was a one-way ticket? I don't believe it! You came and went through the veil and Moss has done it often! He said we were going home.' Indignation was giving way to panic. His obsession that she stay was getting out of hand. 'I don't want you, Watchman,' she said as coldly as she could. 'Not if this now is part of the package. Can't you get that through your head? I *can't* want you and I can't stay here. I want to go home.'

She edged around the wall to the hatch, and pushed against it with her palms as she had seen Moss do. She hoped she might make it through before Gerhardt caught her, but the hatch seemed to be locked, and Gerhardt was coming fast. 'I'll scream!' she threatened. 'I will! I'll scream if you try to keep me here!'

Tell, you don't know what's going to happen if you go.

So? I don't want to know! I want to go home and live my own life.

You won't have a life! There's no place left for you. Not a place you can bear to be.

I want to go home!

'I *can't* let you go!' He had her cornered, now, and he took hold of her upper arms. She tried to pull away, twisting and turning, trying to get her knee up, trying to bite. He had had no idea she would be so strong, or so desperate. A little corner of his mind was registering hurt that she had refused all his persuasion and rejected his idea. It had seemed such a good chance to use her telepathy to give her standing with Hub HI-Q. It would not have given her a lifetime with him, but it would have given another reprieve. Perhaps as much as two years, or even three. If she went home to Trinity Street no-one would notice her exact age. Five years, then, or six. And in that time policy might change. If it did not — then at least they would have had their time.

It might have worked, if he could have convinced her, but Tell had rejected his offer out of hand. He had never wanted to use force on her again, but if force was the only way to keep her, he would use it. Physical force or mental, whatever it took. Jens had used force for love and so would he.

'Tell, listen!' he said again, but she was twisting and squirming and now she did as she'd threatened and began to scream, drowning his voice and hurting his ears, battering his mind. She wouldn't listen, and she wouldn't stop, and he had to get through to her before Moss came back. He had to contact Jens, he had to make some plans — perhaps they could go with Jens to Hub HI-Q and beg there for a hearing.

If only he'd thought of this immediately, he might have done it better, but he had been in shock ever since Jens had brought him the information from Tell's file. It was a very small file, humble and bland, but the final entry had been pure horror. Even if he hadn't cared so much for her he couldn't have sent her home to *that*. He was trying to save her and now she was screaming at him.

Fortunately, telepathy didn't require silence for operation. The signal went straight to the intelligence, by-passing ears and eyes. Gerhardt took a steadying breath, and began, as gently as he could. *Tell, stop fighting me. I won't hurt you, but you must understand the truth. If not from me, you can have it from Jens. You can't go home. I can't let you go home. You will be in an accident . . .*

I know that! she yelled, and his head ballooned in pain. *It's happened already and I survived! Now let me go!*

Not the Kismet *accident, Tell. Another one. Much worse.*

She went momentarily still with surprise and he continued more calmly. *The Kismet was rigged by RI-P for a quick and fairly painless death. The other accident is the one that historically killed Camena . . .* He had to break off there in a vocal cry of pain, for Tell had got her teeth into the back of his hand and was hanging on like a terrier. He let her go, brought round the other hand and slapped her face.

Tell let go with a gasp.

'Das tut weh!' he said, glaring at her in the silence.

She actually bared her teeth at him, then clapped her hands over her mouth and began to laugh, great gulping whoops that sounded worse than any scream.

'Tell, stop that!'

'I w — w — won't!' she gasped, and jumped. It seemed she had bitten her tongue. 'W-watchman, w-w-w . . .'

She was shuddering, and he wasn't sure whether it was because of what he had said about Camena or not. He'd had the impression she hadn't taken it in. Perhaps his efforts on her behalf had simply pushed her too far — she wasn't HI-Q and she was out of her time and her depth. The silence stretched as she wrapped her arms around her own body and visibly fought for control. The shudders began to die and her face went white. 'G-god!' she said, after a while. 'What the h-hell happened then?'

Gerhardt contemplated his left hand. A crescent of tooth-marks showed purple and red and white, and some of them were bleeding sluggishly. 'You bit me,' he said. 'That's what happened.'

'And you slapped me. God, I've got a headache like you wouldn't believe. Now I know how Cammie feels.' She moved over to the couch and subsided.

Cautiously, leaving a good half metre between them, Gerhardt sat down too, blotting his hand with his shirt. He seemed to be suffering quite a few minor injuries in the course of this assignment. The energy he needed to maintain pain blocks was draining his small emotional reserves. He closed his eyes for a moment. Unfortunately, pain blocks were of very little use for non-physical distress.

'You want to put some Dettol on that,' said Tell. She sounded subdued, but rational. 'I really lost it, didn't I?' she said in wonder. 'I really went crazy. I started screaming at you and then I couldn't stop. Sorry, but if you hadn't started babbling on about my staying it wouldn't have happened.'

'Verzeihen sie . . . So am I sorry,' said Gerhardt. 'This has been a nightmare.'

'C-complete with werewolf,' said Tell with a shaky laugh. 'L-lucky I didn't go for the jugular. How *could* I have *bitten* you? That's — ugh! Repulsive.'

Gerhardt put a cautious arm around her. They were still in deep trouble, but at least Tell was back to normal. 'I am sorry I frightened you,' he said, 'but you really can't go home, Estellita. For your own sake, as well as for mine.'

She stared at him, then sighed. 'Okay, what's all this about? And don't worry. I won't go nuts again. Once was enough.' She shivered. 'I scared myself half to death, but you must see you can't just spring things on me like that. It's all too much after yesterday. What is it you've been trying to say?'

'I have been going out of my mind,' he said sadly. 'Trying *not* to say it.'

'I'm not going to like it, then.'

'Nyet, ich . . .'

'English. What is it? Has someone twisted your arm to make me stay on? What for? Am I in for trouble if I refuse? Are *you* in trouble?'

'No-one wants you to stay,' he said. 'No-one but me, and maybe Jens.'

'*Jens*?'

'For my sake Jens would have you stay. He wants me to keep my mind. Do you remember when I told you Camena had a chance to stay?'

'Yes.'

'Jens tells me that option no longer exists. I thought Camena would have a choice. I was led to think it, or perhaps I wanted to think it. But now I know the truth. I wish I had asked questions before! I wish I had spoken to Jens before. I should have trusted him, not Moss.'

'The option to stay?' prompted Tell.

'Yes. I *did* notice there were no Recoverees around here, but I thought they must have been dispersed into the wider community. Quietly, of course, since Hub HI-Q never makes too much noise about their plans. Jens says the Recoverees were not dispersed. They were Returned to their own times. Every one of them.'

'What's the catch?' asked Tell.

'I told you how we Recover childless past HI-Qs, so their genes can be reclaimed. We bring them here, and invite them to donate a child or sometimes ova and sperm — and then they are all sent back to the time and place they left.'

'You don't *force* them to make these donations . . . do you?'

'No,' said Gerhardt.

'Then what's wrong with sending them home? It's only fair to put them back where you got them.'

'What's *wrong* is the places and times to which they return. Suitable candidates for Recovery are very rare, Tell. They must be HI-Q, and in excellent mental and physical health. They must be fertile, but without living children. Their lives must be perfectly documented, so that we operatives can locate them. Our experts research the files, and operatives always observe the candidates in situ for a time to make sure nothing has been overlooked.'

'What if something has?'

'Then the Recovery is aborted. The operative leaves that time and no further contact is made with the failed candidate.'

'So if you'd found something wrong with Cammie, you would have aborted her Recovery.'

'Yes. But something *is* wrong with Camena, Tell, something that was overlooked by all of us.'

'Her migraines,' said Tell.

Gerhardt looked at her with respect. 'These migraines almost certainly render her unsuitable for the Donor HI-Q Programme. They are few, as you say. But if she passed the weakness to her children, they might have more frequent bouts, severe enough to prevent their proper function. There is also the underlying cause, whatever it is. That may have a bearing.'

'Surely you have treatment,' said Tell.

'The aim of Hub HI-Q is to breed out the need for artificial medicine, not to breed it in. Therefore Camena is unsuitable, and must be returned through the veil. I will not be escorting her; Moss won't trust me again. He will probably do it himself.'

'But we still go home,' said Tell.

'Home is the worst possible time and place for you.'

'I don't understand.'

Gerhardt pulled her closer. 'RI-P is against the Recovery Programme. They believe the past should be left undisturbed. They believe it so strongly that they have been going to greater and greater lengths to prevent or distort Recoveries. Usually they wait at the Recovery site to intercept the agent, but in Camena's case they made sure by striking beforehand. First, they tried to remove me from the game as we left the pool. If I had been taken, the Recovery would have been hopelessly compromised. You foiled that attempt by RI-P, so the second was staged on the *Kismet*. It took place several hours before I ever expected.'

'They tried to kill us, didn't they?' said Tell thoughtfully. 'But — how can RI-P believe murder is justified, just to stop Recoveries? Surely killing Cammie would have disrupted things just as much. If *you* took her out of our time you'd probably put her back and she'd go on with her life. If they'd killed her, that would have been it. Her life would have been over. That's a much bigger change.'

Gerhardt sighed. He had explained this before, but she hadn't taken it in. 'They don't see such killings as murder, teur Estellita. They believe they are killing only the dead — and operatives such as myself who know the risks.' He felt her take a quick breath to object or ask a question, and touched a finger to her mouth. 'Listen. I told you the stringent requirements for Recoverees, in the matter of personal history, IQ and health. There is one other criterion, the most important of them all. It is no longer mentioned to the Recoverees.'

'What?' said Tell, her lips brushing his finger in an accidental kiss.

Gerhardt took his hand away. 'Recoverees must be HI-Qs who will never be missed. To return Recoverees to their own times, after allowing them to learn something of ours — we have always known that could be disastrous, for them and for us. Therefore, prospects have been chosen only from among HI-Qs who have died, while young and fertile, as the result of accident or violence.'

He felt her intense revulsion, and knew he shared it. He had once accepted this practice, had even agreed with it, in theory, but theory and practice were step-cousins at best. No wonder so many operatives retired after making a single Recovery. No wonder Jens was sickened and had tried to warn him away. Jens understood that guilt and regret might render him insane.

Saviours? Salvationists? Recovery operatives were carrion crows and scavengers at best.

'The operative waits until seconds before the death will occur and Recovers the subject through the veil,' he said bleakly. 'Recovery cannot affect the Recoveree's future life, because there *is* no future life. If Recovery is aborted, the prospect dies within seconds, just as he or she would have done in the natural order of things.'

'So if you hadn't interfered, Cammie would be dead by now. She'd have died that Wednesday, even without the *Kismet*?'

'The record shows that past HI-Q delta Camena de Courcey died when a gas cylinder exploded in Trinity Street at ten minutes past four in the afternoon of that day,' said Gerhardt. 'Two vehicles collided. One was carrying unsecured cylinders. There can be no mistake about what happened; the accident was reported in the press and the death certificate signed . . .'

'Stop it!' Tell was shaking again. 'She won't die that way now! You'll offer her the chance to stay here instead! You've got to — you promised.'

'That was what used to happen,' said Gerhardt bitterly. 'But Jens says a Hub HI-Q study of earlier cases indicates that an unexplained disappearance can't take the place of an accredited death. Even with a drowning, the effect on the victim's surviving family is subtly different if the body is never found. The past was in danger of changing too much. There was some talk of closing down the programme, but instead the opposing ranks of Hub HI-Q split, and the dissidents formed RI-P. Their brief is to protect the present through protecting the past. They also claim to protect the right of past HI-Qs to follow their destinies.'

'Right to Death,' said Tell with a shudder. 'The right to die — there have been people fighting for that right in my own time, Watchman. But you can only have the right to your *own* death. You can't impose it on someone else.'

'RI-P can. Hub HI-Q has cut the option briefing, but that is not enough for RI-P. It makes every effort to prevent Recoveries, and to make sure past HI-Q deaths occur on schedule,' said Gerhardt. 'Believe me — I didn't know the options had been cut until Jens told me today. Since this Recovery entered the active planning stages, I have spent almost all my time alone with Moss. Jens tried to warn me, but I didn't listen. Moss made sure of that.'

'But — Recoverees could stay until they're ninety, then still go back,' said Tell. 'That way both sides could win. They'd get their scheduled deaths and a life as well. You said they died instantly in accidents. It wouldn't be like asking someone to go home to a lingering illness.'

'To prevent paradox, the dead bodies must match the description of the living victim in all particulars — including physical age.'

'Let me get this straight. Hub HI-Q rescues a girl who is about to die in an accident. You bring her here and breed a few nice clever babies. RI-P says that's interfering with nature. So Hub HI-Q, having got what it wants, takes the girl and *pushes her under a train.* Hub HI-Q is happy. It has its precious babies. RI-P is happy. It has the death it wanted. The only one who loses out is the girl, who thought she'd been saved from a horrible fate. Does she scream when you drag her back through the veil? Or do you drug her first? Watchman — that's *murder.* I'm going to be sick!'

'It isn't murder,' said Gerhardt. 'It's — pragmatism. It's salvaging something from catastrophe. It's taking a woman who's having octuplets and aborting six of the babies to give the other two a chance.' Intellectually he knew he was right, but still he felt as sick as Tell.

'And this is what they were planning for Camena! But — Moss *said* we could go home. He said we could...' Tell's voice ran down and Gerhardt could see that she was struggling to recall exactly what it was that Moss had said. 'He said we could go home a few hours late, so we'd avoid being drowned. He said it would prevent any problems if we were landed in Trinity Street at ten past four. He even made up a story to account for the missing hours...oh.'

'It will prevent problems for Hub HI-Q and RI-P,' said Gerhardt, 'but not for you and Camena. Trinity Street at ten past four is — was — the site of the accident. Camena will be killed instantly, but Tell, she won't be screaming. She'll never know.'

Tell was crying now. 'We can't just let it happen,' she sobbed. 'Watchman, if she can't stay here, we'll have to warn her! If she knows it's going to happen, she can get out of the way before it goes up. Somehow. Can't she?'

Gerhardt was shaking his head. 'It won't work, Tell. If Camena goes home and lives on, she would affect thousands of lives between your time and mine. RI-P would not let that happen.'

'How could they stop it? She'd jump clear of the explosion and after that she'd be forewarned. She wouldn't go on any more bloody boats!'

'No, but she would become — shall we call it — "accident-prone". If Camena lived through Wednesday,' said Gerhardt, 'the chances of her meeting with another fatal accident would become very high indeed. Time would correct the mistake.'

'For Time read RI-P,' said Tell viciously. 'Time doesn't care about us, and I don't believe in bullets with names on them. We could warn her, like I said. I'll be with her, and you can come and be her bodyguard for real. Come *on* Watchman! There must be something we can do. You wouldn't have told me about this if there weren't.'

'The best chance is for Camena to stay here,' said Gerhardt. 'If she lives on in our time, she will have departed from yours on schedule.'

'Will RI-P let that happen? Will Hub HI-Q?'

'RI-P has already interfered too much, and Moss has the say at Hub HI-Q. I think Moss might persuade them all to let the *Kismet* drowning stand as Camena's apparent death. If he will — and I can't see why he wouldn't — Camena will have "died" on the correct day, in an explosion. The only slight differences will be a few hours and a few kilometres, and a missing body in place of one that is badly burned.'

Tell thought he sounded unconvinced and her spirits sank further. Moss had been manipulating Gerhardt throughout this Recovery business, and perhaps for years beforehand. Surely Gerhardt had learnt not to trust him.

'Why should Moss take the risk?' she said. 'He's all set to send Cammie home to die in this explosion. He lied to both of us, just to please RI-P.'

'No, Estellita, he did not lie. Moss never lies, except by omission.'

'We'll have to confront him,' she said. 'Tell him we know what's going on, and have him sort out something with RI-P for Camena. We can use a bit of blackmail. No permanent rescue, no HI-Q babies from Camena.'

'You're forgetting,' said Gerhardt quietly. 'There will be no babies from Camena in any case.'

'Those bloody migraines! Well — we'll have to warn her anyway. It isn't fair to keep her in the dark.

'Unless we can offer some hope, we should say nothing,' said Gerhardt. 'Her death will not be as bad as some. The record says she was killed instantly. Think how much worse if you warned her and she tried to run. She could be — horribly mangled and die slowly.' He swallowed.

'Or she could be quite okay! Or maybe we can talk Moss into letting her stay, even after I go home.'

'You can't go home either,' said Gerhardt.

'But it's Cammie who's going to be killed . . .' In that second, it hit her, the thing Gerhardt had been trying not to say. It had been horrible to contemplate Camena's death, but now Tell was faced with the certainty of her own. She opened her mouth, soundlessly, panic screaming in her mind.

The Trinity Street explosion was going to kill her too.

Camena was seldom bored with her own company, but she was certainly fed up with the situation, and even with Dr Sib's hospitality. She was tired of the sunny room, but when she tried to explore the rest of the house, she met with a polite request to stay put.

'We are a politico/scientific foundation, Camena,' said Dr Sib firmly. 'Some of our work is delicate and classified.'

'I probably wouldn't understand it,' said Camena.

Dr Sib gave her an ironic smile. 'Oh yes you would. And since we have no wish to see our work misused or misinterpreted, you will be staying right here.'

Camena laughed. 'You're pulling my leg. No-one does classified work in Tassie. Look, can I go out for a walk? I'm going stir-crazy.'

For a moment she thought Dr Sib would refuse, but then the woman shrugged and smiled. 'I can't see why not — so long as you stick to the marked paths. I mean that, Camena. We have dog patrols and they're a bit jumpy about people sneaking round in the undergrowth.'

Camena followed her out. 'Can I phone home?' she asked.

'You'll *be* home very soon. And don't worry — all the appropriate people know you are safely here with us.'

Dr Sib led her out through a covered walkway which opened into the grounds. Camena looked about her, seeing trees and more trees. No fences. No dogs. No barbed wire. 'This looks good,' she said.

'We try to keep things as natural-looking as possible,' said Dr Sib over her shoulder. 'There is too much interference in the scheme of things in the world today. Don't you agree, Camena?'

'Is that a trick question?'

'Of course not. The human race has a long history of misusing assets, trying to force more and more so-called productivity. Forests are destroyed, rivers dammed and what is the result? Deserts, where there were none before. Human beings, kept alive long after their natural span is up. Revived, sometimes, when they have been very close to death. Flora and fauna introduced to new areas with scant regard for the damage they might cause, destroying the balance of nature.'

'I can agree with that,' said Camena slowly. 'But sometimes you can go too far in trying to stop it.'

'Certainly. Some younger members of my own organisation have been known to be a little over-enthusiastic! Their motives are good, and they are full of ideas — but sometimes they try to use force when persuasion would be the better choice. I have had to have a stern talk with two of them just today!'

Camena nodded. 'I'm all for persuasion — unless you mean the medieval sort. Thumb-screws and things.'

'Nothing like that, Camena, and no brain-washing, either. Goodness! What a suspicious mind! But I suppose it's typical of your generation. You think there's a catch in everything and sometimes you're right.'

Camena smiled ruefully back. 'If you reckon I'm suspicious, wait till you meet Tell!'

'I look forward to meeting her. Poor child — I wonder what nonsense that misguided young man has been feeding her!'

'Gerhardt might be misguided, but he *did* save me when the boat went down,' said Camena fairly.

'Are you sure?'

'Of course I'm sure! Tell told me all about it!'

'Well-primed by our young friend, I have no doubt. I hate to disillusion you, Camena, but when you fell overboard matters would have been accomplished much more easily if young Watchman hadn't interfered. You were wearing a life jacket.'

'But the life jacket didn't work the way it should have done!' protested Camena.

'Of course it did! Pris assures me the equipment was of the highest standard and performed exactly as planned.' Dr Sib's smile faded as she surveyed Camena's troubled face. 'Forgive me, Camena, but you were unconscious for some time after the accident, weren't you?'

'Yes. I woke up on the beach.'

'Then how can you possibly know what happened?'

'Tell told me — I think.'

'I see! And no doubt young Watchman told her!'

'I thought it was odd at the time,' said Camena. 'Some of the things Tell was saying.'

Dr Sib shook her head. 'I suppose she had some reason . . . but tell me about your friend, Camena. Is she at all insecure? A little resentful, perhaps, of your greater gifts?'

'Tell's the best,' said Camena warmly. 'We've known each other since we were little kids. We go shopping and hang about the mall . . . she drags me along to parties, sometimes.'

'Really?' said Dr Sib. 'That sounds like a lot of fun.'

'Well — it is okay,' said Camena. 'I don't like parties much, but you can't be a hermit, can you?' Dr Sib didn't answer, so Camena went on uncertainly; 'People think you're stuck-up if you don't go to their parties. And they think you're weird if you don't have any friends.'

'And I suppose it's good to have a willing opponent for chess and so on.'

Camena nodded, a little doubtfully. She was good at chess, but Tell had never shown much interest, and just lately, the only things Tell had wanted to do were drag her to the shops and the pool . . . and it wasn't as if Tell didn't know Camena didn't like swimming.

A buzzer chirred discreetly, and Dr Sib smiled an apology. 'I'm being paged, which should mean my brother has come to meet you. If you'll excuse me?'

'Of course,' said Camena.

'When you want to come in, just go back under the walkway.'

Camena nodded, and Dr Sib hurried away.

Light winked suddenly somewhere above, as if the sun's rays had glanced off a mirror. A high-flying plane? thought Camena. It couldn't be a helicopter, because there was no *whupp* of rotors ... Camena shaded her eyes with her hands and spun slowly on her heels, but there was nothing in sight and, although she waited, the winking was not repeated.

Camena glanced at her watch. It had stopped, but according to the angle of the sun and the state of her stomach, it seemed to be past lunchtime already. She wished Tell were with her, but perhaps, after that conversation with Dr Sib, she needed to think about her friendship. Tell and Camena. Camena and Tell. Friends forever, but there was no denying that things had changed. First Gerhardt, and then the accident, and now Dr Sib and her calm rationality. Camena sighed.

Tell and Gerhardt? Impossible ... but perhaps if Tell were to find another friend to care for it might offer a painless escape from a situation which was becoming a little too complicated. They would still be friends, of course, but it wouldn't be so exclusive.

I'm going to die!

'I am, aren't I?' cried Tell. 'I must be. That's why they were going to let me drown. That's why *you*'ve been trying to get me to stay here with you. Not because you really want me. You just don't want me to die.'

I want you, Estellita...

'But if I stay here, what about Maureen? And Betz and David — my library book's in Maureen's car! I've got to — help, I didn't even tidy my locker — there's a rotten b-banana...'

'You've got a choice,' said Gerhardt. 'A rotten banana or your life.' He wished he had never become an operative. He wished he had not been chosen for training by Moss.

He wished he had never been born. And there were his parents — had they chosen the option to become Donor HI-Q, or had they been tricked and Returned to face their scheduled deaths?

'You said there's no choice for Recoverees, and I'm not even one of those,' said Tell. 'How would *I* get a choice?'

Gerhardt pulled himself together, a lifetime of training taking over. 'Jens might help,' he said. 'If he knew about your telepathy.'

'You said Jens would send me back!'

'I know, but I made a mistake. I've seen him since and I know he's on my side.'

'Moss says I must go back with Cammie,' she said uncertainly.

'I'll make contact with Jens now.' Gerhardt went to the terminal, but found it locked into reception mode. 'We'll have to go outside,' he said to Tell. 'There's an auxiliary terminal out where Moss keeps the sol-plane.'

'We can't get out. The hatch is jammed.'

'D'accord. It always seems so. It is a little stiff.'

'It's locked,' said Tell. 'I tried to open it when you were chasing me.'

Gerhardt tested the hatch and found that she was right.

'He's locked us in,' said Tell. 'Is there a key anywhere?'

'Recognition sensor,' said Gerhardt. 'Zut! It's no longer tuned to me.'

'Of course it's not. He wants to make sure I keep my appointment with death,' said Tell morbidly. 'Can you get us out of here, Watchman?'

Gerhardt inspected the auxiliary exit and was unsurprised to find that, too, sealed. Just for a moment, he felt hurt that Moss hadn't trusted him. But this wasn't the simple precaution of a man who wanted to keep a disgraced foster son under control. Gerhardt realised that Moss had to be up to something else, for he had given in to Sib too easily. Unfortunately, since Moss was HI-Q alpha and Gerhardt only HI-Q delta, he knew he had very little chance of working out what Moss had planned.

Two minds are better than one, remarked Tell.

Especially when linked together. Gerhardt was on the point of agreeing with her when it occurred to him that Moss would probably — no, certainly — have left some sort of surveillance in place. He might not bother to monitor it, but that was a poor risk.

He sighed, loudly. 'Perhaps Moss is just giving us time to be together,' he said. 'Perhaps I'm being paranoid. You too.'

Tell gaped at him.

'It's hardly normal behaviour to bite people,' said Gerhardt caustically. 'Moss knows how minds work, so I expect he's making sure we don't do something rash. And Jens might be trying to make trouble between Moss and me. He fostered me as a child, you know. He wasn't pleased when Moss took over.'

'But you were just saying — about Recoverees having no real choice . . .'

Gerhardt raised his voice a little to override hers. 'Even if most Recoverees are being sent back, that needn't apply to you. That bit of telepathy you've got . . .'

'A bit!'

'Well,' he said blandly. 'It isn't all that important. It takes years to develop telepathic talent into anything useful, and sometimes it can never be properly controlled. Yours is all over the place.'

'You said it was extraordinary. You said *I* was extraordinary.'

Gerhardt smiled at her. 'So you are — for an IQ-normal. It didn't work though, did it? You still didn't want me. You said so clearly.'

Tell gave him an incredulous look. *Bloody hell!* Her thought stung his mind like a handful of gravel.

'We're stuck in here until Moss comes home,' said Gerhardt, trying not to wince. 'Sure you won't change your mind?'

'About what?'

'Oh — you know. About me. We could have a good time. Isn't that the idiom of your time?' He moved towards her, adding privately; *About agreeing, loudly, that your telepathy is poor. About agreeing, loudly, that everything's probably fine. Surveillance, Estellita.*

'After you've been stringing me along!' she said loudly. 'Making me believe you could understand what I was thinking!' *How'm I doing, Watchman?* 'Making me think you were a knight in shining armour! And all that about *me* reading your mind — that was just wishful thinking! And all that about my being in danger — Watchman, you're sick! I wouldn't have a good time with you if you were the last guy in the cosmos!'

'It wasn't all that difficult to lead you along,' said Gerhardt. *Estellita, you are more than extraordinary. Totoka cina na butobuto*! 'And don't you get any ideas about biting me again,' he said in a bored voice. 'If you're not interested in having fun, we'll just sit down and wait for Moss. He'll bring Camena here and then we can talk. He *might* think your telepathy is worth cultivating. Even if he doesn't, he's bound to have some good ideas. He always does. Why should he let RI-P have what they want?'

'You're a snake, Watchman. I don't want to stay in here. And I'm sure I could keep Cammie out of trouble. I'll warn her in plenty of time and then she won't tread on whatever it is that exploded. What did you say it was?'

'Two vehicle smash. One of them was carrying gas tanks,' said Gerhardt, and reinforced the words with a silent repetition.

'In that case,' she said thoughtfully, 'you could send us through the veil a minute early, then we can run like mad.' *Can't you?*

'Perhaps. I'll check with Moss if it will be acceptable to send you a few minutes early.'

'Damn Moss! Just do it my way and then tell him you did it his way.' *Is that possible?*

'I can't lie to Moss. I owe him my life. He Recovered my parents, plotted my gene chart, taught me and trained me.'

And your parents owe him their deaths — right? Just like oranges. He took out the pips and picked one to polish up pretty and threw the rest of the orange under a truck.
'Watchman — you won't let me die, will you?'

'Not if I can help it.' Gerhardt heard the doubt in his own voice. He had no way of knowing if Moss really was monitoring the unit. Uneasily, he wondered if he had said too much before discovering the sealed hatch and terminal. At least he had been right when he said Moss knew how minds worked — Moss must have expected some kind of blow-up, and now a gradual return to rationality for both of them would be equally expected. 'I daresay Moss might help,' he added. 'Displeased mit sie, but remember, he hates to waste material and perhaps Camena will be suitable after all. The migraines might be treatable by hypnosis, and perhaps the recessives could be weeded out.' He yawned. *Jens. Mention Jens.*

'What was that you said Jens told you? Who is this Jens, anyway? How did he come to bring you up? I thought you said Moss did that?'

'Jens is the HI-Q beta Moss mentioned. He fostered me for my first decade, then handed me over to Moss when he took up the communicator's chair. He's a bit soft, but he always seemed all right to me. Then I found out he likes to change the rules to suit himself. He tried to force me to muck up this Recovery just to spite Moss. Anyone would think he was working for RI-P.'

That's what I believed. Now I know better.

'He came to see what was going on while you were in here with Moss. I asked him about you in a roundabout sort of way, and he said you were probably just another peripheral who was injured in the smash. He is no friend to Moss, and he's nothing to me these days.' *He is a person you will like. He warned me about Moss. He's been trying to warn me all my life, but I didn't want to listen. I wanted to be like Moss, I thought. I really do think Jens might help us — and Camena.*

'Injured? What do you mean — injured? Wasn't I killed in this accident?'

'I don't have the details, but you were certainly still alive three months later.'

'That's a relief!' *Isn't it?* 'Pity we can't call him here, then he could tell Moss what he told you.' *Is there any way we* can call him?

'We can't call him with the transmitter out of order.'

'I see.' *Watchman, can we call him like this?*

Gerhardt smiled sadly at her hopeful face. *Nein, teur Estellita. Telepathy is short range only.*

Both together? Try?

'Never mind,' he said. He leaned back and closed his eyes. 'Just sit back and relax. There's nothing we can do until Moss comes back.' *Yes, we shall try.*

Where is he? How do I get it to him? I can always find you but I don't even know Jens.

Gerhardt considered. *I know Jens. Remember, you followed me through the veil? I start now seeking Jens, your mind can hold to mine.*

Watchman! That's it! Although soundless, her excitement was almost deafening. *Watchman, take us through the veil! Take us to a time when the hatch isn't locked ... and we're outa here!*

Mentally, Gerhardt recoiled. She didn't know what she was asking. To go back a few hours or days would be to risk finding Moss in the unit. To go back to the short period of time during which Moss was fetching them from the disclosure unit ... it bristled with danger and possible disaster. It wasn't for a whim that Hub HI-Q forbade short-term temporal movement. It had been a reasoned and necessary decision, and not only to avoid trouble with RI-P. The only thing worse than unauthorised short-term hops was slipping to tomorrow — the operative who tried that one would be taken into custody immediately upon his return to his own time, and quickly executed.

The veil is no short-cut ... danger!

Isn't it dangerous if we stay in here until Moss comes?

A vision touched his mind, emanating not from Tell but from his own fears, from the information Jens had given him so reluctantly. A vision of the distant past as it had been once, of Tell's subjective future as it would be if the course were allowed to follow its set path.

Tell, after the explosion.

Camena would be dead and beyond pain but Tell would be screaming, screaming, burned and blind. And Maureen, Tell's casual mother, the calm agnostic, would be praying for her daughter's right to death. And it would be no brief pain and gradual improvement. No merciful coma, and quiet unplugging of a life-support machine. Burned face, destroyed lungs, Tell would be a long time dying.

No, he realised, Tell wouldn't die in the accident. She would linger on for months. And the hands that had held him and then pushed him away — they would be nothing but pitiful stumps she would never use again. He had told her that her future was not a place she could bear to be. It was not a place he could bear for her either. Jens had known, and Jens had warned him well.

RI-P with their death-jackets would have been doing Tell a favour if she had died in the sea. So would he, if he had only helped her to drown.

Gerhardt shuddered, a long, painful, invisible quake from his scalp to the back of his legs. His calf muscles knotted painfully and his skin crawled.

Hold my hand, he said, reaching out to Tell. *We're going through the veil.*

Camena returned under the walkway and entered the sitting room where Dr Sib was drinking tea with an elderly man. 'Oh Camena — there you are,' said Dr Sib casually. 'This is my brother, Dr Moss. Maurie, here is Camena de Courcey.'

Dr Moss rose from his chair and half-lifted his hand. Belatedly, Camena recalled her mother's quaint lectures on manners. It was up to the lady to offer her hand.

Camena offered her hand. 'Hello, Dr Moss.'

'Good afternoon, Camena — what an unusual and delightful name you have! Is it perhaps a variation upon "Camilla"?'

'It's a place-name,' said Camena. She waited uncertainly.

Either Dr Moss was going to sit down, in which case she would also sit, or else he was going to remain standing, which implied they would soon be leaving. 'Are you going to take me home?' she asked.

'That's right,' said Dr Moss. He was a handsome old man, thought Camena, and what her mother used to call 'well-preserved'. He was studying her in a fashion that seemed a bit rude, even for someone old. A curious, almost sly look, like a child peering through a hole torn in the wrapping of a Christmas parcel.

'Where's Tell?' she asked. 'My friend, Estelle Clancy? Weren't you going to bring her here to me?'

'I did offer, but your friend seemed anxious to stay with her companion. A young lad — rather tall. Name of Dotts? Cobbs? Cotch? I'm afraid it escapes me just now.'

'Watchman?' prompted Camena.

'Perhaps. No. No, it was Watts. Gary Watts. She asked me to call for her on our way back.'

Camena nodded, a little put out. Surely Tell could have come straight away! And Gerhardt was *Gary Watts*?

'You look a little pale, Camena,' said the old man, bending forward solicitously and patting her hand.

Camena withdrew. 'I'm okay — I've just had a tiring day or two.'

Dr Moss clicked his tongue. 'Oh yes — you were abducted, were you not, following an accident? A most curious business! I see you were released unharmed.'

'Some young colleagues of mine found her lying abandoned under some trees,' put in Dr Sib. 'Unconscious, poor girl, or nearly so, and wearing only a thin shirt and shorts. If she'd been there overnight she might have suffered ill effects from exposure.'

'Didn't you say she was in a boating accident with her friends?' said Dr Moss.

'With Estelle Clancy and young Watts. Yes.'

'Yet they left her asleep under a tree and wandered off together! How very strange.'

'So I thought, but now I hear young Watts . . .' Dr Sib dropped her voice. 'An unfortunate episode of truancy. His father must be so disappointed in the lad. After all the time he's invested in the boy, to have him break out like that! He'd been missing for several weeks, they say. Of course it isn't really the lad who is to blame. He is under the influence of bad company. His father is very . . .'

'Stepfather, surely?' said Dr Moss.

'These relationships are a little complex,' said Dr Sib. 'Of course the lad is starved for affection. It's no wonder he weaves these romantic fantasies about himself. Compensation, you understand. A common enough syndrome in the under-socialised.'

'Not a dangerous aberration?'

'No — o,' said Dr Sib. 'Although it can lead to bizarre behaviour when the patient attempts to act out his or her fantasies. Often, they are so convincing that they draw in others. And of course they are easy prey themselves for the kind of unscrupulous folk who use them. There was a shocking case not long ago where a young boy became convinced by an aunt that the neighbour's cat was a danger to his baby sister. The boy killed the poor creature rather horribly — I'll spare you the exact details. He needed counselling, of course, but the woman who had incited him was never even questioned. She had a grudge against the neighbour, I believe.'

Camena moved restlessly. She hated talk of illness and

cruelty, and besides, she still felt a little foggy from the sedative.

Dr Sib glanced at her and smiled. 'Poor Camena! No doubt you think us a pair of evil old gossips. I do apologise for our rudeness. It's just that I am a psychologist as well as a doctor of physics and my brother here is a neurologist, as well as a general practitioner — and an eccentric collector of vehicles the like of which were never seen on land nor sea! I fear it's an occupational hazard among the medical fraternity, reducing people to case-histories. But how is your headache now, quite gone?'

'Just about,' said Camena.

'Camena suffers from migraines, Maurice,' said Dr Sib. 'A genetic predisposition.'

Dr Moss shook his head. 'Not necessarily. You have my sympathy, my dear. It is one of the most distressing complaints I know. Fortunately, I have had a good deal of success in treating the condition . . .'

'I have some pills to take,' said Camena rather curtly. She had heard enough miracle cures to last her a year. Inhaling carbon dioxide, drinking feverfew, yoga, positive thinking . . . Unfortunately, none of them seemed to work, for her.

'Drug therapy has its place,' said Dr Moss, 'but I find relaxation and auto-hypnotherapy bring about marked improvement in the majority of cases.'

Camena sighed. 'I tried relaxation tapes,' she said. 'I tried yoga.'

'No improvement?'

'Well — it's hard to say. I didn't have one for six months after the yoga but I mightn't have had anyway. Look, it's no big deal. I only get two or three a year.'

'Which is two or three too many,' said Dr Moss. 'I could teach you a simple exercise in self-hypnosis . . .'

'Now Maurie! Camena doesn't want your advice,' said Dr Sib. She grinned at Camena. 'He can't resist it, Camena! Firing off his half-baked theories! Though I admit some of them have a certain validity . . . the trouble is, he tends to believe anything and everything can be solved by direct intervention. Sometimes, the kindest and fairest thing to do is to allow things to take their course. Let's see — miscarriage is a pertinent example! Back in the 1950s, Camena, spontaneous abortion was a badly misunderstood process. The stock treatment was for the patient to be put to bed, sometimes for months, and to avoid even the most mild exertion in an effort to avoid losing the foetus.

'It didn't work, of course. All that happened was that the patients suffered loss of muscle tone and general fitness and were also afflicted with a great deal of unnecessary guilt and dismay when they failed to keep their babies — babies that would never have thrived even if they had carried them to full term. The treatment — total bed-rest — often so atrophied their muscles that even perfectly healthy pregnancies were lost afterwards. Intervention was positively harmful! And all because of a simple but mistaken assumption that the problem lay in the women. In fact, in the overwhelming majority of cases, it lay in the foetuses. By the time the problem was detectable, intervention was useless.'

Dr Moss cleared his throat. 'Of course, not everyone agrees with you on that, my dear! And medical intervention would surely be warranted in Camena's case, I believe. I wonder . . . I wonder . . .'

'Mau-rie!' drawled Dr Sib.

'I wonder if I might have permission to hypnotise you, Camena? Nothing more than a light trance. I promise you would be aware — at least on one level — of everything and no doubt my sister would stay with us to observe the proprieties!'

'I really don't think so,' said Camena. She had rather liked Dr Sib, but now she and her brother seemed nothing more than a pair of chattering old fogies. She had thought Dr Sib intelligent, but Dr Moss was a fool. He still looked at her as if she was a Christmas present, and she felt uneasy. She hated people poking and prying and she hated going to doctors.

Dr Moss chuckled. 'I fear she thinks I'm going to cause her to bark like a dog or do something embarrassing! Reassure her, my dear, do!'

Dr Sib leaned forward and patted Camena's knee. 'That sort of thing is a parlour trick. The kind of hypnosis Maurie practises is perfectly reputable, I promise you.'

'I know that,' said Camena. 'It's a relaxed state and used in treating panic attacks, addictions and so on. Franz Mesmer was the first to practise it, in the eighteenth century. People thought he . . . sorry. I do run on.'

'Not at all,' murmured Dr Moss. 'Why not relax, Camena? My sister has invited me to have a cup of tea before we leave. You might be interested in seeing this old watch of mine — a pretty thing isn't it? Or perhaps you would prefer to examine my sister's brooch? Perhaps you have noticed it is in the shape of a double helix?'

Camena sighed, exasperated almost beyond politeness. 'Dr Moss, I know perfectly well what you're trying to do and it isn't very ethical,' she said. 'Hypnosis by stealth is as bad as spiking someone's drink.'

Dr Sib laughed aloud. 'She got you that time, Maurie! Next she'll have the medical watchdogs on your doorstep . . . you'll be struck off! And no, you can't use my brooch to hypnotise her. That would make me an accessory to your goings on.'

'I hate to remind you, sister of mine, but I can't be struck off as, officially, I have been retired for some years . . .'

'Some people,' said Dr Sib darkly, 'never do retire. They go on cluttering up their organisations with outmoded ideas, poking and prying and interfering in the lives of innocent people who would be very much better left alone.'

Camena's head was beginning to ache again, and she wished they'd be quiet. 'Oh, all right,' she said ungraciously. 'Go ahead and put me in a trance — if you can. I could do with some relaxation.'

'And some peace and quiet too, perhaps?' suggested Dr Sib.

'Excellent!' said Dr Moss. 'Would you care to examine this watch, Camena? Watch the watch, now. Watch it, watch it — when was the first time you saw one of these watches? Did you like to look at it? Did you want to touch it?'

Camena lay back, listening to Dr Moss's voice. She had never been hypnotised before, but she understood the theory behind it. Altered consciousness . . . once thought to be a kind of sleep, but the brain wave patterns were quite uncharacteristic of sleep. She did wish Dr Moss would stop saying 'watch'. It reminded her too much of Gerhardt Watchman.

'I should have known that wasn't his real name,' she said.

'Tell me all about it,' said the doctor. 'What can you tell me? Tell me about the watch . . .'

'Free association,' said Camena. 'Watch — watchman — the man who watches. People often watch me and I don't like it. I like to be left alone, so I can think. Tell is Estelle and

Estelle is a star, but a tell is a grave — no, a mound or a hill, all hidden. Poor Tell, she can't keep up with me, but we need one another. I expect you think I'm talking rubbish, but free association is a respectable word game though psychiatrists use it to trick people into revealing their obsessions. That's odd. I don't have obsessions, but then I'm not an obsessive personality. I don't have much personality at all, really. Tell saves me from having to — to — I'll tell you a secret, shall I? People think Tell looks after me. She does, but she needs me as well. I don't really need to be needed, and I can't see why I have to pretend to be like them. I — just — wish — people — would — leave — me — in — peace.'

'Picture yourself with a baby, Camena,' said the doctor. 'Picture yourself with a young man — your partner — he is intelligent like you. You want to have his baby, so you have chosen carefully. How does that make you feel?'

'Ugh!' said Camena. She lifted an uncertain hand towards her head. 'My eye is going and I can't see. I'm going to have a terrible pain. I can't look after a baby — not if I have migraine. I can't be bothered with all those things.'

'No, no more pain, Camena,' said Dr Sib's voice softly. 'You will go to sleep soon and when you wake up your head won't ache, not ever again.'

'That's not the way it works!' objected Camena, from her trance. 'It isn't magic!'

'Of course not,' laughed Dr Sib. 'Of course not. It's simply allowing things to take their natural course. Now we must convince Maurice of that ... well, Maurie? Was I right or wrong about the validity of intervention in Camena's case?'

'It appears you *may* have been correct — from your own standpoint,' said Dr Moss, and his voice no longer burbled.

'Migraines are a shocking affliction,' said Dr Sib.

'It is the psycho/personality defect that *causes* the migraines that presents the true obstacle. A contra/survival attitude, inborn and probably ineradicable in the current subject. What a waste.'

'You will take steps to improve her situation, then? There will be no more pain and worry?'

'My dear!' said Dr Moss, and suddenly Camena realised the watch was winking before her again.

'I want to go home,' she remarked.

'Of course you do,' soothed Dr Moss. 'Perhaps a little peace before you leave . . .'

Camena stirred, and stretched. The remnants of her headache seemed to have gone completely, and she felt relaxed and well. Perhaps, she thought sleepily, there was some benefit in hypnotherapy after all. When she went home she must ask her doctor about a referral . . . or perhaps Dr Moss would take her as a patient? He might be an old fool, but he was good at his job. And perhaps he wasn't a fool. Perhaps that was just his manner . . .

Her reflections were interrupted by Dr Sib's voice. 'You will be taking Camena home, won't you Maurie. In your *car*?'

'Naturally,' said Dr Moss. 'Since we cannot leave just yet, perhaps Camena would care to play a game of chess?'

'Why postpone the inevitable?'

'No, Sib, it is you who is trying to stem the tide with a sieve. The Recovery Programme *will* go ahead. Your operative's interference — unpardonable.'

'Pris did what she thought was best. I uphold her purity of intention if not her decision. In any case, her devotion to myself and my cause seems substantially stronger than the devotion of *your* fostern to *you* and *yours*.'

'Then you stand convicted out of your own mouth.' Dr Moss turned to Camena. 'We shall have to schedule the game for some other time, my dear.'

Tell clung to Gerhardt's hand and closed her eyes in concentration.

Do not try so hard.

Sorry.

Remember what I told you? Let the thought float on its own momentum. Don't hurl it around. Now, let your mind shape alpha waves as mine does. It is a state of altered consciousness.

Like hypnosis? Tell tried to obey, stopped trying and let herself drift. Almost impossible, with death stalking Camena and a gruesome danger threatening herself. But Gerhardt was with her and Gerhardt was her Möbius strip. Mentally, as he instructed, she traced the single sinuous curve that so bewilderingly had one surface that was really two. Or two which were one. Up and round and over and under, smooth with tiny whorls or loops or arches. A seemingly simple thing of endless fascination. Her fingertips were curves on curves as she traced the Möbius strip. It shone before her like pewter, dull and bright at the same time.

She wondered placidly how she could be tracing with both hands when one was firm in Gerhardt's, but somehow his fingertips were touching hers and the loops and whorls were the Möbius strip. Then both hands were free and shaping the arches, and the curves faded under her hands and turned coarse and cool and the loops were tiny woven squares . . . She was facing Gerhardt in a loose embrace and her hands were splayed on his back. The shirt was the woven pattern she could feel, with warmth coming through from his skin. And then heat flared through her fingertips, heat and pain and she snatched her hands away. The pain died, and she blinked and focused her eyes.

'What happened?' she asked.

Gerhardt stepped away, avoiding her gaze. His face was pale. 'We're through the veil.'

'It wasn't like that last time,' she said hesitantly.

'Nyet. This time we were touching more than minds. Technically, last time should have been impossible.'

Tell digested that. 'Are we safe now?' she asked, rubbing her fingers to rid them of the phantom of pain.

'Nyet. Come and . . .'

Call Jens? Try the hatch?

Both*, he said.*

Why are my fingers burning? Why do I hurt?

'Over-active imagination,' said Gerhardt dryly.

'Mine?'

Not yours, Estellita mia. Mine. I am very sorry. Telepathy can sometimes bring the impression of pain.

Fire? Is that what's going to happen to me? Am I going to be burned?

Gerhardt didn't answer.

Camena felt relaxed and a little sleepy as she left the house. The grounds she had strolled in before afternoon tea were drowsing in the sunshine. It had been a pleasant visit, and now she was going home. Old Dr Moss helped her into his car and clicked on her seat belt. She sighed languidly. He was one of those elderly people who seemed to think anyone under twenty-one was a child.

'There!' said Dr Sib's voice cheerfully. 'That's fine. Goodbye Camena, my dear. It's been very pleasant.'

'See you later,' said Camena. 'Or is it later than I think?'

The free-association word game seemed lodged in her mind, but it didn't matter. You could play the game any way you wanted and totally cock-up the psychologist's tests. Tests. Testes. Testers. Testers were beds. She'd have to try the test on Tell when they got together.

'What time shall I be home?' she asked.

'I should be delivering you to Trinity Street at precisely 16.10,' said Dr Moss.

'But it seems dark! What's going on?'

'Nothing untoward, my dear. The windows have polarised.'

Camena digested this. 'Can you see out to drive?'

'Quite unnecessary,' said Dr Moss. 'This vehicle has an on-board computer and the latest in automatic direction gear. You might say it's a prototype.'

'I see,' said Camena. She smiled. 'It's one of your collection. When do we pick up Tell?'

'Very shortly,' said Dr Moss.

'And Gerhardt? Gary Watts, I mean?'

'Young Watts will be dealt with for his part in your misadventure. Poor misguided lad — he'll not bother you again. Nor anyone else, I feel.'

'Good,' said Camena. She fell silent, still oddly relaxed.

The whole strange adventure was nearly over and Camena could only blame herself for listening to Gerhardt — Gary. She would have held on to her scepticism if she hadn't wanted so much to believe his story true. Kidnapping — her father — the two letters from her father had been forgeries. Gerhardt — Gary — couldn't have written them, but perhaps whoever had arranged for her abduction had. It seemed that someone had gone to a lot of trouble for nothing. It seemed that someone had put *her* to a lot of trouble for nothing.

The whole thing seemed completely obscure. Nameless kidnappers, Dr Sib's 'young colleagues' who had been a bit 'over-eager'. And Tell's inexplicable support of the rescue story.

Oh well, thought Camena fairly. I believed what I wanted to believe, I suppose Tell did too. She yawned. There were too many things that didn't add up. At the moment, she felt so relieved that she hardly cared. Presumably the mastermind behind all this was someone in politics or society — someone who would presently resign or retire and quietly leave the public stage. It was annoying to be kept in the dark, but if she knew what was really going on, so would others. No doubt then there would be a big inquiry and she'd be stuck with testifying in court. Better not to know ... much better if the whole thing could be hushed over.

'What does Linnie know about this?' she asked after a while. 'My sister, I mean? What do I tell her?'

'It will not be necessary for you to tell her anything,' said Dr Moss.

'But she'll be wanting to know,' she said slowly.

'She will know whatever is necessary.'

'That I fell overboard, was rescued, and spent the night at Dr Sib's house? Fine,' said Camena calmly. 'That sounds good to me. As long as I don't get kidnapped again.'

'The miscreants have been dealt with.'

'Good. But what about Tell? Won't she tell people what happened? I mean, what she thinks happened?'

'Your friend is in a — shall we say — a rather overwrought state, and any wild stories would be disregarded,' said Dr Moss. 'I think in the event she will say nothing.'

'I can't imagine Tell overwrought,' said Camena.

'Stress affects different people in surprising ways,' said Dr Moss. 'I find working out chess problems relaxing yet some folk become agitated when they consider the insoluble.'

Camena felt a stirring of interest, her mind sliding into focus as it always did when presented with an intellectual challenge. 'Do you know a problem that's really insoluble? Apart from the chicken-and-the-egg and the immovable object?'

'Perhaps,' said Dr Moss. 'Most problems have their solutions, but sometimes the time expended in seeking that solution would be spent more appropriately on some other matter. For this reason I sometimes prefer to reason backwards from solution to problem. Consider the chess solution —'

'Yes?' said Camena hopefully.

'Ah — (1) Ke1 Ke4 (2) Ke2 Kf5 (3) Kf3 Ke6 (4) Kf4 Kd6 (5) Ke4. That is the winning solution — where was the state of play when the problem presented?'

'Is there a time limit?'

The vehicle came to a halt. 'Here we are,' said Dr Moss. 'Now, you stay in the car and I'll fetch your friend.'

Camena nodded. She was already grappling with the problem as Dr Moss climbed out of the car.

She was still deeply immersed when she became aware of someone opening the door of the vehicle.

'Tell?' she said.

'No, it's me.' A tall figure slid into the low seat beside her.

'Pris?' said Camena doubtfully.

'Right.' Pris looked tired, but she smiled brightly at Camena. 'I'm glad I caught you,' she said.

'Oh.' Camena smiled back uncertainly. 'Dr Moss is just taking me back now. You rescued me after the *Kismet* went down, didn't you? Thanks.'

'De nada.' Pris waved her hand. 'This whole situation — it shouldn't have been necessary,' she said.

'No,' said Camena.

'Sometimes,' added Pris, 'the only way to prevent evil is to uproot it at the source. If you cut out the tap-root . . .'

Camena didn't really feel like a philosophical discussion right then. She had a chess puzzle to solve, but she supposed she owed Pris something. 'I hope you didn't lose your job when the boat went down,' she put in. 'It wasn't your fault.'

'No,' said Pris.

'Dr Moss said the kidnappers had been dealt with?'

'Not quite yet,' said Pris, 'but they will be. In time.'

After the trial, obviously. Camena hoped she wouldn't be called as a witness. 'Good,' she said. She found her attention wandering again as light winked from the badge on Pris's shirt. It reminded her of the brooch that Dr Sib had been wearing.

'Well — that's it then,' said Pris with another smile. She reached casually into her pocket and pulled out a handkerchief. 'Oops! I've dropped my . . .' Her voice trailed off as she leaned sideways, groping under the seat of the car. 'Ah, there it is. That's better.' She swung out her legs and rose to her feet in one fluid motion. 'Goodbye, Camena . . . oh — by the way — I'd rather you didn't mention this little talk to Moss. You see — I'm supposed to be somewhere else, doing something else.' She grinned. 'You know how it is,' she added, 'there's never enough time for the things you have to do.' She closed the door.

Camena went back to her chess. (3) Kf3 Ke6 . . .

The unit looked no different to Tell, but then it had been abnormally tidy when they had entered the first time. 'When are we?' she asked.

'Moss has just left to collect us from the disclosure unit. We must contact Jens and leave here, immediately. The window is very short.'

Tell nodded, and chewed her lip anxiously as Gerhardt went to the terminal. It was apparently set to normal use, for he touched the keyboards and held a low-voiced and cryptic conversation with the person on the other end.

'We wait here?' she hazarded as Gerhardt dismissed the screen and turned to face her.

'Not here. Jens cannot arrive before Moss comes back.'

'With us. Weird, Watchman!'

'More than weird, teur Estellita. Very dangerous. Come.'

Gerhardt raised the hatch and climbed out, taking Tell's hand to help her. She didn't need help, but she accepted it all the same, and held on afterwards when he would have let her go. She couldn't believe in her own death; no-one could, but she suspected that whatever waited for her in Trinity Street was worse than death. Drowning had seemed bad enough, but fire! She could not face that. 'If I'd been *Jeanne d'Arc* I'd have shut out the voices,' she said. 'I'd have gone mad without a word.'

'Moss will learn of my call to Jens but not yet,' said Gerhardt. 'He did not use the terminal until he contacted Sib.'

'He did — he checked something in a record . . .' said Tell apprehensively. 'Then he was reading for a while.'

'Different mode.'

It should have been pleasant, walking hand in hand across the wide plain of the plateau, but all Tell could think about was the rough footing, the lack of cover — and Maureen whom she might never see again.

Either Gerhardt and Jens would manage to get her out of

this, in which case she was probably never going home, or else they wouldn't. And if they didn't, she would no more escape her burning future than had *Jeanne d'Arc*, the Maid of Orléans.

She had been terrified, now she was simply numb and she clung to Gerhardt's hand as she had clung to David's hand when she had been a little girl.

'You could take me home now,' she said. 'Take me back to four o'clock — and stay with me.'

'RI-P will be there,' said Gerhardt tightly.

'The day after?'

'Tell —'

'Don't tell me — RI-P?'

'Ja.'

'They're ghouls!' she said viciously. 'What have I ever done to them? To any of them? There's so much I want to do, Watchman — I should have had a life.'

'You have never done anything to them,' said Gerhardt. 'They are afraid you may. They work to preserve their present.'

'*They're* afraid!' Tell was silent for a while. 'Why did you have to call Jens?' she asked at last. 'Won't he be coming here soon the first time? The time you met him while I was talking to Moss?'

'Ja, but we must let him come, and go, bring me the information, and go once more. He will return to Hub HI-Q and the message will reach him there.'

'Can't we save time by nabbing him when he does come? It would save him the extra trip.'

'Tell, I cannot interfere too much with Jens's past. Increase paradox.'

'Damn the paradox! So — what do we do?'

'Jens will come to me on the outcrop as he did before. He'll warn me of Moss and the fate of the Recoverees. He will walk away. I will summon him back, and beg for information about you. I will wait. Jens will bring me that information. He then will return to Hub HI-Q. I will die a little.' He drew a shuddering breath, then continued unemotionally. 'You will call me into the unit, Moss will leave us locked in there and everything will happen as it has already.'

'We — don't have to go through all that again, do we?' said Tell nervously. 'I don't think I *could*, Watchman. If I start screaming again I just may never stop.'

'Nyet. We wait out the time in a place I know. Then, just before we reach the time from which we left to cross the veil, Jens will receive my message. He will come to us there. It will not take long.'

'God!' said Tell. 'That's so complicated!'

'Necessary,' said Gerhardt.

'Are you sure he'll come?'

'He will come. I would stake my life on Jens.'

'It's my life you're staking,' said Tell.

It comes, said Gerhardt, *to the same thing.*

The place Gerhardt knew was a tarn on the plateau some thirty minutes walk from Moss's unit. The plateau had always been wild and desolate, and it seemed little changed to Tell. Although the roads had gone, and the guesthouses. There were no stock fences and nowhere did she see a scrap of plastic or an old tyre. 'I used to come here when I was young,' said Gerhardt. 'After I was taken from Jens. It is a good place to be quiet.' He smiled a little. *I used to try to contact him, but my thoughts were never strong enough.*

The tarn was screened from all sides by a huddle of rocks and a stand of the stunted Lakeland trees. Tell sat down on a patch of buttongrass with a sigh. 'It's hard, having to wait,' she said. 'I feel as if I'm treading water. Have you ever re-run time before, Watchman? Your own time, I mean? I can see why you could come to St Saviours — you weren't supposed to be anywhere else at that time. But haven't you ever been tempted to hop back an hour or two to — oh, I don't know! To go on fishing, or to finish a book, or do some homework you'd forgotten? There must be some days when you need an unclaimed slice of time, even in the twenty-seventh century.'

'Never,' said Gerhardt. 'Not for my own reasons. Of course I had to try short trips during my training, but those were carefully planned and monitored by Moss. You cannot even begin to understand the taboo we have against short-term temporal movement. It is as strong as the taboo you have against eating human flesh.'

Tell gulped. 'And we just broke it. God. Did you train at Hub HI-Q?'

'No.' He sat down beside her and clasped his knees, again unconsciously mirroring her own pose. 'I trained here on the plateau, with Moss.'

'How long have you been in training, Watchman?'

'All my life.' He smiled faintly. 'Moss chose me from several who carried the same genetic code, and fostered me with Jens until my first decade was done.'

'Why with Jens? I thought they didn't get on?'

'They do not. Yet Jens is conscientious. Moss knew I would learn to think and to obey.'

Tell made a face. 'Sounds grim.'

'Not grim,' said Gerhardt. 'Jens taught me speech, both

ways, and the courtesy codes for each. He taught me how to be — almost human.'

'But . . . you *are* human.'

'Not by the reckoning of some. But then I went to Moss, and he trained me as an operative. Trained my mind and my morals and my body. Trained me to look forward and never back. You remember, I told you Moss invented me?'

'Yes.'

'He tried to make me in his own image — but I am only HI-Q delta and so I can never be truly like him.'

'Thank God for that,' said Tell. 'If you've been here all these years with Moss, how could you handle life at St Saviours?'

'I have known of Camena de Courcey's world for years,' said Gerhardt flatly. 'Moss is an expert on that period, and so is his sister. In a way, that is why this Recovery was so important to Moss; he hoped to make the twentieth century real in our time. And so — for eight years I have been steeped in the speech, the attitudes, the clothing, the foods — until I am two in one. In a way, I have been at St Saviours for years. I have been to Hub HI-Q occasionally, and sometimes others have come here, but mostly — for the past three years at least — it's been me and Moss. He has taught me everything, taught me to act as he would act, prepared me for every eventuality — or so we thought.'

'Except for me, I suppose,' said Tell.

Estellita mia — nothing could have prepared me for you.

Tell swallowed, hard. 'What will you do when this is over?' she ventured. 'If — if I have to go home?'

'Do? I shall come to Trinity Street and kill you, Estellita.'

Tell gasped, but then understanding dawned. 'Is it going to be — be — that bad for me?'

'No. I'll never let it come to that. I swear it.'

Gerhardt reached out for her, but she shook her head. 'Not now. I'm scared out of my mind and I might fall apart. Talk to me instead. So — what about Moss and telepathy? He tried it on me, but it seemed pretty foggy. Was that because I'm not tuned to him, or isn't he as good at it as you?'

'Moss is able to send and receive very little. I learned what I learned from Jens.'

'Are any of your friends telepathic?'

'What friends? The natural-born have very little use for my kind.'

'Is that what they're called. What about other Donor HI-Q kids?'

'Most of them are far away. Far beyond my range, even if I knew them.'

Tell was disinclined to ask any more. All they could do now was wait while time unrolled. She looked at the sky and tried to think where she would be by now — her other, subjectively earlier, self. Conversing with Moss? Comforting Gerhardt? Screaming?

Oddly, there was no feeling of déjà vu, perhaps because she had spent this piece of time inside the unit. Otherwise she would be seeing the same cloud pass over the sun, the same butterfly on the twig. 'I feel as if we should be *doing* something,' she said. 'Anything but sitting here.'

'While we sit here we affect nothing and no-one.'

'Except a few insects,' said Tell, as the butterfly flew away. 'We could stay here, Watchman, until then catches up with now. Then we could go back and stay here again. We could live this hour forever — no, don't say it.' She sighed. 'Impossible. Watchman? I don't want to die . . .'

Gerhardt reached out in silence and this time, she didn't turn away.

The transition from then to now, as Tell had termed it, came quite suddenly, the two moments sliding together and mingling as drops of water mingled. Gerhardt was aware of the tiny temporal shift in his brain and looked up superstitiously. A second ago in real time, he and Tell had stood in one another's arms and crossed the veil. He wished he could go on holding her forever, but what place had his uncharted wishes in a situation like this one? *Nothing* could have prepared him for this.

'Jens will be here quite soon,' he said.

'If he comes.' Tell's voice was muffled against his shoulder. 'What happens to us now?'

'I don't know,' said Gerhardt. 'I have never been here before.'

Tell began to laugh. 'I was thinking of the banana in my locker,' she said. 'And the library book in Maureen's car. I guess I shouldn't worry about anything. Whatever happened, happened long ago, and you're not going to let me burn. Do you think Camena's all right? Do you think she's frightened?'

Gerhardt had almost forgotten Camena, for during the past few hours his attention had been painfully focused on Tell. He was still considering his answer when Jens came through the trees.

'Regret recall,' said Gerhardt. 'Tak return.'

Jens waved a hand. 'Bitte.'

Gerhardt rose, and placed Tell's hand in Jens's.

'Estelle Clancy — mein leman, Jens.'

'HI-Q Communicator Beta Jens — my first fosterman, Tell.'

If Jens was surprised at this formal introduction, it didn't show. What did show was a terrible sorrow which turned his swarthy, wide-lipped face into a tragic mask. He held Tell's hand for a moment, then released it with a tiny bow. 'Daichcue Forn — Recover?'

Before Gerhardt could answer, Tell cleared her throat. 'He didn't Recover me,' she said. 'He Recovered my friend Camena de Courcey and I — sort of came along for the ride.' She turned to Gerhardt. 'Does he understand?'

'Ja, compre,' said Jens. *Ill-done, Daichcue Forn — warned.*

You warned him too bloody late. He'd already done the deed, said Tell.

Jens blinked. *Telepathic?*

'Highly,' said Gerhardt. He heard the pride in his own voice and so did Tell. For a few seconds they simply gazed at one another.

Your fault, Watchman. I never was before. You must have stirred up something in my brain . . .

You were always gifted, teur Estellita, but there were no others in your range.

Jens shook his head. 'Lord, what fools these mortals be,' he said softly, as if quoting in a foreign language. He smiled at Tell. 'Ja, compre. I understand. Have post versiation Auseuro. I speak a later version of your language.' The smile died, and his eyes were bleak as he contemplated Gerhardt. 'What?'

'What — what?' asked Tell.

'Jens wants to know what I want him to do about it — about you,' said Gerhardt. His spirits were low. He knew Jens would help if he could, but what could he do, after all, if Moss had made up his mind? Quickly, he switched to his own dialect and explained the situation. He didn't know how much Tell understood, but when his voice began to shake she took his hand.

'Telepathy,' said Jens, putting his finger unerringly on the point of hope.

'Hub HI-Q develop?'

Jens shook his head decidedly. *Unregarded,* he commented with a shrug.

Gerhardt sighed. He had known Moss thought telepathy a fairly useless accomplishment, because so few active telepaths existed and those who did were short range and often incompatible. Such an unreliable mode of communication could not be held to have much practical value, especially since Moss was unable to make good use of it himself. *Offspring?* he offered. *Reinforced telepath?*

Jens made a wry face. *Donor. Return.*

'Watchman thought I might be able to stay on here and learn how to do it properly,' said Tell. 'Telepathy, I mean.'

'Learn?' Jens's amusement was bitter. *From?*

'He means . . .' began Gerhardt.

'I *know* what he means. He means I'm already better at it than him, and he's the best there is. But need Hub HI-Q know that?'

Jens shook his head regretfully. 'Recovery Programme — Donor Past HI-Q — finis,' he said. 'RI-P risk unacceptable.'

'What's that?' asked Tell.

Gerhardt squeezed her hand. 'The Recovery Programme is in bad trouble,' he said. 'Jens says Hub HI-Q will probably wind it up completely — when they know what happened with you.'

'But no-one knows I'm here!' said Tell. 'No-one but Moss and Jens. And Sib, I suppose.'

'And the two RI-Ps who took Camena. RI-P has been playing games, Tell. Forcing Hub HI-Q's hand. Perhaps their bungling was deliberate; an object lesson to show what *can* happen if Recoveries go wrong. Jens believes that too — nein, Jens?'

'Never mind who believes what,' said Tell tensely. 'What's going to happen now?'

Despite the interruption from Pris, Camena had worked out the chess puzzle and had the answer waiting when Dr Moss returned to the vehicle. She was about to expound the problem that fitted the solution when she realised Dr Moss was alone. 'Where's Tell?' she demanded.

'There seems to have been a slight misunderstanding,' said Dr Moss. 'Your friend and the boy have left already.'

He sounded put out, and Camena wasn't surprised. It was too bad of Tell, first asking him to come back later and now not being ready when he came.

'Where have they gone?' she asked.

Dr Moss sighed. 'I wish I knew. But now we must go. I promised my sister I'd take you back to Trinity Street without delay.'

'Can't we wait a few minutes for Tell?'

'I am a busy man,' said Dr Moss reproachfully. 'No, I shall take you now, Camena.'

'But — what about Tell?'

'Someone will bring Estelle to Trinity Street a little later.'

'Are you sure?'

'You may be certain of it,' said Dr Moss.

'I wonder why she's gone off?'

'Estelle was not at all rational when I saw her last,' said Dr Moss austerely. 'I think she will need medical treatment upon her return. Excuse me one moment, Camena. I must contact my sister and warn her of the change of plan.'

Camena frowned, trying to work this out. It was unlike

Tell to be unreliable. It was also unlike her to be hysterical. Something was very wrong. She wondered if it was possible that someone had administered some drug to Tell. It seemed unlikely, but the whole recent situation had a surreal quality about it. *She* had been drugged at some point during the past two days, so why not Tell? Of course, Tell had not been kidnapped, but Gerhardt's — Gary's — actions had been rather peculiar.

'Tell is usually very rational,' she said. 'There must be something wrong. I wish she had waited for us.'

'So,' said Dr Moss, 'do I.'

Tell saw the closed expression on Jens's face and the greyness of Gerhardt's. 'I'm going to be sent back,' she said numbly. 'Aren't I? I'm going to be sent back with Cammie. RI-P will insist and so will Hub HI-Q. To try to sort things out. I'm nothing to them but a sort of — of pawn, to use as an example.'

'No,' said Gerhardt. 'Jens?'

'D'accord,' said Jens. 'What?'

Gerhardt's arm closed firmly around Tell's shoulders. 'We go.'

Tell felt a rush of relief, and dread. 'To my time?'

'Not your time, Estellita mia. Impossible.'

'Another time?'

'Another time is just as dangerous. It must be in this now. But we leave this place. Go where no-one will find us. Jens . . . ?'

Jens nodded. 'Silence, I. Daichcue Forn —'

'No more,' said Gerhardt.

Jens raised one eyebrow. 'Then —?'

'Watchman will do.'

Jens nodded.

Tell licked her dry lips and offered him her hand. *I wish I could know you better,* she sent carefully to Jens.

And I, you.

It seemed the only way to leave the plateau was to walk. Jens had arrived in a single vehicle which looked very much like an enclosed bicycle. Tell could see at a glance that there was no way of begging a lift. Besides, vehicles could probably be traced more easily than people on foot. But still, her back crawled at the thought of walking halfway across Tasmania and a wild, scarcely populated Tasmania at that, with a vengeful Moss searching them out in his sol-plane. And what if RI-P joined the hunt? It seemed unfair that no-one was on their side. No-one except, perhaps, for Jens.

And even Jens, she thought, believed she should not have crossed the veil.

'We're not going to make it, are we?' she said. 'Unless we can do the time thing again?'

As she had expected, Gerhardt shook his head. 'No time to plan,' he said tersely. 'Before crossing the veil, I must know precisely what will be happening in the time of arrival.'

'You did it in the unit.'

'Aye. Moss was collecting us from the disclosure unit. This I knew, and the unit was locked against intrusion by others. There was little danger of paradox. But who knows who or what may be abroad in the Wild Zone?'

'We're not going to make it without being discovered,' she said again. 'And even if we reach the bay, how would we get away from here? Are there ferries? Or planes? Do we need money to travel?'

Gerhardt didn't answer, which alarmed Tell more. He had no plans, except to get themselves as far from the site of

Trinity Street as he could. 'And what about Cammie?' she asked fretfully. 'I want to bring her with us.'

'We can do nothing for Camena.'

'*Nothing?*'

'Estellita mia — it is you I must shield this time.' *I cannot betray you again.* 'I cannot help Camena. I probably cannot help you . . . but I try.'

'But we can't just leave her!'

'Moss will find us gone from the unit. He will be looking for you. Do you understand? To Moss, you are now an inconvenience. And I am expendable.'

'After eight *years?*'

'I failed him,' said Gerhardt simply. *And now I fail myself.*

They hurried on over the rough, uncertain ground, but it was not Moss who came for them. It was a sol-plane, but this one had a silver insignia in the shape of a double helix.

'Jens?' said Tell hopefully. 'Jens has come for us?' But Gerhardt shook his head.

The sol-plane landed and two passengers disembarked. The woman was very dark, and the man had red hair. His face was badly bruised and one arm was strapped up.

'Oh no,' said Tell. 'Oh *no.*'

'Good afternoon, Estelle,' said Pris. Her smile flashed with triumph. 'DHQ number 49 — stand away from the subject.' She raised a small, stout bar. It hardly looked big enough to do much damage, but Tell was aware of Gerhardt's sudden hopelessness.

'You can't kill me here,' said Tell, with more bravado than she felt.

'No. However, there is some damage which will need to be inflicted in order to avoid paradox. If you give me no trouble it can be postponed.'

'I wish you'd fallen off the life-raft and drowned,' said Tell viciously. 'And you — Red — I thought you'd been blown up. I was sorry about that. For a little while. Talk about being hoist on your own petard!'

Red looked embarrassed and shrugged his good shoulder.

'You're a yes-man, right? You don't make the decisions? You're only doing your job?' she remarked nastily.

'Come along, Estelle,' said Pris. 'You're going home.'

'Moss wants me sent home and your lot's against Moss, right? Right? Why are you climbing into *his* bed now?'

Pris raised her hand as if to slap Tell across the mouth, but visibly controlled herself. She even managed to smile. 'This one time we are in accord,' said Pris. 'Moss is no more eager than RI-P to have his present changed. As to his future — that will be as it will be.'

'If my being here would change your present, it would have happened already,' said Tell desperately. 'I *am* here, and nothing's changed.'

'Since you are bound to be Returned,' said Pris implacably, 'you are *not* here in any real sense. The operation is still in fluid state but once we gain Trinity Street time will normalise. Right, Donor HI-Q number 49?' She paused, and actually spat on the ground. 'If I had *my* way, I'd Return you too,' she said viciously. 'But the puzzle would be where you should be sent. He's not a real person,' she told Tell. 'Merely a genetic mistake. Half of him should be in the twenty-first century and the other half in the twenty-second. Which means he shouldn't exist at all. He is a perversion. A symbol of paradox. A symbol of Hub HI-Q.'

Tell looked at Gerhardt to respond, but the blind look was back in his eyes.

'So bigotry's alive and well in the twenty-seventh century,' she said bitterly. 'It's still the good old us-and-them.' *Watchman — Watchman? Can you get us out of this? Through the veil again?*

As Tell formulated the appeal Pris stepped forward and detached her from Gerhardt, menacing him with the black bar. But it wasn't quite black any longer. The tip was glowing cherry-red. 'Right,' she said to Red. 'In mit her.' Tell saw Gerhardt tense for action, but Pris brought up the glowing bar until it almost brushed Tell's face. The heat was unbelievable, and she flinched, convinced her face would craze like a broken windscreen.

'You cannot reach her,' said Pris, thrusting Tell at Red. 'Try, and I burn her now, before we go to Trinity Street.'

'Paradox,' whispered Gerhardt.

'Paradox! Remember, number 49 — this one is dead already these seven hundred years. You, on the other hand, should never have been alive.'

'Inept!' said Gerhardt.

'Nyet,' said Pris. 'Red, perhaps, triggering detonation five seconds early. But not so inept as you, number 49. You really made a mess. Because of *this*, was it?' She prodded Tell. 'Sib said you'd run true to type, number 49. Being of primitive retro stock. Of course, if Red had not been inept, *this* would have been burned before it hit the water. Why didn't you leave it to drown, number 49? Kinder, really. I was bound to rescue it, but maybe by the time I got there it would have been too brain-damaged to feel the pain. Now it has to be Trinity Street.'

Tell made a sudden effort, kicking out at Red, but he was holding her in an impossible position, turned away and bent back so she could scarcely keep her feet. There would be no bending back of fingers or biting this time. It seemed that Red was just as determined as Pris that Tell would not escape. Or was he simply afraid of what Pris would do to him if she did?

Pris gestured and Red sidled towards the sol-plane, thrusting Tell along with him. Tell forced herself to go limp, and make herself as heavy as possible, but Red simply hoisted her up and flung her into the vehicle. He jumped in beside her, holding her with his one free arm. He seemed horribly strong, and all the wind was knocked out of her. She struggled for breath.

The windows were opaque, but Tell could hear Gerhardt and Pris grappling outside. Once the sol-plane rocked violently as if they had fallen against it, and she could hear their voices, raised in a jumble of contention. There was a curse from Pris, and now Red was nudging a control. When she had travelled with Moss she had felt no vibration, but this sol-plane was a little less smooth. There was no sound, but she felt the engine coming to life. She gulped for air, and screamed.

'WATCHMAN! WATCHMAN! HELP ME!' She was still screaming in and out of her mind when Pris, scowling and breathing hard, and rubbing her head, got in and closed the door. She clapped a hand across Tell's face, silencing her.

'Number 49?' said Red.

'I should have burned him when I had the chance.'

'The Returnee?'

'Soon,' said Pris. 'I adjust the thermo-wand to broad band diffusion . . .'

So that was what the thing was called. A thermo-wand. It might as well have been a blowtorch.

Gerhardt watched the sol-plane vanish. He knew where it was going — back to the disclosure unit and the site of Cockatoo.

Trinity Street.

Because of his mistakes, his lack of trust and foresight and courage, Tell would suffer Trinity Street. The sol-plane would be on-site within minutes, so at least Tell would not be terrified for very long. Pris would take her through the veil to Trinity Street and, a split second later, the crash and explosion would rip the air. All he could do now — if he were able — was to go to Trinity Street himself and kill Tell quickly.

Paradox. But what was the use of all his training, all his talent, if he could not make use of it when it really mattered? *That* would be the paradox. To have the means and to be afraid to use it.

He had a long walk ahead, but it didn't matter when he arrived. He could get there a year from now and still be in time when he passed back through the veil to Cockatoo. The long agony of suspense would be his, not Tell's, to suffer. He knew he would never be able to snatch her unharmed from the explosion. RI-P would expect him to make an attempt and operatives would be waiting at the site to make sure the accident went ahead. They would act swiftly to prevent his interference, perhaps trying to kill him in the confusion. They might succeed, but they would not be able to prevent his acting to readjust that already tangled strand of time. It might have been cruelly ironic that he held a mental weapon that could destroy a person he cared for while leaving most others unharmed. It might have been cruelly ironic . . . but it was now a camouflaged blessing.

It didn't matter when he got to Cockatoo, but he couldn't forgive himself until it was done. Afterwards — when he had killed Tell — if he were still alive himself — he would face the wrath of Hub HI-Q and RI-P. The change would have been made for good, then — there was no going back to tamper again. How had RI-P meant to handle Tell's slow cruel dying? They wouldn't have let her drown; he knew that for certain now. They must have known she'd fight free of the life jacket — Pris herself had checked the fastenings. So how would it have been managed?

She had not been burned when the engines blew, but had she not become an unscheduled Recoveree, he had no doubt Pris would have 'rescued' her, and brought her to shore in her own time to live the last few months of pain and decline. The injuries would have been there, just as the record stated. Pris would have managed them, probably by using her thermo-wand. Anything else, to an agent of RI-P, would have been a perversion of reality.

Dr Moss returned to the car and sprang into the driver's seat. 'Your friend has been found,' he said to Camena. 'My sister will bring her to meet us, then you can both travel on together.'

'Is she okay?'

'Physically, yes. Her mental state ... frankly, I am not happy with that. However, she will be taken to the hospital when she gets back to Cockatoo. It is all arranged. She will be collected from Trinity Street.'

He started the car, and drove a short distance. Camena became aware of a dreamy acceptance. That seemed odd, since she was worried about Tell. 'Did you give me a post-hypnotic command, Dr Moss?' she asked suspiciously.

The old man chuckled. 'Ah, there is no fooling such a one as you, Camena. But relax. It was for your own comfort, only. You have suffered an abnormal amount of stress in the past few weeks, and relaxing your anxieties can only do you good.' He chuckled unexpectedly. 'Yes, Camena de Courcey, I think we can safely say that before today is over you will be a different person.'

Tell had been living in an agony of terror ever since Red had forced her into the sol-plane. She knew Gerhardt couldn't help her, but she couldn't help screaming for him in her mind. There was nothing else she could do. Pris had tired of her struggles and enveloped her in what felt like a coarse blanket. She could hardly breathe, let alone scream aloud. All she could do was lie there sweating and sick with terror.

The sol-plane landed, briefly, and she became aware of someone else embarking. There was a murmur of voices, and then they were airborne. It seemed both hours and a matter of seconds before the vehicle grounded again. Pris stripped off the blanket and dragged Tell out of the sol-plane by the shoulders. Tell heaved and twisted, lashing out with any limb she could free. She made successful contact with Pris a few times, and received a clout that knocked her dizzy. Better not to struggle, perhaps, but how could she help it? She seemed to feel the white-hot pain of the explosion already. And if not that, it would be the thermo-wand. She screamed until her breath had gone, then went on screaming in her mind.

Pris hit her again. 'Stop that!' she panted. 'Or I burn you now! Red!'

Vaguely, Tell heard Red fumbling around with something, then he was handing it to Pris.

Tell struck out, but Pris had her in an arm-lock, and a short, red-hot bar was suddenly in front of her eyes. Any movement would bring it into sizzling contact with her skin . . . Tell stopped struggling.

'Good!' said Pris. 'Now stand still.' She turned and spoke

over her shoulder, apparently to someone else. 'Es verdad, Sib, she's crazed!'

'Enough,' said a precise voice, and the woman Tell had last seen on the screen in Moss's unit came into her line of sight. She looked calmly at Tell. Just as a school principal might regard an erring pupil. 'Estelle Clancy,' she said. 'Be still and listen to me. Your friend Camena will be here in a moment, and you will *not* alarm her. Do you understand?'

'Go to hell!' said Tell, and followed it up with a vicious mental jolt.

Sib's eyes narrowed, and she shook her head. 'And no more of that, either. You make it rather obvious, Estelle, that you have somehow learned too much about your future. That is unfortunate for everyone, most of all, for you. You may take my word for it, however, that Camena de Courcey has no idea of anything that is to come.'

'She's going to be killed!' spat Tell. 'Murdered.'

'Her death and its manner is inevitable,' said Sib calmly. 'However, it will be instantaneous and quite painless. She will be unaware — or almost unaware — that anything is amiss. She will simply cease to be. I am sorry you cannot go out in equal ignorance, but this being so, I appeal to your sense of friendship.'

Tell swallowed, hard. The saliva was gushing in her mouth and she was going to be sick.

'You are very fond of Camena, I know,' said Sib. 'So fond that you followed her to this time.' She held up a hand. 'I know my foolish brother believes you have formed some attachment with that retrograde fostern of his, but you and I know better. Love between friends and equals, such as yourself and Camena, supersedes any consideration of physical attraction.'

'Equals!' cried Tell. 'You stupid old woman!' She broke off

with a choked cry of pain as Pris touched her face with the burning metal. Her stomach heaved and she retched.

'Equals,' said Sib. 'Pris, my dear. Put that thermo-wand away. If you frighten her any more, she will become incoherent.

'Yes, Estelle, you are Camena's equal. In many ways, in fact, you are the stronger. If you think about it, you must agree that to distress Camena with news of her impending death would be cruel. She is going to die. That is unavoidable. It is up to you whether she dies in an agony of terror or in the happy expectation of going home.'

Tell's gorge rose and she retched again. Her face burned sickly, and she felt sweat prickling all over her body. 'Damn you,' she said to Sib. 'Damn you and your stinking RI-Ps to *hell.*'

Sib shrugged. 'Better to damn DHQ number 49 and my brother Moss, perhaps,' she said.

Camena was surprised, when Dr Moss helped her out of the car, to find herself in a bush clearing. 'Why are we here?' she asked. 'This isn't Dr Sib's place.'

Dr Moss laughed at her observation. 'No, but we are here to meet my sister and to take charge of Estelle,' he said. 'And there is my sister's car already.'

Camena turned expectantly, her eyes narrowed towards the slanting sunlight. A long, low vehicle was parked over beneath some trees.

'She seems to have brought some young friends with her!' exclaimed Dr Moss. 'Why not come along and say hello, Camena? I think you have all met before!'

Camena shook her head. 'I think, if you don't mind, I'd rather wait here. Tell can come and sit in the car with me. I don't suppose you'll be long?'

Dr Moss chuckled. 'Not too long. I have, after all, recently spent time in my sister's company. I have great respect for her, but, as you may have noticed, we do not always see, as the idiom has it, eye to eye.'

'No,' murmured Camena.

She turned to get back in the car and blinked. She hadn't noticed before just how odd it looked. 'What kind of car *is* this?' she asked.

'My sister told you, Camena, that I have an interest in unique vehicles.'

'Yes — so she did.'

'This is the pride of my collection.'

Footsteps crunched, and Camena turned back to see Dr Sib approaching. Dr Moss touched her arm and then moved unhurriedly to meet his sister, who nodded cheerfully across to Camena. 'You concede?' she said to Dr Moss.

Dr Moss sighed. 'I cannot deny you appear to have won this round.'

'Won what?' asked Camena.

'Just a little bargain I made with Maurie, Camena,' said Dr Sib. 'A round in an ongoing game of forfeits, you might say. He wins a little, I win a little, and so it goes on.'

Camena wasn't very interested in whatever games these elderly eccentrics were playing. 'Where's Tell?' she asked.

'She's over by my car with two of my young friends,' said Dr Sib placidly.

Camena peered across the clearing. She could see Tell now, apparently standing arm in arm with Pris. Camena sighed inwardly. She was tired of being sociable. She hoped Pris would not come over and start talking to her again.

'Tell?' she called. 'Are you okay?'

Even at that distance she could see that Tell looked

terrible. Strained, almost ill. Camena thought she had been crying. And she was dressed in a horrible sort of prison outfit — baggy mottled shorts and a shapeless top. Whatever Tell had been doing since they had been parted on the beach it looked as if she'd had a much rougher time than Camena. But of course — she'd been with Gerhardt. Camena felt a wave of anxiety, tinged with exasperation. Surely Tell hadn't been stupid enough to get too involved with *him*?

At the sound of Camena's voice, Tell looked up, and made a sudden movement as if to break away from Pris, who bent down and seemed to be saying something soft but emphatic. 'Hey, Tell!' called Camena, and beckoned to Tell to come over.

'I should warn you, my dear, your friend is in a very unstable state,' said Dr Sib in a low voice. 'I have just been telling Maurie — she seems to have quite lost touch with reality.'

'*Tell* has?' said Camena. 'But Tell is the most stable person I know!'

'Even the strongest psyche can sometimes warp under intense emotional strain,' said Dr Sib. 'However, perhaps you *should* go to her. You may be able to help her.' She raised her voice. 'Pris? Thank you, dear. Camena will keep Estelle company now.'

Tell broke away from Pris and stumbled over to Camena, hugging her fiercely. 'Cammie — Cammie, are you okay?'

She was shaking and sobbing, and Camena was appalled. 'What on earth has that creep done to you, Tell? He hasn't — hurt you, has he? I mean — look at your face!'

'Watchman? Oh no . . .' said Tell. 'But listen, Cammie — Oh God, there isn't time to explain. We've got to get out of here!' She grabbed Camena's hand and tugged, trying to drag her away.

Camena resisted. 'It's all right, Tell, really it is. Dr Moss is taking us home right now. You can have a bath and a hot drink and they'll check you out in the hospital . . .'

Tell interrupted with an hysterical sobbing laugh. 'The hospital! No way! Cammie, *listen* to me. These people are RI-P — except for Moss — he's Hub HI-Q. Don't you understand? *They're* the ones who kidnapped you. The ones Watchman warned us about. We've got to get away from them.'

'No,' said Camena, 'you've got it all backwards.' She glanced appealingly at Dr Moss. She had been warned that Tell was upset, but she seemed to be positively nuts. She was dragging at Camena's arm, her fingers digging in painfully.

'Come *on*!' said Tell. 'I'll explain later!'

'Yes, of course,' said Camena. 'Later. But for now, we should be getting you home.' She took a deep breath and put her free arm around her friend. It felt all wrong to be the comforter instead of the comforted. 'It's all right, Tell,' she said. 'It's nearly over now. Dr Sib's been looking after me — ever since you and Gerhardt — Gary I mean — left me near the beach. We're quite safe now — we're going home.'

'Cammie, we've got to get away!' Tell's voice rose to a hoarse shriek.

'All right, Camena,' said Dr Moss. He stepped forward, smiling. 'Now, Estelle, that's quite enough. You need not be afraid any more. You are suffering a psychotic episode — that's all. Soon it will be over. Now, why don't you calm down and look at this watch? Camena found it very interesting, didn't you, my dear?'

'Very,' agreed Camena. She looked uncertainly at Dr Moss. The glint of his watch caught her eye and she felt the strange calm spreading over her again. It was really very relaxing, and she wished she could let herself float . . . No! She must help Tell listen to this man. She pulled herself together. 'Tell,' she said persuasively, 'why don't you do as Dr Moss says? It really will help you.'

'No!' shrieked Tell. She flung herself at Camena and started shaking her. 'Cammie — can't you understand? This isn't what you think! There's a sol-plane and in a minute we're going to be sent through the veil! For God's sake — just for once — *open your eyes!*'

Camena jerked away, profoundly shocked. She stumbled a little, and Dr Moss came forward to put a reassuring hand on her arm. 'The best place for your friend is in the hospital,' said Dr Moss. 'You come along with me, Camena, and my sister can look after poor Estelle . . .'

'No, Maurie,' said Dr Sib. 'That is not part of the bargain. Both girls must be dispatched together. That's what we agreed.'

'No!' shrieked Tell. She lunged at Camena again, but Dr Moss moved around to stand between them.

He smiled genially at Dr Sib. 'Checkmate, Sib,' he said, and then his face changed. 'Merde!' he said softly.

Tell's nightmares were surging about her. Death for her best friend, lingering agony for herself — and she couldn't even warn Camena. That woman Sib, damn her, had been right about that. It would be wanton cruelty to warn Camena if there was no way out. Perhaps she should have smiled and made small talk and stepped out gaily to meet her own grim future . . . but that was beyond her. Early Christian martyrs might have gone singing to their deaths, but Tell knew she could never match their courage. She would be more like the queen who had tried to run away from the headsman and been horribly butchered as a result. And it wasn't only herself and Camena who would suffer. Maureen and David and Linnie and Justin would all be hurt as well. And Gerhardt might be hurt the worst of all — she wished she had been able to say goodbye properly instead of screaming. A brave smile would have been a nicer way for him to remember her. And he had promised her a quick death. She must cling on to that. He wouldn't let her suffer long, and she would see him just once more when he came to kill her.

And now Camena was turning away from her, turning to Moss.

Her eyes were blurring with terror, and she felt a faint touch in her mind.

Watchman???

Nein — I.

Her mind fumbled. *Jens?*

Ja. Where?

I don't know! In a clearing — oh, the disclosure unit must be somewhere near.

There was a terrible moment of uncertainty, then Jens stepped into view.

Tell heard Moss cursing, shocked out of his usual urbane calm.

Estelle — we strike, ja?

Strike? For a second, Tell had a ridiculous vision of a picket line, then she understood that Jens meant they should somehow strike at Moss and Sib. They might have been a physical match for two elderly people, but there were Red and Pris . . .

Mit minds, said Jens. *Overload.*

Yes! Her enthusiasm must have startled Jens, for he pulled a wry face. She took a deep breath, but Sib and Moss had already turned to stare at the intruder.

Tell had no idea what to do, so she took a stab in the dark and summoned a mental shriek, which she directed squarely at Sib and Pris. She saw Sib wince and for a wonderful instant she thought it was going to work. But it was Jens's face that was creased and sweating with pain, while Sib was merely uncomfortable.

It seemed that her efforts were causing Jens more distress than they were causing Sib ... and Pris was not affected at all.

Sword — double-edged, said Jens with irony.

'Stop them!' snapped Sib.

Camena watched in bewilderment as the stranger stepped into the clearing. She had no idea who he was, nor how he could have arrived. He was simply there. There was an oddly breathless moment, and then she felt Dr Moss quiver, as if a cold draught had touched him. She looked up at him, startled, as his arm came heavily down on her shoulder. Could he be having some kind of seizure? She put out an instinctive hand to support him.

But Dr Sib was snapping some kind of an order and then Red was bending to pick up something from the ground and long-legged Pris was hurling herself across the clearing and ...

There was a shimmer in the air — and Moss and Camena were gone. Tell screamed, aloud this time.

Run Estelle!

The tone was unmistakably Jens's. And Jens was trying his best for her, directing all his mental power at Sib. But Red was coming fast again, and so was Pris, and then Pris flung herself at Tell, tumbling them both on the rocky ground. Perhaps there had been a chance to break away, but it had simply happened too quickly.

A second later Moss reappeared, without Camena. He looked white and very strained, but there was an air of triumph about him.

Run, Estelle!

I can't! screamed Tell.

Run.

Tell shrieked again, at the top of her mind's power, then, desperately, heaved over and bit Pris's arm, grinding her teeth back and forth energetically. Pris hit her a ringing blow on the ear.

Run.

But she could not run. She couldn't even stand. She could only huddle there, watching in terror as the roller coaster of action swept around her. Her head was spinning, but occasional scenes stood out like ragged snapshots.

Sib holding her head in her hands as if to shut out the light.

Red weighing a chunk of rock in his hand.

Pris shrieking something at Red.

Red pivoting on one foot to fling the rock at Jens.

The aim going wild and the rock striking Sib instead.

Run.

Sib toppling sideways, the silver brooch flashing a reflection from the lowering sun. Her neat grey hair soaking through with blood.

Red wailing with terror at his mistake, and bolting — straight for the RI-P sol-plane.

Pris flinging herself after him.

Pris dragging at Red, then the vehicle suddenly flipping sideways.

Swooping drunkenly over the clearing.
And away.

In the sudden silence, Tell dragged herself up on hands and knees.

Jens?

Safe, Estelle . . .

Jens's face was a mask of exhaustion. He was shaking as he stumbled over to Moss, who was standing looking down at Sib.

'Condition?' said Jens.

'Alive,' said Moss judiciously. 'However, she needs attention if she's to avoid permanent damage. I could bear it with fortitude if she were to be removed from the arena, but to have her live on dulled — I think not.' He glanced at Jens. 'You disgust me, Jens. To use that undisciplined skill of yours in such a way . . .' He actually clicked his tongue. 'So very inefficient. Nothing to say?'

Jens shrugged.

Leave us, Estelle, he said, and Tell realised, numbly, that Moss had forgotten her. And that Camena was dead. And that . . .

But her body and mind hurt too much to take in anything else. She retreated slowly, step by step. Behind her, she was aware that Jens was helping Moss lift Sib into Moss's sol-plane. And then Moss was gone.

Jens?

'Estelle?' Jens turned to face her, and she saw the pallor of his face beneath the swarthy complexion.

Are you . . . The pain deepened in his face and she realised her thought-sending was hurting him. She wondered if her own brain should hurt, and came to the conclusion that it felt no worse than the rest of her. 'Are you okay?' she said, very quietly.

'Nyet,' said Jens. 'Soon, bitte.' He smiled.

Tell touched her cheek. It throbbed and she felt a blister blossoming. 'What now?' she asked.

Jens turned out his hands, swaying. He was almost unconscious on his feet.

'The disclosure unit,' said Tell. 'You can rest in there.' She had no idea how to find the disclosure unit herself, but she supported Jens until he had located the concealed hatch.

It seemed extraordinary that the unit had not changed. It was exactly as it had been when Gerhardt had guided her there, even to her discarded clothes and ruined shoes in the hamper. Jens lay down on the couch, much as she had done, and was almost instantly asleep. There was nothing much wrong with him, she thought. It was probably only exhaustion.

There was nothing much wrong with her. Only numbness, and shock, and misery. But if — no, *when* — Moss remembered and came back there would be more wrong with her than shock. When Moss came back, he would take her to Trinity Street. And Moss knew precisely where the disclosure unit was...

She had to get away from here. Somewhere quiet, where Moss wouldn't find her. A place where she could wait for Gerhardt.

Tell drank some water, and swabbed the burn on her face. There was no point in waiting. Moss might be back at any minute — she climbed out of the unit and replaced the hatch, leaving Jens to sleep. Moss wouldn't hurt *him*, surely.

Outside, she stood wavering, almost as exhausted as Jens. There was a blackness crowding her vision, she supposed it was like one of Cammie's migraines — *don't think of that.*

The grief for her friend was fresh and raw, and when the shock wore off it would hurt very much. Now, all she could do was find Gerhardt and tell him she was still alive. She took a step forward. Her feet seemed a very long way away, but that was the way to go. Step, by step, by step. The thought of so many steps was appalling, but she would go on.

Totoka cina na butobuto! she whispered. *You are a light in my darkness.*

That was what Gerhardt had said to her, and that was what she must cling to during her long journey. Step, by step, by step.

And after all it was not too many steps before she was seen. She was no more than halfway across the clearing when someone emerged from the gathering dusk, not three metres away. A figure which resolved itself into Pris. Pris had a new bruise on the side of her face, and she was looking wildly around the clearing. There was no escape this time. Her gaze touched Tell and closed in with an almost audible snap. She strode forward and raised the thermo-wand, the tip already glowing red.

'Where is Sib?' she asked.

Tell blinked. The question might have sounded innocuous, but the expression on Pris's handsome face was not. The nightmare was beginning again.

'Where is Sib?' Pris demanded again, and brought the thermo-wand towards Tell's face.

'Gone!' said Tell blankly. 'And if you touch me with that, I'll be sick all over you.'

'Gone?' Pris sounded staggered at the news. 'Gone where? I have come back to her.'

'She's gone with Moss,' said Tell.

'Gone with Moss.' The words were barely above a whisper, but the whisper curdled Tell's blood.

'Yes,' she said, trying to speak calmly. 'Moss took her in his sol-plane. He was going to get her some treatment for concussion...'

'No!' The word seemed ripped from Pris in an almost animal howl. 'No...'

'He's not going to hurt her,' said Tell. 'They don't get on, but she's his sister, after all.'

'She went in the sol-plane...' muttered Pris.

'She could hardly walk!'

'Then — Sib is dead.' Pris's voice was chilled and hopeless. 'Do you not understand, you deadling? Sib is gone with Moss. I thought to finish him for her... and now they're both gone together. I could laugh.'

And she did laugh, horribly, and sank to her knees, still clinging to Tell.

'You did something to that sol-plane,' said Tell. It was not a question. It was a certainty. Nothing else made any sense. 'You planted something...'

Pris lifted her face and her eyes were points of black. She rose, letting go of Tell in the process. Her face was swelling, but she showed no sign of pain as she lifted the thermo-wand with a new sense of purpose and twisted the end. A fan of light sprang out, throwing shadows across the clearing.

'Burn, Estelle,' she said. 'It is your destiny. We go to Trinity Street.'

Jens!

But Jens was asleep, unconscious. There was no way he could help her. Pris lunged for her arm, but somehow Tell began to run, with Pris so close behind her she could smell the odd coal-burning smell of the thing she held. She could hear the sighing flutter of the invisible flames.

Watchman! Watchman! she screamed. But telepathy was only good for short distances, and he was far away. He would never even know she was crying out.

She ran. Her lungs were hurting and she had hardly the breath left to scream. Pris would catch her soon; she was taller and stronger, and in a murderous rage. No matter how long it took, Pris would catch her and burn her, and then send her back to the horror awaiting her on Trinity Street. There was no point in running now, no hope of final escape, but still she ran. There are some things that cannot be faced.

The sun was slanting into the hills but Gerhardt didn't hurry. He had a long way to go and all the time in the world. He wondered what he would do after he had done the only thing he could for Tell. Perhaps he should do himself the same favour, although he would have to find a different means. He could hardly send a mental jolt to shock his *own* mind into death. It would be as impractical as strangling himself with his own hands ... If Hub HI-Q was winding up the Recovery Programme, his usefulness was over and he wanted to be far away from Moss. How *could* Moss have given in to Sib? It didn't seem to gel — those two had been rivals forever, probably since the day of their joint birth to their HI-Q alpha parents. But Moss was incalculable, and Gerhardt couldn't think of him now.

Gerhardt felt inhuman, unfit to live at all, as Pris had implied. Real time. He was in real time, and Tell's real time was running out — had run out long ago. Perhaps she was burning now. If only he'd had the courage, he might have saved them both. There had been one way out. Forbidden.

Dangerous. Perhaps as lethal as Trinity Street. He'd thought it an impossible risk, but now he wished he'd tried. If Tell were dead and he were finished he might as well have tried. There was a chance he could have dodged Pris and still reached Tell in time . . . she might have been burned, perhaps even blinded, but she would have been alive . . .

Watchman! Watchman!

Gerhardt raised his hands to ward off the terrible cries. He could *not* be hearing Tell.

Watchman!

He was hearing Tell. And hearing her was worse than imagining.

If only she were here, or he were there, he'd try the impossible route. They'd linked minds once to pass the veil. Difficult and dangerous, but they'd made it back in the unit.

No, he thought. They must have done it twice. Once in the unit, once in Kestrel Bay. The second time they had been touching, as traditionally they must. *Only* a trained operative could pass through the veil from now to now. *Only* a trained operative and the Recoveree he held in contact with his body.

He had held Tell so the second time, but he had not held her the first. The first time he had been holding Camena in his arms, and Tell had been only in his mind.

Tell. Estellita ma —

It was no good. She was not calm, she was screaming.

Listen, Tell! We're going for broke, he said, trying to project calm and certainty. *We're going where they can never find us. Totoka cina na butobuto!*

Watchman — Pris is going to burn me! The cry was terrible with fear.

Don't let her touch you! he thought in alarm. *Don't let her touch you again! Come to me instead.*

Where are you?

He caught his breath and lied. *Here. Behind the rock, so close to you. Come to me. We're going through the veil.*

She was running. She must be, but he couldn't hear her feet. How could he, when they were still so far apart?

See the rock? he said.

Which — rock?

The one that's nearest to you. So close to you.

Yes.

Behind the rock, Tell. Come and take my hands!

He lifted his hands and pressed the air, reaching for the alpha state. He felt her mind touch his and thought he felt her hands. Whorls on whorls, Möbius strip, her hands were whole and warm. *Now!* he cried. *We're going through the veil!*

He was falling. The plateau was changed and he hit the rock with a thud. The sky spun, the clouds stretched like honey in the sunset. He sat up and looked around. Silence.

He was bruised and shaking, but he was still alive. *Tell?*

Watchman! Where the hell are you? They've killed Cammie! Jens came and tried to help, but Moss was too quick. And Sib and Moss are dead . . .

I'm here on the plateau, he said. *Close to our quiet place.*

Bloody hell! I'm still near the disclosure unit only — Watchman, no-one's here!

I'm here.

There was a pause, and the air caressed his arms and face. Mist on the moon, he thought. He should not have been breathing this air.

They'll find me, she said. *Pris will take me back to Trinity Street.*

No, teur Estellita. Now they'll never find you.

Why not? They can go back to any time. They'll only have to check.

They can go back, he said, *but they can't go forward. Nobody goes forward; it's far too dangerous.*

So?

So. That's why we came forward.

Another pause.

When are we, Watchman?

Gerhardt thought about that. *I do not know, precisely. Shall we call it now?*

Camena's gone, said Tell. *She hasn't got a now.*

Gerhardt felt a stab of sorrow, but there was nothing he could think or say.

Life's not bloody fair, said Tell, and he knew that she was crying.

At least you are alive.

I know, she said, *and I know you gave me back my life. But what about Cammie's life?*

Perhaps, sometime . . . he said.

Yes? Her hope was deafening.

It's only perhaps, he said. *Sometime we might find the way to save her.*

But what about the others? What about Jens and Red and Pris? Where are they now?

They're all gone long ago. But you and I — we have our now, and we have a future, too. He bit his lip, still bruised from contact with the rock. *I love you, Estellita.*

Blast you, Watchman! Why the hell aren't you here?

I am here.

But I'm there. How shall I ever find you?

Her exasperation was plain, and he could see her in his mind. Pale and shabby, grief-stricken but whole. Gloriously, wonderfully whole. And somehow, soon, he would see her with his eyes.

It wouldn't be easy. He didn't know when they were. He didn't know how they would live, nor what she would want of him. But now at least they had a chance. Technically, he supposed, they were dead . . . surely they'd be dead if they returned to the time they'd left. That put him on par with Tell — it was a curiously liberating thought. And what *about* Camena? Wherever she was, he hoped she would be at peace. Until her sometime came. If it ever did.

He took a deep, shuddering breath. *Start walking, teur Estellita*, he told her. *I'll meet you in the middle.*

AUTHOR'S NOTE

I like writing sci-fi.

Why?

Because it's interesting. Because it gives me a chance to explore other dimensions . . . Because it can be mixed with adventure, romance and mystery.

I like writing books where the characters have to think on their feet, think fast, and make the right decision.

I like writing books where the stakes are bigger than popularity, bigger than being cool.

I like writing books that keep me awake at night, planning and worrying for my characters.

I like writing books where the characters learn and grow.

I like writing books where the dividing line between right and wrong is sometimes blurred.

I like writing books where the ending is really the beginning.

Sally Odgers
1997